Book 3
Revised Edition 2019

By
Andrew Dobell

The book is Copyright © to Andrew Dobell, Creative Edge Studios Ltd, 2019.
No part of this book may be reproduced without prior permission of the copyright holder.

All locations, events, and characters within this book are either fictitious, or have been fictionalised for the purposes of this book.

Welcome to the Magi Saga

This is book three of a long, sprawling adventure over several series of books, of which, this is the start.

This book has been through various editions, with this being the latest.

I hope you enjoy reading about the adventures of Amanda and the Magi, as much as I've enjoyed writing them.

Acknowledgements

For my Grandfather, who was a continual inspiration and support. I miss you, and this is for you.

Thank you to my wife and family for their love and tolerance and help. You make everything worthwhile.

Thank you to my old gaming friends, you guys have inspired this story more than you can know. I have some of the best memories from those hours sitting at the gaming table.

Thank you to my Editors Julie Hall, CP Bialois, and Hanna Elizabeth. Your input has been amazing, thank you.

Thank you to Vicki Blatchley for being my cover model.

Dedication
For my boys, my kids, I love you!

Language
I'm a British author living in Britain, and I write in British English with British spellings.   ;-)

Booklist

For full list of Andrew Dobell's Books, visit his website at;
www.andrewdobellauthor.co.uk/booklist

Table of Contents

Welcome to the Magi Saga 3
Acknowledgements 3
Booklist 3
Table of Contents 5
Prologue 7
Fallen Angels 12
Working Girl 22
Opening Salvo 39
Is the grass greener? 57
Jade Crusade 70
Holy Plans 84
Orb 98
The L.A. Gambit 111
Park Life 133
Curiosity 144
Generals Gambit 159
New Management 173
Cold News 178
Ball of Destiny 187
New Lead 216
Promotion 221
Meltdown 228
Home again 246
Cold Trail 255
Under the Sea 273
Dark Information 287
Black Dawn 295
Epilogue 1 334
Reawakening 334
Epilogue 2 337
Taking stock 337
Author Note 341
Review 341
Booklist 342

Prologue

American Midwest

Dust slammed the Arcadian up against the wall. Gripping him by the neck, Dust held him a good foot above the floor as the Arcadian struggled and clawed at his attacker's hand.

"Please, don't kill me, you can take it…" he whimpered, struggling to get his words out through the Nomad's iron grip.

Dust had no idea who this Arcadian was. He only knew that he had something he wanted, something he'd been hunting for a very long time.

"Where is it?" Dust demanded, his voice rough and deep. He loosened his grip on the Arcadian's neck a fraction, just enough so that he could speak.

"It's… It's in my pocket. Here, take it," he said, rummaging in his jacket pocket. He pulled out a rolled-up piece of paper bound with a leather tie. It looked ancient.

Dust snatched the scroll away from him and stuffed it in the pocket of his tan-coloured leather duster.

"There, you've got it, you've won. Please, can we talk about this now?"

"No," said Dust. Tightening his grip, he pulled a blade from his belt that he slashed across the man's belly. Blood poured onto the packed earth floor of the ramshackle building.

The man choked and struggled as his eyes went wide in panic. His hands tried in vain to keep his ropey insides from spilling to the floor, without success.

Dust smirked, one side of his mouth pulling back in a half-smile as he dropped the Arcadian to the floor. He landed on his knees and looked down in horror at his guts, piled all around him like slimy red snakes.

Standing back, Dust watched the man try one last desperate use of Magic. But he calmly called on the Essentia and dissolved the healing Magic the Arcadian had attempted.

Blood bubbled up into the Arcadian's mouth and dribbled over his chin as he slipped into the cold embrace of death. He pitched forward, his face hitting the floor and kicking up a small cloud of dirt.

The Nomad pulled the scroll from his pocket and held it up for a closer look. Small and unassuming, it seemed wrong that such a tiny thing would be so valued by Arcadians and Nomads alike. The rolled-up parchment was only about eight inches across and felt as light as a feather. The paper was creased and discoloured, taking on a tan hue that made it appear like it had been dunked in coffee. But Dust knew better than to judge such an item by its mundane appearance. This happened to be one of the most infamous and powerful Magical items known to the Magi world.

Known as the Lazarus Scroll, the tales of its power were legendary, including its ability to resurrect the dead. Dust chose not to undo the leather strap at this moment. He'd look at it later when he had more time to sit and study it. For now, he wanted to be on his way in case the Magus he'd just killed had friends nearby.

He looked down at the body, slumped on the floor and gave it a kick. At least, he'd been entertaining and put up a bit of a fight.

Turning from the body, he walked across the room that was little more than four brick walls and a pitched, corrugated iron roof over a dusty desert floor to reach the exit.

Opening the door, he frowned at the sight that greeted him.

The exit had been bricked up.

Had it been like this when he came in here? He found he had difficulty remembering. He pushed on the bricks, but they held firm. Suddenly, an intense feeling that he wasn't alone anymore washed over him. He spun on the spot and fell back against the bricked-up doorway in shock.

The man he'd just killed was no longer dead. He stood with his arms wide, blood pouring from his eyes and mouth. His intestines writhed and curled around each other like snakes extending from the man's stomach, reaching for him.

Dust scrambled to get away, but it felt like he was submerged in treacle—his every movement slow and ponderous.

As he watched, the man's belly opened wide to reveal rows and rows of wicked-looking teeth as blood and ichor oozed from its horrendous maw.

The snake-like intestines whipped out and wrapped around Dust's legs, dragging him back towards the mouth from which they'd come.

Dust clawed at the floor. He reached for anything that might help him pull himself away, but nothing presented itself. The tentacles flipped Dust over onto his back. Looking up, another length of intestine whipped out and wrapped around his neck, pulling him headfirst into the tooth-filled mouth.

He screamed as the jaw distended, opening wide enough to fit his head into it, before slamming shut with a final chomp.

***

Dust woke up. His eyes snapped open as he sat bolt upright on a metal-framed bed.

The building didn't look dissimilar to the one in his dream, apart from the few bits of furniture it had in real life and the light streaming into the interior through holes in the walls and roof. He swung his legs off the bed and looked at the scroll that sat on the small cabinet next to the bed.

He still had it, the Lazarus Scroll, right where he'd left it when he'd drifted off to sleep the night before.

He'd killed a man for this artifact—an Arcadian Magi. He forgot the name of the man now, not that it was important. Who had it before him was of little consequence. He owned it now. He controlled its power, and with it, he could bring Horlack back from the Abyss.

Dust had visited the alleyway in New York. He felt sure that Horlack had not been killed, but instead, transported out of this realm and into the Abyss.

He didn't really know how he knew this, he just did. Just like he also knew that he had to bring him back. But for that, he needed the Lazarus Scroll. He'd been searching for a year, following up clues as to its whereabouts which had ultimately led to his favourite hunting ground. The desert.

These dreams had been happening ever since he'd found the scroll. Every night he went to sleep, and every night he woke up screaming at least once. He had no idea why and he supposed it didn't really matter.

The artifact was his now. He could complete the ritual and bring Horlack back.

He just needed to find the right place to do it. He needed a Pooling. A place where two Ley Lines crossed and the Essentia from the crossing streams of energy weakened the barrier into the Abyss.

Rising from his bed, he picked up the scroll and his wide-brimmed cowboy hat, and stepped from the shack out into the morning light. Already warm, the Arizona desert looked dry and inhospitable. But Dust loved these places. He loved to wander deserts and focus on his hobby when the mood took him. He'd not seen anyone for a few days now, so he'd not had the chance to indulge himself. Shame, really. Killing a pretty girl always seemed to pass the time quite nicely. What is it the Arcadians called him? Dust Devil, wasn't it? He didn't mind the name, not really.

Looking around and putting his hat on his head, he wasn't really sure which way he needed to go, so he just picked a direction and walked, the wind whipping his coat about him as he went.

Fallen Angels

Los Angeles

Toni stood at the edge of the terrace at the back of the mansion and looked out from her vantage point over the tens of thousands of lights that shone in the darkness. Yellow, white, blue, and red. The lights glowed from windows, cars, and buildings in the vast sprawl of Los Angeles on this balmy November evening.

Turning away from the view, she looked across the grounds. Ahead, a large swimming pool glowed from within, while other lights lit up the decking and gardens closer to the house.

She wasn't alone. Four other Magi were with her on the terrace, while the rest of the coven remained inside.

Jonas, Tybolt, and Melissa chatted idly as they enjoyed their drinks. The two guys wore their swimming shorts—Jonas looking like a blond surfer dude beside the dark-haired Tybolt with his designer stubble and a towel wrapped around his shoulders.

Melissa looked as classy as ever, wearing a dark bikini and cover-up skirt that didn't hide much at all. All three of them had bodies to die for; like most Magi, they took pride in their appearance.

As they watched, the fourth Magus wandered over carrying a pair of drinks. Toni smiled at her, enjoying the view as Tabitha approached.

Before Tabitha, Toni had always been a little bi-curious, even though she'd only ever been with men. But joining this coven had changed all that.

Apparently, Tabitha had taken an immediate liking to her, or so she said. Over several weeks, they had grown closer until one night after a drink or two, one thing had led to another, and that was that.

Soon, she'd fallen in love with Tabby, and it had been the most passionate and intense relationship of her life so far.

Tabby's bob of platinum blonde hair complemented her orange bikini perfectly. She had quite striking features, not least of which being her Magically-altered golden eyes that had a vertically slit pupil, just like a cat's. Tabby reached Toni's side and handed her one of the champagne flutes.

"Thanks," she said, giving Tabby a kiss and then taking a sip of the bubbly.

"So, you didn't say one way or the other. Do you want to go?" Tabby asked.

"To the ball in New York? Sure, sounds good."

"It should be. I hear it's going to be a hell of a celebration. It's been a long time since the Arcadians had a presence there."

"This is them staking their claim to it," Toni agreed.

"Who can blame them? The Nomads controlled that city for decades."

"Lucian. Wasn't it?"

"Yeah. Glad he's gone. I'm sure there's a particularly hot part of Hell waiting just for him," Tabitha mused.

"Who killed him?"

"Don't know. I think they're keeping that one quiet."

"That's probably wise," Toni agreed.

"Absolutely, unless that person wants Nymira after them. If it were me, I'd be keeping it quiet, as well."

"Maybe we'll find out at the ball?" Toni asked.

"I doubt it, but it would be good to see some of New York while we're there," Tabby said. "Come on, let's sit down," Tabby said, leading her back to the table.

"Sounds good," Toni agreed. "So who do you think killed Lucian? I heard that it was a Council task force that acted on a tip-off from a Nomad defector. They found out where Lucian was hiding and stormed the place."

"The council *has* wanted Lucian dead for ages now," Tabby agreed.

"I heard it was a Nomad who wanted to join the Arcadians," Jonas joined in. "One of Yasmin's coven who wanted to prove himself to the Council."

"That's a bit far-fetched," Tybolt said. "The rumour I heard was that a Magi named Amanda killed him. She moved from Europe to New York about a month before or something."

"Amanda, I've not heard of her," Tabby commented.

"She's not been a Magus long. Red-headed girl, I think," Tybolt answered.

Toni suddenly had a moment of recall. She thought she remembered seeing a red-head at the Liberty's Children Coven House, back when she'd visited Victoria after her coven had been wiped out by Nomads. Could that have been Amanda? She couldn't be sure. She'd been quite upset that day.

"You read that online?" Tabby asked.

"Yeah, on the DWeb forums."

"Of course, the home of reliable news," Tabby commented, a hint of sarcasm in her voice. She turned and handed her drink to Toni, "Here, hold this. I'm going to do a couple of laps."

Toni watched her walk away to the edge of the pool, enjoying the sight of her lover in a bikini. Damn it, if they were alone out here she'd be joining Tabby in the pool for a little alone time.

BOOM!

Toni's head snapped up. She looked in horror at the explosion that blossomed out of the back of the house. Debris and fire rained across the garden. A charred-black dead body landed in the pool with a giant splash. Tabby screamed. Melissa and the boys cursed and jumped up.

Shifting her vision into the Magical spectrum, she watched the Aegis on the house flicker and fail as bright lights and explosions sounded from within. Toni ran and met Tabby in an embrace as she moved away from the pool and the burnt body that floated in it. Melissa, Jonas, and Tybolt followed.

"I think it's Osmond," Toni speculated, indicating the body in the pool. She recognised the clothing.

"It is. What the fuck?" Tybolt cursed.

"Nomads?" Jonas asked.

Not again, thought Toni. She shivered as the memories of the attack on her coven played in her head. The images of those three Nomads slaughtering her friends would be with her forever. She'd never seen such carnage and bloodshed.

She thought she was safe here. It had been six months since the massacre.

More lights danced inside the house as smaller explosions echoed through the night. Essentia flared and a figure in black Ported onto the lawn. Toni felt her stomach drop as she recognised the woman. She wore latex fetish gear and had the same long black hair, pale face, and deep dark eyes that haunted Toni's nightmares.

It was the same group—the same Nomads—and they'd found her again. On instinct, Toni pumped Essentia into her Aegis.

Jonas pushed Melissa towards Toni and Tabby. "Get out of here, we'll deal with this."

"Hey, don't be so..." Melissa began, turning to challenge their macho bullshit. But they'd already Ported across the garden to stand in front of the Nomad.

Toni saw Melissa call on the surrounding Essentia and boost her Aegis. "Mel, please, stay here," Toni said in a panic.

Melissa looked back at Toni and Tabitha and hesitated. They all looked back at the three figures. Essentia flared from the Nomad, and suddenly the two guys disappeared. The Magic the Nomad used seemed odd, different to what Toni was used to, but she also thought she recognised it, maybe.

"What the…" Toni said.

"Holy shit!" Melissa exclaimed.

The Nomad disappeared as well, using the same kind of effect she'd just used on the guys.

"What was that?" Tabby asked.

Melissa looked back at them. "I have no idea," she muttered.

More explosions rang out inside the mansion, making the girls pause in their conversation.

"What do we do? What do we do?" Tabby asked, her voice warbling with panic.

"We leave. We Port out of here now before we're killed too," Toni said.

"It's just one girl, how bad can it be?" Melissa said.

Magic flared again, and the woman in black reappeared, this time holding two decapitated heads by the hair—one in each hand.

Toni put her hand to her mouth. She felt sick to her stomach as she recognised the two heads as Jonas and Tybolt.

"Holy fuck," Melissa whispered.

"We're leaving," Tabby said, "right now."

Toni felt a thought pass into her mind from Tabby, details of a location in L.A. as her girlfriend's Essentia flared. Toni followed suit, Porting to the same location, and hoping that Melissa did too.

A heartbeat later, Toni appeared next to Tabitha, followed immediately by Melissa. They stood under a bridge in the concrete channel known as the L.A. River. Apart from a small, thin stream of water that ran down the middle of the enormous artificial riverbed, it was bone-dry.

She grabbed onto Tabby, holding her tight and not wanting to let go.

"It was her, wasn't it?" Tabby muttered.

"What do you mean, it was who?" Melissa asked.

Toni nodded as she blinked her tears away and tried to get her emotions under control.

"What?" Melissa pressed, confused.

"The Nomad we just saw, it was one of the trio who killed Toni's coven six months ago. Am I right?" Tabitha asked.

Toni sniffed and took a few deep breaths. "Yeah, it was her. I'm sure of it."

"Shit," Tabby cursed.

"Well, that's just awesome," Melissa added, sarcasm lacing her voice. "Fuck. And what the hell are we doing here?" Melissa asked, waving her hands around at the drab concrete environment.

"What do you mean?" asked Tabby.

"Here. Why are we here, when our coven is being massacred? We should be back at the house, helping them."

"Then we'd die too," Toni whispered. She understood Melissa's frustration, but she knew what these Nomads were capable of, but she knew this was the right choice.

"That's right," Tabitha agreed. "You saw her. You saw what she did to Jonas and Ty. If she can do that to them, then we wouldn't stand a chance. We'd be dead within seconds."

"Arrgh! God damn it! I just... I feel helpless," Melissa snarled. She walked to the nearest support column for the bridge and slammed the bottom of her fist into it before turning and leaning against it.

Toni followed Tabitha as she walked over to Melissa and did her best to comfort her. "Hey, we'll be alright. We'll get through this."

"So, what are we going to do? We can't stay here, look at us?" Melissa said, gesturing to her bikini. Toni had to agree, they did look odd, standing under a bridge in their swimsuits.

"I don't know, maybe we should tell Victoria?" Tabitha offered.

"What will she do?" Toni asked.

"She can help. She can track down who did this."

"You mean like last time? She didn't do anything," Toni replied. "The Nomads are still out there, still killing."

"So, what do you suggest?" Melissa asked, sounding slightly accusatory.

"We go to New York. We find this Amanda Tybolt mentioned. If the rumours are true, maybe she'll help."

Tabitha raised her eyebrows and nodded. "That sounds like a bit of a long shot."

"Do you have a better idea?" Toni asked. "If she's set up shop in New York, then either she was the one who took out Lucian, or she'll know who did. Either way, she sounds like she'll do more than Victoria has."

"Fuck it, why not?" Melissa said as she stood up.

"Our best bet to find her will probably be at the party tomorrow night," Toni said. Raising her arms, she added, "but I think we need some street clothes first."

Essentia flared up from around Melissa, and a pile of clean new clothes appeared in her hands.

"What about the mansion?" Tabitha asked. "Maybe we should go back in the morning and see if anyone survived?"

"Agreed. I need to know too," Melissa said.

"I don't know," Toni said hesitantly, her stomach flip-flopping at the prospect.

"We'll be quick, just in and out, no one will even know we were there," Tabitha assured her.

Toni sighed. She wanted to know as well. Going back to the house felt like an unnecessary risk and one which might get them killed. But she did want to know if anyone else had survived.

She hated that they'd run out on their friends, leaving them to who knows what fate. But she'd seen these particular Nomads in action before. She'd seen how they operate and how they'd slaughtered her coven. There was no fighting them, not as they were. They needed someone who knew what they were doing.

Maybe this Amanda Magi might be the one to help them.

Mansion first though, and then they could Port over to New York.

"Okay, sure. In the morning, when the sun's up. We'll head back and take a look," Toni said.

Melissa threw her a set of clothes. "Awesome. Get dressed, let's find somewhere we can wait out the night and get some breakfast."

- Lyonesse, UK.

Trevelyan rose from his desk and walked over to the window. He gazed out through the glass and into the ocean beyond, looking across the gothic rooftops of the sunken city of Lyonesse. He felt troubled. Things were moving quicker than he had expected, but he also trusted his friend.

"So, the time is nearly upon us. The truth of the prophecy will soon be revealed." He saw his guest nodding to herself in the reflection of the window, agreeing with him. "This is a critical time, how will the Council react?"

"There'll be a period of adjustment. Some challenge it, but I'm sure you already knew that," she said.

"And young Amanda, how will she react?"

The woman smiled. "She'll cope."

Working Girl

Manhattan, New York

Amanda sat back in the reclining office chair, listening as Victoria addressed the group, talking about recent events. Sitting sideways to the boardroom table with her legs crossed, Amanda played with the frayed edge of one of the holes in her ripped jeans.

"The Magi Legion is still unhappy with the situation. They've met with me a few times, and they're still pushing for the Council to have you removed from the city," Victoria recounted.

Amanda sighed. "I'm not the new Queen of New York. I won't be declaring this Legacy territory and defending my borders against anyone who wants to live here," she protested.

Victoria nodded. She wore her usual tailored business suit and looked as pristine as ever and the total opposite of Amanda's scoop neck sweater, skinny jeans, and knee-high boots. She had her scarlet hair tied back in a ponytail today with just a couple of loose strands falling over her face.

"We know that, but the Legion is playing politics again. They see you, a Legacy Magus setting up in New York, as a threat."

"I presume you are trying to calm their fears?" Amanda asked.

"I believe this is all for show, but yes, I am talking to them," Victoria said.

"Do they want New York for themselves?" Trevelyan asked.

"They may make a play for the territory, but I think it's more likely they dislike a European coven claiming it, rather than wanting the city for themselves."

"Okay, thanks for the update," Amanda said.

"No problem. How about you, how are you coping with all this?"

"It's certainly different. I never wanted to be the custodian of the city, that wasn't my intention at all. But these new covens come here, and they want to see me. Then they ask me if they can stay, and I'm not going to say no, am I?"

"You know why they want to see you, don't you?" Trevelyan asked.

"Oh, to be sure. They think I killed Lucian. The rumours have spread despite our best efforts."

"It was going to come out eventually. Something like this is always going to spread."

"I know. I don't confirm or deny it. They can think whatever they want. But apart from the rumours, it's going well. We've turned The Jade Palace into our meeting spot when they arrive in the city. We're trying to keep track of everyone who moves here, but it's not easy. We're certain that there are covens in the city we have no idea about. Maybe even some Nomads."

"The Inquisition?" asked Trevelyan.

"Not yet, but I doubt they'll be far behind, and no trouble from the Nomads yet, either."

"Good," Victoria said.

"Do you think Nymira will try to find me?" Amanda asked. "She must have heard the rumours by now."

"She will certainly have heard the rumours. But will she come here? I'm not so sure," said Trevelyan.

"How come?"

"Well, there was our warning to them. But also, very few Magi want to upset someone like Yasmin. So if Nymira knows Yasmin was protecting you, and I think that's possible, then she might think twice about coming for you," Trevelyan said.

Amanda nodded, taking it all in. She hadn't thought about it like that. Nymira certainly seemed to be well connected, so it wasn't unlikely that she knew about Yasmin and her involvement in the events that happened six months ago.

Amanda's life had become a lot busier now that the news of New York's liberation had been made public. After Lucian's death, the Council had decided to keep things quiet for a while and to downplay Amanda's involvement in it all. But before long, the Haitian Nomads realised something was up, and a coven was sent to New York to ascertain the reason behind Lucian's disappearance. The Magi Council were here to meet them and made it clear that New York was off-limits. Amanda had been there for that confrontation in the abandoned Pit Club. The meeting had been tense and aggressive, but the Nomad coven didn't want to take on the might of the Magi Council, not with a couple of Arch Magi there to back the Council up.

The Nomads had retreated to Central America, and they hadn't been heard from since.

The Council had kept things quiet for a few more months. But before long, the rumours started to spread, and it became clear that they had to go public with the liberation of New York. That had been a few weeks ago, and since then, countless covens had been coming to New York, mainly to visit, but a few stayed, choosing to make New York their new home.

The last thing she needed was for Nymira and her covens to storm in here and make trouble.

Amanda turned and addressed the other two people in the room.

"Anything else to discuss?" Amanda asked. "What about the ball on the twenty-ninth?"

Kai, a Japanese Magus in a prim business suit, said nothing. She hardly ever spoke, but was a regular at the meetings Amanda had with the Council. Amanda wondered if her presence had anything to do with Black Lotus and her assassination attempt on Yoh.

Harry Fleming sat forward at her question and nodded

"The observation deck at One World Trade Center has been booked for the ball and everything is progressing well, we should have quite the night up there. I'll keep you informed, but everything is in hand and on schedule."

Harry, unlike the others in the room, was not a Magus. He was a normal Riven human and represented the Arcanum. The UK based organisation worked with the Magi Council and used their contacts around the globe to help keep the Magi hidden from the masses.

Any time the Magi world and the Riven world crossed paths, the Arcanum were there to make sure things ran smoothly. But when they didn't, they had their Black Ops division to clean things up.

This time though, they'd been brought in to organise the New York Ball.

"This is a little out of your usual area of influence, Harry," Trevelyan said to him.

"A little, sir. Kristal had other matters to attend to and sends her apologies. I came in her stead."

Trevelyan turned to Amanda. "Harry here, looks after some of the more tactical elements of the Arcanum."

"Um, sir…" Harry stammered.

"Don't worry; Amanda is no threat to you. I'll vouch for her."

"If you say so, sir," Harry replied.

"I… I didn't mean to cause…" Amanda said, feeling like she'd stumbled into a conversation that wasn't meant for her.

"Don't worry. Harry worries enough for all of us," Trevelyan said to Amanda with a wink. "Anyway, I think that's everything. I'm sure you have a busy day ahead of you. You know how to reach us if you need to. Otherwise, we'll see you at the ball."

Everyone stood up. Trevelyan walked to Amanda and shook her hand warmly.

"Lovely to see you again, my dear," he said before turning to the others. "Ready?"

They all nodded, said their goodbyes, and moments later the Magi Ported from the room, leaving Amanda alone.

These four Magi had become Amanda's primary point of contact for the Magi Council, and the only ones from that body that she'd really spoken to.

During the confrontation with Nymira's Nomads a few months back, she had seen several more Councillors and two Arch Magi, but she'd not spoken to any of them.

Trevelyan was her main point of contact. A British Magus who usually wore the kind of robes you might expect a modern wizard to wear, she always found him to be friendly and kind. Even when she'd first met him, he greeted her like an old friend, and she felt very much at ease around him.

Happy with how the meeting went, she walked from the room and through The Jade Palace. She had a few people she wanted to speak to. She'd arrived just prior to the meeting with the Council and hadn't had time to see her friends. Downstairs, she found Liz sitting in the Japanese rock garden going over a couple of things on a clipboard.

"Look at ye, all organised. Ye have a busy day ahead?"

Liz smiled up at Amanda as she joined her on the bench. She looked very business-like in a smart-looking suit, which suited her role as Stella's new assistant.

"Yeah, I have a few meetings today with some of the covens who've recently arrived. Just to make sure they're up to speed on what's what," she said.

"Well, I need to add to your list," Amanda said. "Victoria just told me we have a new coven arriving here today from L.A. Not sure when, but they could be here any moment, I suppose."

"Okay, thanks. Who are they?"

"They went by the name of The Coven of Angels."

"Okay, great," Liz said.

"Are you around later?" Amanda asked.

"No, sorry. I'm on a mission with the boys tonight," Liz said, referring to Orion and Xain. They'd been helping Amanda improve Liz's combat training, and nothing beat actual missions to really hone those skills.

"No bother. I get a night off from training then, excellent."

Liz smiled. "You can pay me back later. You could try hunting for Alicia some more," she suggested.

Amanda pressed her lips together and looked away, trying but failing to hide the pain that Liz's comment brought up.

"Aah, sorry. Still no luck, then, I take it?"

Amanda had looked everywhere for Alicia, even returning to the orphanage every week since Alicia's disappearance. Her friend had just fallen off the face of the Earth, and despite all of Amanda and Shaun's efforts to find her, they'd come up emptyhanded. Amanda had pretty much given up on trying to find her. If a new lead presented itself, she'd follow it up, but otherwise, she felt like she needed to focus on the here and now and not get too distracted by what amounted to a wild goose chase.

"We've looked everywhere for her," Amanda said. "I don't know if we'll ever find her."

"Never give up hope. She'll turn up someday. Stranger things have happened."

"Yeah, I know," Amanda sighed. "Thanks,"

Liz stood up. "No problem. I'll see you later. I really have to get on. Oh, by the way, Yoh's here today if you wanted that chat?"

"Thanks." Amanda smiled as she watched Liz disappear into the building. She barely recognised the young girl she'd taken as her apprentice two years ago. These days, Liz had much more confidence in herself and way more independence as well. Feeling proud of her apprentice, Amanda got up from the bench, banishing thoughts of Alicia from her mind and looked up at the windows that surrounded the garden on all four sides.

Windows to Yoh's private quarters.

She'd been meaning to see Yoh and try to rebuild some bridges with him for a while now. Things had been going so well when she'd first moved here. Images of the passionate one-night-stand she'd had with him still burnt strong in her mind. But everything had changed since Kimi Takahashi, the Black Lotus, had attacked and basically killed him, which led to Maya turning him into a Scion to save his life.

Going from a Mundane human to Vampire would be traumatic enough, but going from Magus to Scion, and potentially losing your Magic... Well, Amanda knew that she would feel utterly lost and confused if that ever happened to her.

Since that day, Yoh had seemed to withdraw into himself and they'd hardly talked in months. She'd meant to visit him, but he'd not really spent much time in New York, or at least, not in The Jade Palace or anywhere else she knew of. So, maybe now would be as good a time as any.

She left the garden and made her way upstairs and into Yoh's apartment. She soon found him in the library, sitting with Maya, who he'd grown increasingly close to since the attack.

She walked into the dimly lit room, her heels clicking on the polished hardwood floor announcing her presence.

"Hi, guys. Sorry, hope I didn't interrupt anything."

"No, no, come in," Maya replied and rose from the leather chair she'd been sitting in opposite Yoh. Maya always looked stunning to Amanda. They were the same height but Maya had lustrous, wavy, dark hair that framed her pale face and dark eyes and ruby lips. Today, she wore a long-sleeved black turtleneck dress and approached Amanda with her hands out, pulling her into a hug as they reached each other. "It's lovely to see you. It's been too long, I think," she said, looking back at Yoh as she said that last sentence.

Yoh had also stood to greet Amanda and walked over to her, offering his hand. "It has, it's been way too long."

Amanda took his hand and pulled him in for a hug. "Do you have time to have a chat? I'd love to catch up," she said as she pulled away and looked at them both.

"Of course, he does," Maya answered. "I'll leave you two alone." Maya smiled before walking away, showing the rear of the dress and its plunging backless cut.

"Thank you," Amanda said to the retreating Maya, who raised her hand in acknowledgement. She looked up at Yoh and smiled. "You okay?"

Yoh gave a half-smile and sat in his chair. Amanda followed suit, the leather creaking as the two chairs took their weight.

"I'm fine, thank you…" Yoh said, and paused.

"Look, I know…"

"I just wanted to…"

They'd both spoken at the same time, and both of them stopped as quickly as they'd started.

"You go," Amanda said.

"I know I've been distant, and I'm sorry, that must have been confusing after our… thing."

"The sex."

"Yes, that. I didn't mean to become so distant. I just... I'm different now. What Maya did to me, saving me, but changing me… I'm not the same man I was. I mean, I'm technically dead now, and my Magic is… different. It took a long time for me to get my head around it. I'd been a Magi for years. My Magic was part of me, as I'm sure you're learning yours is part of you. It helps define you, it shapes your life."

Amanda just listened, she could see his pain and how much the change had affected him, and she hated herself for it.

"What I'm saying is, I just needed time to figure things out. I needed to re-evaluate my life, and Maya-san has helped me do that."

"I understand. But I feel so guilty. They asked me, you know, Maya and Liz. They asked me what to do. I didn't know if I could use my Magic to bring ye back, I didn't know if that would be considered Necromancy or not and get me branded as a Nomad. It wouldn't have, as it turns out. I could have brought ye back, but instead, I gave Maya the go-ahead to change ye into a Scion. It's just... I'm so sorry. I didn't know. It was a crazy situation, and it should never have happened. Can ye forgive me?"

Yoh sat forward and took her hands in his as tears fell down her cheeks. She felt guilty and sad, but also foolish, both for not knowing the law and also for crying here in front of him.

"It's okay. I was dead. You weren't to know that you could use your Magic. All is well now. I'm here."

"I know, I just feel guilty and, God love ye, but I just can't imagine what ye've had to go through. I've tried to put myself in your shoes, and the thought of it kills me. What ye've been through is horrific, and yet ye've come through it. I'm not sure I could be that strong."

"I think you underestimate yourself, Amanda-san. You're stronger than you think you are."

Amanda smiled. "Thanks," she said, blushing slightly as she relished the feel of his large hands holding hers. She still didn't quite know what their relationship should be, going forward; she felt she needed some clarification. She needed to know what this was. "So, I hope ye don't mind me asking, but, where do we stand? I mean, after that night we had."

"Friends. We're friends, Amanda-san. I don't want anything more."

Amanda let out a breath and relaxed. She'd not been sure where things were for a while, but knowing where Yoh stood on this whole thing felt like a huge relief.

"Is that... okay?" Yoh asked.

"That's totally fine, so it is. Perfect, in fact. I feel like a weight has been lifted."

"Come here," he said as he stood up. She went to him then, and they hugged. Everything felt right with the world, and she enjoyed the feeling of love and friendship she got from his powerful arms wrapped around her body. They pulled apart and sat back down, Amanda dropping into her chair and enjoying its cool embrace.

"So, how about Raven?" Yoh asked. "I thought you and him were close."

"Yeah, so did I. I don't suppose I ever mentioned to you that I caught him in bed, well, in his room with another woman. I mean, we were never a thing, we've never done anything, but we seemed close, and I felt like he'd returned some of the signals, but when he opened that door half-naked and I could hear someone giggling behind him... I don't know. I felt a little led on by him. But maybe that was just me. It's not like we'd done anything. Maybe I just read the signs wrong."

"Aww, that's a shame. Sorry to hear it," Yoh said.

"Ah, it's no bother. No offence, but I don't seem to have much luck with men. I'm thinking I'll just give up on them for a while. It's not like I don't have enough other things happening anyway without a man to complicate matters."

"Sounds like a plan."

"Maybe… So, we're good, then?" she asked.

"Grand," he said, mimicking her Irish accent.

"Hah! Happy days," she replied, smiling. Suddenly, she felt the presence of someone's thoughts wanting to talk to her. Concentrating, she recognised Liz's Magic, so she opened the link.

~Amanda, we have that coven from L.A. here, would you like to pop down and say hello?~ Liz asked her telepathically.

~Yeah, sure. I'll be right down,~ she replied before closing the link. She looked at Yoh. "I'm needed downstairs, but I'll be sure to see ye soon, okay?"

"Of course, Amanda-san."

They rose from their seats, kissed cheeks, and parted ways, Amanda feeling a spring in her step after finally smoothing things over with Yoh. It had been a long time coming. In fact, she felt a little silly having put it off for so long. This should have been sorted a long time ago, but then, she knew that sometimes in life, these things never get sorted, so better late than never.

She walked through the building and came to a ground floor meeting room. It was much smaller one than the one upstairs, but big enough for meeting most of the small covens that came here. Inside, Liz sat at a table with three other young-looking women, although, with Magi, looks could be deceptive and they could, in theory, be of any age.

"Hi," Amanda said as she entered the room.

Liz stood, "Hey, so this is Melissa, Toni, and Tabitha. They're from L.A, and they're interested in possibly settling here."

Amanda greeted each of them, shaking their hands and saying hi. "So, what brings ye to New York?" she asked and watched as they all hesitated and glanced at one another. Amanda immediately had the feeling she'd put her foot in it, that she'd mentioned something raw and emotional for the three of them. She noticed that Toni had even started to well up, the first hints of tears glistening in her eyes.

"I'm sorry, did I say something…" Amanda asked.

"No, no, you didn't do anything wrong, it's just, the reason for us being here, it…" Melissa paused and took a breath, seeming unsure how to proceed.

"Our coven was attacked by Nomads," Tabitha said, picking up the thread. "We think… we're pretty sure we're the only survivors."

Toni sobbed while Melissa took a moment to herself, looking at the ceiling and dealing with her emotions. Tabitha pulled Toni in close to comfort her. Amanda noticed how comfortable they were with each other and guessed that Tabitha and Toni might be more than just friends.

"You're from the Coven of Angels, right? You must have had over ten members?"

"Seventeen, actually, not counting our affiliate covens," Tabitha answered.

"Jaysus, and they were all killed?" Amanda asked.

"We believe so."

"Any idea who the Nomads were?"

"We don't have any names, but for the past, maybe six or seven months, Arcadian covens in the Los Angeles area have been attacked again and again by what we think are the same three Nomads."

"Just three?"

"We saw one of them. They're powerful and they're using Magic that I don't recognise," Tabitha explained.

"You saw one? May I see?" Amanda asked.

"Sure," said Tabitha, who sent a mental image to Amanda. She felt the rush of Essentia and accepted the telepathic thought and could suddenly see the memory of the Nomad from the attack.

Amanda let the memory fade after a moment and brought her focus back to the room. "Thank you. Firstly, I'm sorry for your loss, and for what it's worth, you're very welcome in New York."

"Thank you."

Amanda sent a request for a Mental Link to Liz, who immediately allowed Amanda's thoughts to pass through her Aegis.

~What do you think?~ she sent to Liz.

~They're genuine. Victoria's been in touch and vouched for them in very strong terms. They're young, but they're loyal Arcadians,~ Liz sent back.

"Have you got a place to stay?" Amanda asked the trio of girls.

"No, we've only just arrived," Tabitha said.

"Then come stay with me. I can have some rooms made up for ye at my place. Can ye see to that, Liz?" Amanda asked. If Victoria was vouching for them, she felt sure she could trust them in her house for a few days.

"Of course," Liz said.

"Are you sure? We don't want to be any trouble," Tabitha said.

Melissa smiled. "Thank you. We appreciate it. We'd love to accept."

"Good, I'm happy to help. Any friend of Victoria's is a friend of mine." Amanda said.

Toni, still staying close to Tabitha, nodded and mouthed the words, "Thank you," through her tears.

Amanda nodded back and smiled. "I'll also have a think on the whole Nomad situation in L.A. Might be that we can do something. Leave it with me."

- The Vatican

Mary signed the document, authorising the order which would now be carried out. She looked over the open file next to her and the photos that spilt out of it. She recognised that face.

Amanda-Jane Page. Her actions and the actions of her coven had caused Mary's plans to become the next Witch Finder General to be put on hold while she rebuilt her reputation with the Conclave of Grand Inquisitors. As the only woman in that group of twelve, she had to prove herself above and beyond what the others had to. But she'd come back even stronger than before.

Amanda might have disappeared for two years, but as it turned out, that worked out quite well her. Now, she would start to take some well-earned revenge.

She looked over the order to send a squad of Crusader Knights into New York and smiled as she handed it to her secretary. This would be phase one.

Opening Salvo

Brooklyn, New York.

Jessie stood at the island in the kitchen, pulling out groceries from the box in front of her, ready to put them away in the cupboards behind her.

When Alex had first suggested the coven should move down to the city, Hayden, Roxy, and herself were all a little unsure. They'd lived in Upstate New York, on the edge of Lucian's territory for a long time. They'd always wanted to live in the city, but it had never been possible until now. But making that jump and moving down here had taken some confidence. She'd heard the reports that Lucian was dead, killed by an Arcadian and that the city would now be under the Council's protection. She'd also listened to the rumours that the King of New York had been killed by a Magus she'd never heard of before. A young lady named Amanda. They'd discussed it for a week or so before they started to hear of other covens moving into the city, which quickly convinced them to make the trip.

Looking back on that choice, now that they'd been here for a few days, she felt they'd made the right decision. They'd met Amanda on their arrival, along with Liz and a couple of others at The Jade Palace. She found them all very welcoming, and she wasn't sure she could believe the rumours that Amanda had killed Lucian. She seemed too ordinary. She wasn't sure what she'd expected, maybe some sort of hardass?

Well, maybe she'd killed him, or maybe not. Who knew? There was no official word, after all.

She loved their new house as well. It made for a very welcome change compared to the dump they'd lived in Upstate. A beautiful suburban house on a quiet road in Brooklyn was a significant change from the dusty, cramped old loft in the middle of some nowhere town.

She watched her coven mates in the main living space towards the front of the house. They were laughing over something. Jessie had missed the joke, but she didn't mind. She wanted to get this food put away.

When the Aegis over the house fell away, it took her a moment to realise what had happened. It felt like a tension in the air that suddenly grew and then snapped away to nothing. She frowned at the sensation, not sure what to make of it when a second later, the lights went out.

"What's going on?" Jessie called, while her friends made similar comments.

The window smashed as something sailed through it and clattered to the floor, trailing smoke.

"What the hell?" Hayden exclaimed.

"Shit," yelled Alex.

Jessie looked at it from the kitchen door. It was a curious metal canister that sat in the middle of the living room smoking wildly. Her friends did the same, and a moment later, with a loud bang, it exploded, filling the room with smoke. Jessie dropped to the floor just as the front door got kicked in and slammed open.

She could hear voices shouting and the sound of heavy boots running into the house.

"Go, go, go!" they shouted.

They came through the back door in the hallway next to the kitchen as well, their gear shifting on their bodies as they moved into the open-plan living room, their weapons at the ready.

From where Jessie crouched behind the island, she realised that the intruders couldn't see her. She was hidden. Her friends, however, were not.

"Get down, get down now. On your knees, hands on your heads. Do it NOW!" the men shouted.

Jessie gingerly moved to the edge of the island and readied herself to peek around the side into the room as the men shouted at her friends.

Were these policemen? A SWAT team, maybe? What the hell were they doing here? She and her friends may be Magi, but they'd done nothing to warrant this.

She could hear her friends, their voices shrill and wobbly. They were scared, and she couldn't blame them. It wasn't often that you had an assault rifle pointed at you.

Jessie slowly peered around the island and looked into the room beyond. Through the thinning smoke she saw her three friends on their knees with their hands on their heads, looking terrified.

She also laid eyes on a few of the men for the first time. Initially, she thought they might be a SWAT team. They were dressed in black tactical gear, carrying silenced machine guns, with balaclavas on their heads, and they worked as a unit. But a couple of things made her question her initial assumption. One of them had his back to her, and she could quite clearly see a large sword strapped to his back. She felt fairly certain that the police did not carry swords around with them.

But what she noticed next sent a chill racing up and down her spine and all of a sudden she knew who they were.

A small insignia on one of the shoulders of the men in the shape of a shield with a crucifix on it meant one thing and one thing only—these guys were the Inquisition.

"Keep still, don't move!" the men shouted. "You three, secure the rest of the house. Make sure there's no one else. Go!"

Jessie listened as several of the men left the room and ran upstairs, she could hear them quite clearly as they moved around above her.

Jessie cursed to herself; what could she do? She felt helpless and knew she'd be discovered in a matter of moments should just one of the men head towards the small kitchenette.

As it stood, her friends were beyond help, from her at least. She'd only recently become a Magus and hadn't progressed beyond the rank of Apprentice yet. Taking on however many Inquisitors, all of them heavily armed, would be suicide. She could surrender herself, she thought, and maybe she'd survive this. Maybe.

Hell, who was she kidding? This was the Inquisition. She felt reasonably confident that her friends would be dead in a matter of moments.

No. She needed to get out of here. She needed to find Amanda and warn her that the Inquisition was in town. Looking up, just across from her, the glass patio doors at the back of the house were invitingly close. The key rested there in the lock, waiting to be turned and the doors opened.

But she couldn't just walk up to the doors and unlock them. She'd be seen and likely killed.

Scared and frustrated, she looked around the edge of the Island again and saw her friends, helpless in the clutches of the Knight Inquisitors.

As she watched, another man, dressed similarly to the others, walked into the house.

"Report," the man said.

"Three Witches apprehended, sir. The rest of the house is being searched."

"Our Intel said there were four. Where's the other one?"

Jessie shivered. They were talking about her. She needed to get out of here.

As she watched, she suddenly noticed that Alex was looking in her direction. His face hadn't moved, but his eyes looked right at her. Suddenly, she felt a faint, gentle presence start to slowly press on her mind. It might have been there for a while, but the casting had been so subtly done that she just hadn't noticed it. It was Alex, he wanted to create a Mental Link with her, and he'd been careful to make the working as covert as possible to avoid detection. It had worked so far. But had she not seen him looking at her, she wasn't sure she would have noticed it.

Jessie opened her mind and allowed Alex to Link with her.

~Jess, you have to get out of here,~ Alex told her.

~I know, but how?~

~I'm going to create a diversion. The moment I do, get out through that door. Keep low and run like hell. Trust no one and find Amanda, they have to know about this.~

~But what about you?~ Jessie asked.

~Forget about us. Just get ready, okay?~

Jessie shifted her crouch to one she could move from quickly. ~Ready,~ she said.

She peeked around the corner once more, wanting to see her friends one last time. She saw the man she assumed to be the leader step forward, pull a gun, and put it to Roxy's head.

"Where's the other one?" the man asked.

"What other one?" Hayden replied, defiant.

Jessie felt a sense of pride that her friends were being so strong and standing up to these bullies, but she knew the Inquisition's reputation, and she knew what was probably about to happen.

"So, it's like that, is it?" the man asked. "Well, consider this your final warning."

She could see Alex had closed his eyes. He had started to psych himself up for creating a distraction; he knew what it would mean for him.

The man continued to speak, "I'm going to ask once more, and then I will start redecorating, understood?"

"Crystal," Hayden said, as Alex suddenly stood up and with a surge of Magical energy, sent out a shockwave of Kinetic force at the men.

It caused the Inquisitors to stagger backward, and in one case, fall over.

The shockwave blasted through the ground floor of the house in a heartbeat. It smashed most of the windows, including the glass in the patio doors that fell out into the garden. Shouts of shock and surprise sounded in the room from the men while gunshots rang out.

Jessie didn't look, she just ran for the patio doors as hard and as fast as she could. She slipped through them, cutting her arm on a shard of glass still in the doorframe, but she didn't stop.

More shouts and gunfire rang out as the door behind her was shot up in her wake.

They'd seen her.

In the garden, she bolted towards the nearby fence. Jumping from a garden chair to a table, she vaulted over the fence. Gunfire from suppressed weapons sounded behind her and peppered the fence as she disappeared over it.

Located in the heart of suburbia, their home had houses on either side of it and behind it, each with a similar backyard adjacent to theirs.

She heard shouts and movement behind her, back in their own garden. She sprinted for the next fence at the side of their neighbour's yard. She glanced back and saw one of the Crusader

Knights come into view, no doubt standing on the table that Jessie had used to vault the fence.

Jessie didn't think, she just let her Magic flow and do its thing. Following her instincts, she let her Magic show her the best route.

She adjusted her course and got some cover from the well-maintained bushes and trees in her neighbour's yard as bullets, fizzling with Magical energy zipped past her, hitting the trees and mud.

She jumped the next fence and landed in another garden. Jessie veered right as a dog started barking at her. She didn't hang around. Instead, she vaulted the next few fences and hedgerows before heading to the street.

She had no time to think. With a glance down the road, she ran to cross diagonally, following her instincts.

She had a sudden urge to turn left. She did, just as a car turned onto the road behind her, its wheels screeching as it fought for grip. She caught a quick glance at it as she ran, seeing someone lean out of a window and fire their weapon at her. She ducked behind a car sitting in a driveway. She could hear the *pfft pfft* of the shots before they slammed into the sides of the vehicle with metallic bangs.

She didn't stop for long though. Running down the side of a house she started leaping fences again.

Jessie kept to her strange route through the streets of Brooklyn for as long as she could but didn't see any more of the Inquisition.

As soon as she could, she hailed a taxi and took it into Manhattan, heading for The Jade Palace and hopefully some protection.

***

Amanda appeared beneath a tree in Brooklyn just opposite the house Jessie had fled a couple of hours before. Amanda had been at her townhouse when the call from Stella at The Jade Palace had come in, saying that one of the new Magi in the city had come to The Palace in a state of shock and that Amanda should come down to see her.

Jessie had been upset, but not as distraught as Amanda had feared, given the situation. She'd sat and listened and comforted Jessie, taking in everything the young Magi said. Amanda had remained calm and had done her best to be supportive and yet measured in her responses. Afterwards, Amanda made sure Jessie was taken care of, before undertaking her own investigation. Her first order of business—checking out the house where the coven had been attacked.

Looking at it now, on the quiet street with no one about, it seemed fairly innocuous, apart from a few blown-out windows on the ground floor.

Using the local Essentia, she Ported over the road and appeared on their front porch. Examining the front door, she could clearly see it had been forced open and would not close anymore.

Pushing the ruined door open, she walked inside and into the open-plan living area. Slightly off to her right, close to the front of the house were several pools of blood, no doubt where the rest of Jessie's coven had been killed.

Ahead, at the rear of the house was the kitchen and the shattered patio doors just next to it. The whole room looked a mess with broken glass and furniture scattered about, while bullet holes perforated the walls everywhere she looked.

The bodies of Jessie's coven were missing, but Amanda knew the Inquisition well enough by now to know that they usually disposed of the bodies themselves, usually through cremation. The cleansing fire purged the Magus of the demon within, or so they believed.

Concentrating, she pulled on the threads of Essentia once more and cast her mind back through time to watch the attack take place.

Partway through, she paused the action and sent her senses around the building to count up the number of men who had been here. She wanted to know the size of the problem.

She counted nineteen men, in total, both in and outside of the house. As she watched the rest of the confrontation play out, she felt fairly sure that none of the men in this group were Magi. They all seemed to be Initiated but they carried Magical items that would allow them to take on Magi such as Jessie and her coven mates, especially when they were caught by surprise. As they left with the dead bodies of Jessie's coven, an Aegis sprang up around their van, blocking it from Amanda's Scrying Magic so she couldn't follow it back to their base.

Amanda scowled. She'd come to hate the Inquisition early on when one of their number, someone she later learned was called Mary Damask, had killed Liz's sister, Francesca and Fran's boyfriend, Stephen. They had hunted down that Magical Gold Book with a single-minded determination that had been scary to see. She'd also since learned that a different Inquisitor had interviewed and tortured some of her old friends from New York to find out more about her.

She had foiled Mary Damask's plans for the Gold Book that day, and although Mary had fled the scene, she felt sure that she might one day try to exact her revenge. Given that her presence here in New York had been made common knowledge and with Lucian's death making New York a place of interest, she felt reasonably confident that it was only a matter of time before Mary showed up.

Was this raid the start of it?

Finishing her sweep of the house and satisfied she'd seen everything, Amanda walked out into the back garden through the patio door.

As she stepped outside and ruminated on her previous run-ins with the Inquisitors, she thought back to her beginnings and the attack in the alleyway. She'd never been back there, she realised, and the urge to see it again grew inside her.

Amanda Ported from Brooklyn to a familiar alleyway in one of Manhattan's red-light districts. In the darkness of the alley, flashes of memory came back. She'd been walking past here on her way to the shop at the end of the road. She'd been grabbed and thrown down the length of the alley. Rolling through dirt and puddles, she'd ended up covered in scratches. She remembered the terror she'd felt like a visceral thing, as the Demon had stood over her, readying itself to kill her.

Some Magi are introduced to Magic and monsters gradually and with time to take it in. Amanda had been thrown into that world without warning.

Walking down the alleyway, she arrived at the scene of the attack and of her Epiphany when she first used Magic.

The alley widened, and Amanda came to a stop next to where Stuart, her protector while she worked the streets, had died. Punched by the twelve-foot-tall, hideously powerful Scion, he'd been pulverised and buried beneath crumbling brick. Amanda looked at the rebuilt section of wall and ground where Stuart had died, its colouring different from the brickwork and concrete surrounding it. She wished she could have saved him; Stuart had been a good man and didn't deserve to die in such a horrible way.

She turned and looked at the burn mark on the opposite wall where she'd blasted Horlack with an outpouring of raw Magical energy, and remembered the intense gut-wrenching terror she'd felt that night.

Seeing that electrical energy shoot from her arms had been both a miracle and, at the time, scary as all hell. But she'd destroyed Horlack, vaporising him into nothing.

"You alright there, little lady?" a fragile voice asked from behind her.

She turned and looked at the bearded face of a homeless man sitting amongst the rubbish piled up between two dumpsters. He'd made a little den for himself and peered out from it, looking curiously at Amanda, no doubt wondering what a young girl like her might be doing wandering an alleyway at night. "Hmmm?" she answered him.

"Are you okay? You look lost," he said.

She smiled. "No, I'm not lost. I'm just... remembering a few things."

"Well, creepy alleyways are no place for pretty girls like yourself."

She could see he had no connection to Essentia. He was a typical Riven mortal and no real threat to her. "Thank you," she said and walked over to him.

He looked scared as she approached as if he expected her to attack him or something. Instead, she scanned his mind telepathically and quickly knew that he was just down on his luck. He wasn't a threat to anyone and just needed a helping hand to turn his life around.

Working a bit of Magic in her jacket pocket, she conjured a suitably large roll of cash into her hand. "Peter, is it?" she said.

"Uh, yeah, how did you know?"

"I'm your guardian angel, and I'm here to help you."

"Yeah, right."

Amanda pulled out the roll of cash and offered it to him.

"This is a joke, right? This is a joke. I can't take that." he stammered.

"It's yours. Here, take it."

Gingerly, Peter reached out and offered his hand, into which Amanda dropped the roll of money. "What's the catch?" he asked, staring at the cash.

"Just promise me you'll go to the bank, deposit the money and start to get yourself sorted," she said.

"Oh, I promise. I will."

"You'd better. I'll check on you tomorrow, and if you've started to sort yourself out, I'll double it with another deposit into your account," she said, smiling. "Deal?"

"Deal!"

She smiled at him once more, and in full view, Ported away with an extra flash of light for the man's benefit, leaving him aghast.

Amanda appeared in the basement garage of her brownstone in Greenwich Village with a soft pop of air.

She really did hope that Peter sorted himself out.

But there were other more pressing matters for her to deal with. First, she needed to speak with Shaun.

She approached a frosted glass door to one side of her basement, passing her custom Fireblade Motorbike and a couple of cars they kept down here. The room beyond these modern glass doors had been created by Amanda only a few months ago to Shaun's specifications. She stepped inside to the hum of computers and servers working away in this pristine space, the door swinging silently shut behind her.

To her left, several cabinets held more computer power than most spy organisations had, while to her right, the wall had been covered in banks of monitors, below which sat several workstations where Vanessa sat in her large, comfortable-looking leather office chair.

At the back of the room, opposite Amanda, Shaun sat facing her behind his desk, engrossed in something on his trio of screens. She couldn't see his face, only the top of his head, distinguished by the ridge of bone that ran over the top of it.

"Hi, Mandy, how're things?" Vanessa asked. Both Shaun and Vanessa had expressed stipulations about joining her coven. The main one for Vanessa had been to deal with a criminal gang that wanted her dead because of some hacking she'd done before she'd ever met Shaun. Amanda had managed to call off the group, meaning Vanessa could walk the streets safely once more.

"Hiya, I'm grand, thanks. Although things out there are becoming a little troubling," she said, waving her hand absently towards the street.

"What's up now?"

"The Inquisition is in town and they're not playing nice." She noticed Shaun's head pop up from behind his monitors. He looked like the classic Nosferatu Vampire with his white skin, sharp teeth, and talons. She'd procured him a Magical item though, that when activated would hide his appearance, but he wasn't using it right now.

"The Inquisition?" he asked.

"That's right."

"Well, shit, that didn't take them long."

"No, it didn't, but I suspect it might be personal," Amanda confessed.

"Really?" Shaun asked, his curiosity piqued. "And what makes you say that?"

"I fought… well, *we* fought them a couple of years back, killed a couple of their men, and stopped them from getting their hands on an artifact."

"That would do it. Who did you piss off?"

"A woman by the name of Mary Damask apparently, she's the only…"

"…the only female member of the Conclave of Grand Inquisitors," Shaun finished for her, "Yeah, I know who she is. Her reputation is well known. She's out to prove herself and to prove her dedication to their cause. Rose through the ranks very quickly and some tip her to be the next Witch Finder General. Certainly, her ambition alone could get her there."

"Feckin' excellent," Amanda said. "I always get the bat-shit crazy ones."

"So, what's happened?"

Amanda related the story of Jessie's encounter with the Crusaders and of her subsequent visit to the house. "So, can you look into it? Try and find them?"

"Won't be easy. The Inquisitors are good at this. It might be that they find you first."

"Then, I'll be ready," Amanda said. "I wouldn't want to disappoint them."

- Nowhere

Alicia sat naked, leaning up against the vertical steel girder she'd been left bound to, in what looked like a warehouse. How did she get here? Her memory was all fuzzy and she had trouble making sense of anything.

There had been a voice in her head. The voice of the thing that was inside her. The spirit. But it was gone now. Where had it gone?

Looking up, she saw a figure in black stood nearby. How long had she been there? The figure approached her and smiled, but the expression was cruel.

"Who... Who are you?" Alicia asked.

"Hello, Alicia," the woman in black replied.

"You know my name?"

"I know a lot about you."

Alicia swallowed in fear. She did not like this woman.

Is the grass greener?

Greenwich Village, Manhattan

Amanda sat up in bed with a start, breathing hard. Around her, the room remained empty and quiet, with only a thin strip of light from the gap in the curtains spilling into the room from the ever-present lights of the city that never slept.

She sat up properly and ran her hands through her hair, massaging her scalp as she did so. She'd had a bad dream, although she couldn't remember any of it now.

The room sat in relative darkness apart from the meagre light from the window. She loved her house and her bedroom. She'd decorated it in a somewhat haphazard way with various bits and bobs from her travels. She was never the neatest person in the world and her room always looked a little unkempt. Clothes hung off the backs of chairs and in a couple of piles on the floor. Makeup and trinkets were scattered over several surfaces, the wardrobe door sat half-open. Yep, she needed to tidy up.

She yawned and stretched, and came to the conclusion that she needed a drink. Her mouth was dry. For a moment, she considered just conjuring one in her hand, but then thought better of it. She could do with the walk to stretch her legs, so she pulled the covers off and swung them over the side of the bed. She wore a large baggy t-shirt, a pair of fluffy socks and had a minor fright on seeing the state of her hair in the mirror before she shuffled to the door.

She left her room behind and walked along the corridor, passing the rooms of her coven mates and house guests as she went.

As she neared the stairs, she heard noises coming from one of the rooms. Someone gasped. She paused to listen for a moment to make sure all was okay, thinking someone might have hurt themselves.

The room was Toni and Tabitha's, and she suddenly realised the sound was not of pain, but of pleasure. She could hear one of the girls moaning in delight. Amanda's eyebrows rose a good inch as she suddenly understood what she was listening to. They were having sex. Amanda felt a little flustered and quickly looked around, feeling embarrassed at having heard them and hoping no one had seen her.

The corridor remained dark and quiet, however, and she stood here alone. Biting her lip, she went to continue walking, only to hear more moans and heavy breathing, this time from both girls, and it made her pause mid-step.

She couldn't help it. She felt intensely curious and stepped closer to their door to listen.

The sounds from the room painted a picture in her mind and almost unconsciously, she placed herself within that mental image. She felt incredibly horny and suddenly all thoughts of going to get a glass of water vanished from her mind. Instead, she padded quickly back to her room and lost herself in those fantasies.

***

The following morning, Amanda finished her breakfast and ambled back up the stairs of her house towards her room. She didn't have many plans for the day, as far as she knew no new Magi were coming to the city today, and Stella had the issue with Jessie under control. Only the related issue of the Inquisition needed to be dealt with, but Amanda had nothing to go on for the time being. Shaun had started to look into it, so she hoped he would turn something up in the next few days before there were any more deaths.

In the meantime, Amanda had to play the waiting game.

Instead, the sum total of her plans was meeting with Maria to catch up. They'd been meeting for drinks every few weeks for the past few months. Amanda always enjoyed seeing her friend. She'd grown close to Maria and really enjoyed her company.

She knew that Maria wanted more than just friendship, though. She'd not made a secret of it and had made several advances over the last couple of years. Amanda had grown used to these playful touches or comments though, and just laughed them off, not really taking them too seriously. Maria continued to flirt with her, but it was always on a playful level, more friendly than anything else.

In recent months, she'd found out that Maria practised a kind of free-love lifestyle, keeping multiple partners of all genders and persuasions. She just wanted to squeeze every last drop of juicy fun and pleasure from the orange of life, and for her, being monogamous just wasn't in her nature.

If Amanda ever did choose to be with Maria, she knew she would be one of several, like the rest of Maria's lovers.

Amanda had never been with a woman. She'd played with the idea in her head and remembered Georgina had experimented with it, but Amanda had always refused. She found it hard to admit to herself why she'd resisted the temptation exactly, but did wonder if it had anything to do with her Catholic upbringing and the idea of a same-sex relationship being a sin.

She'd never been very religious though, and in recent years, especially after becoming a Magus, considered herself to be agnostic at best. During that time, her view of things like being gay had softened. She'd always found both men and women to be attractive, but it was only recently that she'd allowed herself to begin to explore those thoughts and ideas.

Having Toni and Tabitha in the house and seeing their very loving relationship, and then hearing them last night had certainly been something of an eye-opener and had served to further break down that taboo in her mind.

The men in her life had been something of a let-down, she supposed. Was this a sign? Did she need to start looking elsewhere? Was the grass greener on the other side? She didn't know and wasn't totally sure whether she wanted to find out or not.

As she continued up the stairs, Toni suddenly appeared at the top and started down. Amanda saw her and immediately blushed. A fine sheen of sweat broke out on her brow, as the embarrassment of what she'd inadvertently heard last night washed over her.

Amanda took a breath and a moment to calm herself before looking back up and smiling at Toni as she approached.

"Hiya," Amanda said, feeling underdressed in her bathrobe compared to Toni's black dress.

"Hi, how are you?"

"I'm grand, thanks. What are ye up to today?" she asked, silently cursing herself for asking a question which would prolong the conversation and allow Toni to see her discomfort.

"Well, we're going to have another look at a few apartments we saw yesterday. We just need to figure out which one we like."

"Oh, wow, that's grand."

"We've seen some nice ones. That is to say, we really do appreciate what you've done for us. Letting us stay here has really helped, and I know that Tabby and Mel feel the same."

"It's no bother, it's been a pleasure to have you," Amanda said.

"I don't want you to think we're not grateful, is all," Toni said, sounding a little flustered herself.

"Don't worry, I wouldn't think that," Amanda smiled.

"Good, thanks."

Amanda smiled. "Good luck, then."

They parted ways, and Amanda continued up the stairs, quickly entering her room and sitting on her bed. She cringed. Why had she listened to them last night? It was such a pervy thing to do. She sighed and flopped over, burying her head in her pillow, her red hair spilling over the white sheets.

"Aaaaaaagh," she shouted into the bedsheets, her cry muffled to nothing. Why did love and relationships and stuff have to be so frustrating? She felt more than a little confused by it all. Did she like men? Did she like women? Maybe it was both, like Maria? Hell, it wasn't like she didn't have enough to deal with, without her emotions clouding her judgement.

She sat up and looked in the mirror opposite her that was inlaid into the door of the wardrobe. Sitting slouched on the edge of the bed, her white bathrobe falling off one shoulder, her deep red hair just one big mess falling over her face, she thought she really did look like a feckin' witch today.

Why would anyone want to date this? she thought as she eyed her reflection.

She fell back onto the bed again and sighed. She could afford to waste some time. She wasn't due to meet Maria for a few hours yet. She also wanted to shoot into town for a quick follow-up on the homeless man, Peter, and see if he'd done as she asked.

After a few moments, she sat back up and thought better of just lying there doing nothing and bemoaning her love life. She'd feel better after a shower. Everything looked better after a shower. She could stand under it for a while and let it hammer away on the back of her neck, massaging her shoulders. Maybe she'd lose some of the tension she'd already built up this morning.

***

Her brief trip into the city to find Peter proved fruitful and served to lighten her mood. She found him sitting on a bench at the edge of one of the city's parks. Today, he was dressed sharply and his beard and hair had been trimmed. A quick read of his mind from a distance revealed that he'd done as she'd asked and opened a bank account.

Amanda sat down next to him. "How are ye, Peter?"

The man jumped at her question, surprised by her sudden appearance. "Oh my God, you scared me to death."

"Sorry," she said. "So, you opened the bank account. Well done."

"I did, yes, thank you. Thank you so much. I can't tell you how much it means to me."

"My pleasure. Now, I made you promise," she said as she worked a little Magical effect. "If you check your inside jacket pocket, you will find a little something for you."

Peter looked away from her and dug about in his pockets. As he did so, Amanda Ported away, so that when he looked back a second later with the huge stack of cash in his hand, she had disappeared into thin air again.

She watched him from afar as he looked around, trying to spot her and failing, before he returned his attention to the money and quickly hid it.

She smiled to herself, feeling good about this little act of kindness. She wouldn't follow up on him again. He was on his own now, and she wished him all the best.

***

Amanda met Maria in London, England. Together they walked along Oxford Street, picking up a few bargains before they headed over to Fortnum & Mason's restaurant on Jermyn Street. They sat on a red leather circular couch that surrounded a round table and enjoyed a delectable steak dinner with a salmon and soda bread starter.

They talked about the recent events in New York and the Inquisition's latest attack. Maria agreed that Amanda needed to find out where they were, so she could deal with them as soon as possible.

Talk soon came round to her new lodgers Tabitha, Toni, and Melissa. Amanda recounted the tale of the attack they'd suffered at the hands of the Nomads using Magic that they hadn't seen before.

"There's plenty of Magic that isn't used regularly," Maria said. "Necromancy for instance, and Astral Magic. Maybe that's what they saw?"

"Maybe. Tabitha said that the Nomad disappeared using it and then came back moments later."

"Disappeared? Using Magic they hadn't seen before?" Maria looked off into the middle distance, her eyes unfocused, and concern pinching her eyebrows together as she considered this.

"Why, what are you thinking?"

"Only of the old Nomad legend of the Magnus Transitus. The great crossing."

"I've heard of that," Amanda said. "Isn't that when they pass into the Abyss?"

"I'm no scholar on the subject, but as far as I know, apart from a few rumours, no one has ever managed it before."

"Until now, perhaps?"

Maria shrugged. "Maybe. You said you can get in touch with Trevelyan anytime these days? Maybe ask him? The Council is probably your best bet for that kind of information."

Amanda nodded and looked at her glass of wine. Could it be that this Nomad or this trio of Nomads had discovered how to pass into the Abyss? It seemed unlikely. But then, Magic had seemed unlikely to her a few years ago, so maybe it wasn't so far-fetched after all.

She made a mental note to send a message to Trevelyan to see if he knew anything.

"So, these girls are staying with you now, then?"

"Yeah, they're lovely. I do like them. I feel sorry for what they've been through, but Toni and Tabitha have each other, they're all good friends, and have a good craic at life from what I can see."

"Toni and Tabitha are lovers, then, I take it?"

Amanda blushed, suddenly thinking back to last night again. "Um, yeah. They are."

Maria raised her eyebrows at Amanda. "You're holding something back, I can tell. What is it?"

"Nothing. I'm not holding anything back."

"Amanda-Jane Page, I know you well enough to know when you're lying to me."

Amanda sighed.

Maria raised her eyebrows expectantly.

"Alright, fine. I walked past their room last night and heard them, you know, at it," she said, feeling a little self-conscious telling Maria about it, but she knew she could trust her.

"Hah!" Maria laughed. "Is that all? So what? It's only sex, Mandy."

Amanda sat back, surprised by Maria's reaction, but also relieved. "Heh, yeah, you're right," she said, and all of a sudden she had a totally different perspective on it. It had turned on a dime, and just like that, Amanda wondered what she'd been worried about.

Maria placed her hand on Amanda's where she rested it on the back of the sofa. "Are you okay? You seem a little uptight."

"I'm… I'm fine. I just have a lot on my mind right now." Wasn't that the truth, she thought. There always seemed to be someone wanting to kill her these days. The feeling of responsibility she felt for the Magi in New York also weighed heavily on her shoulders. And with the Inquisition here, targeting Arcadians in what she thought must be a way of getting to her somehow, that weight had grown much heavier. Sitting with Maria, though and talking with her, made her feel so much better. She felt more at ease than she had done for a few days now.

"Well, if you need to share, you know where I am."

"I do and thank you. I think I needed my bubble burst." She laughed. She'd been so wrapped up in things, that she couldn't see the woods for the trees. She'd been too close to it. She'd been terrified that hearing Toni and Tabitha meant something profound. But all it meant was that she was only human after all, and it didn't really matter who she liked, male or female. Feelings didn't care about such things. You either had feelings for someone, or you didn't. Maria had given her that perspective in a few quick words and made her realise what she actually knew all along—to just follow her heart.

Amanda smiled at Maria and left her hand under hers, enjoying her touch and her smile. Maria looked gorgeous, like she did every day she supposed, but for some reason, she noticed it today. If she were honest with herself, she did find Maria attractive. Perhaps, just maybe, she quite fancied her. She looked at her friend, eyed her up and down surreptitiously, looking at her with different eyes.

Maria wore a fitted skirt with a slit up the side, which showed off her legs quite nicely, which Amanda had caught herself admiring a few times this dinner. Those legs, clad in thin hosiery, looked particularly inviting today and she caught herself wondering what it might be like to run her hand up the inside of Maria's thigh, feeling her warmth, her heat.

Amanda flushed and felt kind of weightless, as she thought about touching Maria. She couldn't help but admire her and let her gaze lock with Maria's over her wine glass. She found herself enjoying looking into those deep blue eyes and feeling like she might drown in them.

Maria's fingers caressed the back of Amanda's hand, gently tracing patterns on her skin. The softness of her touch, her gentle manner caused Amanda to feel very relaxed and to get a pleasant tingly sensation in her head and neck.

Amanda couldn't help but caress Maria's hand in return before interlocking their fingers.

Had Maria caught her looking at her? Maybe. But she realised she didn't really care if Maria had noticed. Amanda went back to her drink, feeling a little more at ease with things as the waiter approached, asking if they would like anything else. Their hands separated and they finished their drinks.

Had their relationship just changed?

To my Grace, Mary Damask,

God has blessed us once more and seen fit to gift us with precious knowledge. It seems that the Witches in New York use a meeting place called The Jade Palace. Amanda-Jane Page greets new arrivals there upon entry into New York. We seek to know your orders regarding this nest of Satan worshipers.

God bless you,

Marco Di Antonio, Knight Inquisitor

Jade Crusade

The Jade Palace, Manhattan, New York

"So, they've moved out?" Liz asked.

Liz eyed Amanda, who sat opposite her on an identical barstool as the one she sat upon. Looking as scruffy as ever, thought Liz. And yet, she made it look good. Ripped Jeans, sneakers with laces undone, and a fitted top that looked like it might be a size too small stretched over her bosom, all fairly typical for Mandy, and no matter what Liz suggested as a good wardrobe choice, she always went back to these kinds of clothes.

Over the past couple of years, Liz had worked it out but wondered if Amanda had ever realised it herself. Amanda had told her a few times of the shapeless frumpy clothes she'd been forced to wear in the orphanage. The starched shirts, the drab sweaters, and the hideous ankle-length skirts that barely revealed the flat shoes that looked like they might have been from the 1940s.

Her mentor's disdain for those clothes was clear and as soon as she'd been able to wear something different, she had. In fact, she'd gone to the other extreme.

Where the nuns had forced her to wear shapeless things, now everything was fitted, showing off her shape. The nuns liked long, frumpy skirts, so Amanda wore jeans, and as an extra "feck you" she usually liked them to be ripped or distressed. Where the nuns made Amanda wear what she often called "orthopaedic shoes" with neatly tied laces, she preferred trainers and didn't worry about the laces.

If Amanda did wear skirts, they were also something the nuns of her childhood would have seen as scandalous. They were nearly always short, well above the knee, and paired with spiked heels that looked like torture instruments to Liz.

To some extent, Liz envied Amanda's carefree attitude. The way she seemed to breeze through life and never let things get to her was something of an inspiration to Liz. So when Lucian's men had taken her to Columbia earlier this year, Liz had thought about Amanda and tried to imagine how she'd react. She'd been determined to be strong. She wouldn't allow them to get to her the way the Nomads and Inquisitors had in London and refused to let them win.

She'd been scared, terrified even, but she knew that Amanda would come. Liz felt that she'd come out of that ordeal a good deal stronger, and from that point on, she knuckled down with her Magical and martial arts studies. She wanted to be strong. She wanted to be able to defend herself and not to have to rely on the strength of others. It had almost been embarrassing being the damsel in distress in Columbia. Even in the fight at the Pit Club with Lucian's gang, she'd only barely escaped with her life.

Over the past six months she'd worked hard, training with Amanda, Xain, and Orion. She'd even progressed enough in her Magic to be officially classed as an Adept. Amanda seemed impressed with her progress and agreed that Liz's experiments with Magic with her sister had probably helped and maybe even had kick-started her learning.

"To be sure. The other day, in fact," Amanda answered.

"Jesus, I've been so busy that I didn't even notice they'd gone. Do you know where?"

"To be sure. They picked out an apartment close to the Dark Side Night Club. A nice place from what I saw."

"You saw it?" Liz asked.

"I did. I helped them settle in. I wanted to be sure they were okay, so I did."

"So, they're not heading back to Los Angeles?"

"They'd rather not, I think. They seem awfully spooked by the attack. We talked about it again and they asked if I would go to L.A. and look into it for them."

"And will you?" Liz asked.

"Yeah, I think so. I'm curious about what happened," Amanda mused.

"And you know what that did to the cat."

Amanda smiled. "Hasn't stopped me before."

Liz raised her eyebrows briefly. "So, what are you waiting for?"

"They contacted Victoria, on my suggestion so they did, and they're waiting to see if the Liberty's Children will do anything."

"Well, I'm sure *you'll* do a good job in L.A. for them," Liz answered.

"Heh. Yeah, I doubt they'll do anything, either. You never know, though."

"Will Toni and Tabitha go with you to L.A.?"

"I'd prefer it if they did. I've never been there and wouldn't have any idea where to start. I could use their guidance."

"Hmmm," Liz mused. Her mentor's good nature was once again getting her into possible trouble. In Liz's opinion, as much as she admired Amanda's willingness to help others, sometimes she needed to learn to say no. Her escapade in Ireland six months ago meant that she'd been out of the country when Liz had been kidnapped by Lucian's men. Would things have been different if Amanda had been home when that happened?

Probably not. What difference do a few blocks, as opposed to a few thousand miles, make to a Magus?

So, it seemed that Toni, Tabitha, and their celebrity friend, Melissa, had left them and headed out into the world once more. She wished them well. They had been friendly and the perfect guests while they'd been there.

"What?" Amanda asked, no doubt seeing the consternation on Liz's face.

"Oh, nothing, it's just you're too kind sometimes, Mandy. You need to learn when to say no."

Amanda sighed. "Maybe. But these girls have been let down by the system. If Victoria is mired in politics again and can't do anything, then it falls to us to see that justice is done."

"That's admirable, but it sounds like a dangerous situation out there," Liz replied.

"What's dangerous?" said Yoh as he and Stella walked into the bar.

"Amanda is thinking of heading to L.A. to look into the Nomads who attacked Toni and Tabitha's coven."

"Bold move, Amanda-san. You want to kick the hornets' nest again?"

"I'll just be having a look round, that's all. I'm not heading over there looking for a fight. I want to help, sure, but I'm not planning on hunting the Nomads down. At least, not right away."

"Your crusade is an honourable one, Amanda-san."

"What do you think, Stella?" Liz asked.

Stella looked up from tidying a few things behind the bar. Liz had taken a liking to Stella since working for her. She'd thought Stella might be something of a jobsworth at first, but she'd mistook pride in her work for being a bitch, and felt bad that she'd misjudged her. She might be a Magus, but she seemed content to stay out of the politics and manoeuvring that had been going on in this city recently, preferring to stay focused on her job. Liz could sympathise. She could see Amanda getting drawn into it more and more each day. Hob-knobbing with the Council and now, potentially interfering with an issue that should really be handled by the American Arcadians did not bode well for her mentor.

"I honestly couldn't say. I don't think I know enough about the situation, really."

"Some Magi from L.A. want Amanda to head over there and look into the Nomads who attacked and killed their coven mates," Liz explained.

"Well, I'm not sure I could do it, but sure, if you can help?"

"Looks like I'm outnumbered," Liz said.

"Not at all, I value your opinion," Amanda reassured her. "I'll bear it in mind."

Screeching tyres from several cars sounded outside in the darkened street as headlights from at least three black 4x4s lit up the inside of The Jade Palace.

Liz had barely registered the noise before Amanda shouted, "Duck!" She body-slammed Liz off the stool and onto the floor as high calibre Essentia-charged bullets slammed into the building. Three huge machine guns, mounted inside the front passenger seat space in each car, fired with a deafening sound, releasing streams of metallic death into the restaurant.

Liz landed on her back with Amanda on top of her, the wind knocked out of her lungs as furniture and fittings exploded around them.

"Aaagh," Liz moaned in pain.

"Feck me," Amanda said on top of her. "It'll be grenades next, and then they'll come in. Get your Aegis up and get ready."

"Right," Liz said through gritted teeth as Amanda rolled off her. Liz could feel Amanda's Magic grow. The local Essentia flooded into her mentor as she fuelled her Aegis and prepared to fight.

Liz called on the same energy, strengthened her Aegis as the machine guns emptied their magazines into the building. To her right, Amanda sat up in a crouch, the last few bullets ricocheting off her shield with a whine and slamming into the walls.

Liz looked to her left, past the end of the bar where she'd been sitting and saw Yoh and Stella also on the floor. Stella was also powering up her Magic and getting ready for the fight which was sure to come.

Yoh looked furious, but continued to hug the floor as he waited for the guns to stop firing.

Just as it ended, several canisters and tennis ball-sized objects sailed into the room through the smashed windows.

"Cover your eyes," Amanda called to them and protected her own as the grenades exploded. Two or three burst open, filling the room with thick choking smoke. A couple more were flashbangs, exploding with a powerful blinding phosphorous flash meant to blind and disorientate the enemy. The rest just blew up, sending deadly shrapnel through the room.

Liz stayed down for these few seconds of chaos, her Shields doing their job and protecting her from harm.

"They're coming," Amanda warned, and disappeared into the hazy smoke. Liz caught some quick shadowy movement from Amanda as she took out the first enemy she happened across.

Liz still didn't know who was attacking them, not for sure, anyway. She suspected it might be the Inquisition. Maybe one of the Magi the Inquisitors had tortured and killed recently had divulged the location of the Magi meeting place at The Jade Palace during their interrogation.

Liz got up and backed away from the entrance, feeling shocked and more than a little disorientated. She'd been on a couple of missions with Xain and Orion, but this was another level entirely.

The smoke grenades had done their job well, and Liz couldn't see more than a few feet in any direction, but she could quite clearly hear the sounds of fighting and the occasional burst of gunfire from within the mist.

She flinched with each gunshot, afraid she would be hit by stray bullets at any moment. She edged around the back of the room, not really sure where she was going until she saw the shadows in the haze of two soldiers closing in on her. She turned to look the other way, the direction she'd come from, but her escape route had been blocked by a third figure.

She'd have to fight her way out of this one. She quickly pulled off her business jacket and reached down to the side of her pencil skirt. Pulling on either side of the seam, she tore it open, exposing her leg and giving her more freedom of movement.

She ran towards the two in front of her, bounded onto a chair, then a tabletop, before leaping into battle.

Both figures were dressed from head to toe in black tactical gear with body armour, helmets, gas masks, and holsters holding weapons.

Leaping into the area between them, she kicked out in mid-jump. Ripping her skirt further as she sent a foot each way, she smashed their guns out of their hands as Essentia slammed into their bodies.

As she landed, both men recovered quickly and they dropped into a fighting stance. Liz could be just as quick, though, maybe quicker and delivered a spinning kick to the man on her left. The attacker spun away and stumbled, allowing Liz to concentrate on the other one.

Her movements fluid, she followed her momentum and delivered an Essentia-laced punch to the second figure. It hurt him, but it didn't stop him from throwing punches of his own. A couple of them connected, but they didn't register much through her Aegis. She caught the next one and quickly twisted him forward and off-balance. She bent the man forward presenting the handle of the sword he wore strapped to his back to her. She grabbed it with her right hand and drew it out of its scabbard.

Sensing the second man was once again approaching her, she spun as she drew the sword. Swinging it in a wide arc, it clanged against the blade of the second man's sword.

He stepped back. She twisted the weapon in her hand and brought it low, under, and up into the first man's belly. Continuing to turn, she spun around, withdrawing the sword from his abdomen and forcing it up as she did so.

As she turned to face the second man, she saw the thin line of blood smudged upon her blade.

She didn't have time to think about it as the other man charged in. They exchanged blows, their swords ringing out as they clashed.

Seeing movement from the corner of her eye, she turned to move around her opponent and put him between her and this new threat. The third man raised his gun and fired.

Liz ducked. The bullets slammed into the back of the man she fought, into his Kevlar vest. The force of the gunfire threw him forward with a shout of pain. Liz dodged around him and launched herself at the third man swinging her sword into the man's gun.

It connected perfectly and sent his weapon tumbling from his grasp. Liz twisted and brought her sword around to slash at him again. He caught it in his gloved hand and struck her across the face with the other.

His gloves discharged Essentia into her Aegis and Liz staggered back from the attack, dropping the sword.

Spitting blood on the floor as it filled her mouth, Liz said, "Ah, Jesus Christ."

The man grabbed her by the throat with one hand and slammed her against the rear wall. Pain flooded her mind as her vision swam. She grabbed his wrist and clawed at the hand that gripped her neck.

"Blasphemy! You will die tonight, Witch," he spat as she heard him draw his sidearm.

A single gunshot rang out to Liz's left. Blood splattered across her face as a bullet slammed into his head. He went limp. Letting go of Liz's neck, he dropped to the floor like a sack of potatoes.

Liz looked left and saw Stella there with a gun pointed at where the man had been.

"Why you..." said the Inquisitor who'd been shot in the back, looking at his colleague. He tried to reach for his gun as he got to his feet.

"Try it," Stella warned him, aiming her gun at him.

The man looked around. The smoke had thinned and it was painfully clear that the Inquisitors had lost. Yoh stood in the middle of a pile of bodies, blood soaking the huge claws on his hands. Amanda stood in the middle of the room, her Magic holding an Inquisitor up off the floor by the neck.

The last of the Inquisitors to attack Liz backed off, and along with a couple of other survivors, moved gingerly out of the building.

Liz rubbed her neck and turned to Stella. "Thank you. You were just in time."

"Of course," she replied.

"Who's that? Liz asked, indicating the man Amanda held up with her Magic.

"No idea," Stella answered.

Liz approached her mentor through the debris, noticing an illusion had been cast over the front of the building to hide the attack from the public.

"You leave this city today, and if Mary has a problem with me, you tell her to come here herself rather than send more feckin' idiots like you. Got it?" Amanda said.

The man barely managed to nod, but it was clear he agreed.

Her Magic let him go and he dropped to the floor. He started to get up as Amanda looked down at him.

"And take your dead and wounded with you," she ordered him.

The man nodded and hobbled out of the room towards the waiting cars. Liz stood with Stella and they watched in silence as the survivors helped remove the bodies from the building under Amanda's watchful eye.

No police came, no one saw the events that night, and within moments of the Inquisition leaving, between them all they had cleared up the mess, fixed the furniture and décor, and made the place look as good as new with their Magic.

Liz helped, but as they finished off, she had to leave the others to it. Wandering out into the Japanese rock garden in the centre of the building, she felt she needed some time alone.

She sat on one of the small stone benches and looked at the ground. She felt exhausted and mentally drained from the fight.

Amanda had been right, the Inquisition was back, and they didn't seem to like Amanda or her coven.

Liz looked at her hands and turned them palms up. She realised they were shaking a bit. Maybe the adrenalin in her system caused it, but looking at her dirty, battered hands she couldn't help but think back to the events surrounding the deaths of her friends and family. Both the Nomads and the Inquisition were to blame, but Liz felt the Inquisition were most at fault. The Nomads were unapologetic in their approach. They were evil incarnate and made no bones about it. The Inquisition, however, should really be the good guys. The way Vito had been friendly at first had put them off their guard, and then when Mary killed Stephen and her sister right there in front of her, it just made her feel incredibly angry.

She knew now that she hated these Inquisitors just as much, if not more than the Nomads and she felt a burning need to make them pay. Mary Damask, especially.

-The Dark Side of the Moon Nightclub, New York.

Tabitha embraced Toni and gave her a lingering kiss on the lips.

"We've bought it. I can't believe it. We're the owners of a night club!" exclaimed Tabitha.

"I'm so glad you're happy. I know you've been thinking of getting a club for a long time."

"Looks like we're staying in New York, then," Tabitha said.

"Looks that way. I hope Melissa doesn't mind."

"She'll be fine. I think she'll fall in love with this place as much as we have."

"Toni and Tabby's Dark Side of the Moon Nightclub. It's got a good ring to it."

"Tabby and Toni's, I think you'll find," Tabitha said, teasing her girlfriend.

The sudden whip-crack of air and the powerful Magical presence brought Tabitha up short as she looked to see who had Ported into the room while she brought her Aegis up to strength in an automatic reaction. Toni had a similar reaction as they looked at the man standing nearby.

"Who are you?" Tabitha asked.

"My name's Trevelyan, and I'm a member of the Magi Council, much like your coven mate, Jonas was before he passed."

"Jonas was a member of the Council?" Tabitha said incredulously.

"He never mentioned it," Toni backed her up.

"Hmmm, he did like to keep things quiet. Can you tell me what happened to him?" Trevelyan asked.

Both girls looked at each other. The memories of their friends' deaths were still raw.

Holy Plans

The Vatican

Mary strode down the corridor, walking with purpose, and approached a door partway down. She had someone she wanted to see and she despised waiting. The fact that Marco had returned to the Vatican and had come here, rather than straight to see her, annoyed her enough that she felt he needed to be reminded about how things worked.

The door she walked up to had a simple figure of a man on it, right above where it had "Changing Room" written on it. She didn't wait, she didn't knock, she just walked straight through the first and then the second door, and scanned up the first aisle in the room.

Three men stood down the aisle, each in some state of undress. They talked like men do, in that macho way that Mary disliked. One of the men saw Mary and did a double-take before snapping to attention. None of them were Marco though, so she walked on.

As she moved along the end of the aisles, the realisation that someone of rank had walked in spread quickly and they all came to attention, no matter their current level of undress.

Three rows in, Mary spotted Marco with his back to her, chatting with one of his team.

"It was a massacre. Those Magi crippled us. The redhead, Amanda, she's a nightmare, man…"

Mary walked right up to him and saw when the man he spoke to noticed her. He went silent and saluted her.

His sharp movements surprised Marco, but he'd been surprised by officers before, and he wasted no time in turning and coming to attention himself.

"Miss Damask, I apologise, I didn't see you…"

Mary didn't have time for this, so she punched him in the gut with a fist filled with Divine energy and doubled him over. "Grand Inquisitor Damask, to you. That's for coming here and relaxing before coming to see me and being debriefed."

"Ma'am," Marco said, his voice struggling through the pain of the punch.

"Get your clothes on and get yourself up to my office," Mary ordered him. He pulled himself up to his full height and did his best to salute, given the circumstances. Marco was a big man, well built, powerfully-muscled, with a military-style haircut and a powerful chin. He stood before Mary buck-naked, holding his towel in his hand. But Mary didn't care, she hated his lazy attitude, and he needed to be taught a lesson.

"Now!" Mary shouted at him, and he quickly started to dress.

Mary turned around and stalked from the room, fury radiating from her in waves. He'd only been working for her for a little while, but he should have known better.

She marched back up to her office—a few floors up in the same, huge building—ignoring everyone she passed. People she knew looked up, saw her, and parted before her like the Red Sea parting before Moses–Grand Inquisitor Demask was in a mood.

She'd sent Marco over to New York to stir up some trouble. But within just a few days, he'd returned. She'd spotted the bruises and grazes that covered his torso during the confrontation in the changing room. He'd no doubt been in a fight. Maybe he had confronted Amanda directly. She wanted to know; she needed to know. That flame-haired Witch had killed her most promising apprentice, and she wanted nothing more than to cause her some pain in return.

Within five minutes of reaching her office, Marco walked in. He wore a utilitarian outfit, combat trousers, fitted top, and military boots all in black, but all of it hastily put on. Even his hair still looked wet.

He stood before Mary's desk in an at-ease position. Mary finished what she was doing and looked up at the man.

"If you ever return from a mission again while I'm available in my office and don't bother to come see me immediately, being embarrassed in the locker room will be the least of your problems. Now, give me your report."

"We arrived in New York as planned and followed the Intel we already had from our agents within the city. The first coven we cleansed fell easily, although one of their number escaped."

"Excuse me?" Mary interrupted.

Marco gulped. "One of them escaped my men. She fled the scene and we believe she reported back to the primary target."

"You mean Amanda." Mary sighed. "Go on."

"During our interrogation of the other three Witches, we discovered that a place of business called The Jade Palace was being used by Amanda to meet with new Magi as they arrived in the city. So, we made our plans to assault the target."

"Let me guess, judging by the number of men in that changing room, you lost some of them during the operation?"

"That is correct."

"What happened?" Mary asked as she sat back in her seat. She had already guessed what had happened, of course—a full-on assault by Marco's team, who were not amongst the blessed and could not call on the power of the Divine, didn't go well. She wasn't surprised, just disappointed.

"We used our highest calibre weapons and used the element of surprise to carry out the operation. But we underestimated them and lost several good men. Amanda herself confronted me and asked me to deliver a message."

"Please, do enlighten me," Mary said, feeling deflated by the apparent failure of Marco's squad.

"She said you should go to New York yourself, rather than send us.

"I'm sure she did. Anything else?"

"No, ma'am. We returned here after that."

"Tail between your legs," she said.

"Pardon me?"

She wasn't sure if he either didn't hear her or didn't understand her. Whatever, she didn't care.

"So, you let one Magi escape and then screwed up your second mission. Correct?"

He went to say something, but didn't and nodded his head instead, letting his eyes fall to the floor.

"Get out, and I want your full report on my desk in an hour."

Marco turned and walked from the office, leaving Mary alone. She slammed her fist down onto the table in frustration. She'd been reliably informed that Marco and his team were some of the best, but they'd just been made fools of by Americans. What was the world coming to?

His report ended up on her desk in less than forty-five minutes, during which time she went back through her records and pulled out Marco's file. He was a capable agent on paper, but he lacked experience in the field against actual Magi. She concluded that he'd benefit from some further, and more intense, training. She made a note to inform the relevant people.

Right now, though, she had another worry—a Conclave meeting this afternoon, during which she would undoubtedly be asked about the mission in New York. She wasn't looking forward to that.

***

Mary strode along the corridor, her secretary at her heels, carrying her bag that was bursting at the seams with files and reports. The statues, paintings, and murals that had been inspired by God, and which lined this main corridor, were breathtaking. She marvelled at the imagery and wondered how the Spirit of God Most Holy must have filled the artists and inspired them to create these beautiful works of art.

The meeting room was located on one of the lower levels and had been where the Conclave of Grand Inquisitors had met for decades now. They were occasionally graced with the presence of the true leader of the Catholic Church, Simeon Cephas, who the Witch Finder General reported to directly. Better known as Simon Peter, he was one of the original Disciples of Jesus, who, through the Grace of God, still lived within the walls of the Vatican. Mary had met Simeon a couple of times; he'd even attended one of the meetings while Mary had been a member.

He was an old man, infirm and weak, but his mind remained active and sharp, and his Divine power radiated from him, setting him apart from all the other blessed.

Simeon was one of the most closely guarded secrets of the Holy Curia, only the Conclave, the Pope, and a handful of the most senior Cardinals knew he existed. These days, he didn't take a hand in the day-to-day running of the Disciples. Instead, he acted as an advisor and a guide to the Witch Finder General and the Pope.

However, the mere thought that he might attend, made everyone dress to impress. Mary approached the room and saw a few of the other Grand Inquisitors standing around outside. There were twelve Grand Inquisitors in total, and although officially they each took responsibility for a part of the globe, in reality, they never really stuck to operating within their designated areas. Mary's assigned area of influence was the East Coast of America, but she operated globally, going wherever her work took her.

She saw Francesco Acardi walk in, the man who had been Vito's original mentor before he'd graduated to the level of Inquisitor and been assigned to Mary, at which point she had taken over his training. He hadn't really spoken to her since Vito's death and she suspected he felt the loss as keenly as she did.

Marcus was there as well, the oldest Inquisitor she knew, apart from Simeon, at nearly two thousand years old. He'd turned down the role of Witch Finder General many times, preferring to be out there fighting the good fight.

She always marvelled at how the Grace of God granted such miracles as long life to those most devout.

She walked in, nodding to some of the men she passed, and settled into her seat while her secretary prepared her notes before leaving the room.

Only the Grand Inquisitors were allowed in these meetings. Aids and secretaries had to wait outside.

Valerio Rossi, the current leader of the Disciples of the Cross, the Witch Finder General of the Inquisition, sat down at the head of the long table. Each time she saw Valerio, he looked more and more infirm. He moved slowly, with a walking stick these days. Picking up the gavel, he banged it on the table and brought the meeting to order.

Mary sat listening to the reports from the other Grand Inquisitors. Each talked about their own efforts against the Witches and Warlocks of the world, the missions they had won or lost, and their strategies for future operations were discussed in detail. Mary enjoyed listening to these reports and always felt she got a clearer understanding of the world at large and where the current battles in the war were being fought.

Soon, Valerio reached Mary and rested his gaze upon her. "Mary, please update us on your current work."

Mary looked up at Valerio. He'd always supported her in her bid to join the Conclave amidst a lot of objection from the other members who disliked the idea of a female Grand Inquisitor. The Inquisition had remained a mainly male domain, with very few women advancing to the level of Inquisitor. And to date, only Mary had reached the level of Grand Inquisitor, although there had been other women in the past who were more than qualified for the role.

It didn't help that Simeon was a bit of a misogynist and didn't seem to approve of Mary being here.

But the support of Valerio had been enough to sway the vote. Since then, Mary had been careful to become useful and valuable to the majority of the Grand Inquisitors since she'd need to have the support of as many as possible should the role of Witch Finder General become available.

Mary had always had lofty goals, and being a Grand Inquisitor was never going to be enough for her. She'd always wanted more and had her sights set firmly on the role of High Inquisitor and Witch Finder General.

Valerio might have taken her under his wing and supported her—she suspected he even liked her—but he'd never shown real affection for her and had been a tough taskmaster. Mary had no real love for him either. Valerio was just another step on the ladder, another obstacle that she needed to surpass.

"Of course, General. As you know, New York had been under the control of the Warlock known as Lucian for many years and had resisted any attempt to be liberated from him. Recently, however, it came to light that a Witch called Amanda had moved to the city, and around the same time, it was made public that Lucian had been killed. This Witch had then opened the city to other Satanists, and there has been something of an influx of Witches since then. It was decided that we should send in a squad to test her defences."

At least, that was the official line. For many, the attack on New York, and specifically Amanda, had a more personal angle.

"The mission in New York has been a partial success, as we have discovered the location of the main meeting point for new Witches entering the city," she said.

"You mean it's been a partial failure, as well?"

"Unfortunately, yes. Marco's team, under their own initiative, chose to strike at the Witch Amanda and her coven. They underestimated the Magi and suffered several losses before retreating with a message from her."

"What message?" Valerio asked.

"According to Marco's report, she told him that I should go to New York rather than send another squad in."

"Well, she can say what she likes, our choices are our own."

"Of course, General," Mary replied.

"Suggestions, please?" Valerio asked, opening the issue to the table.

"If she's willing, Mary should take the Witch up on her offer and go to New York with a show of force," Francesco said without looking at her. This made Mary both smile and feel suspicious of Francesco. She agreed with his suggestion as she wanted to go to New York and show Amanda the true might of the Inquisition, but at the same time, she wondered what his motives were. Did Francesco hold a grudge against her for the death of Vito and want her dead, after all? Was he gambling on Amanda killing her? She had no way of knowing, but resolved to watch Francesco a little closer from now on.

"I volunteer to go to New York. This Witch needs to understand that we won't take such threats lying down," said Nico Orsini, a large man and the youngest of the Conclave. He had a hot-headed attitude and always volunteered for any operation that looked like it might end in a fight.

Mary rolled her eyes at his comment; she should have expected such a thing from him. "I would like to make the chair aware that I would like to go to New York, just as the Witch has asked and finish this mission myself," Mary said.

"Duly noted, Inquisitor Damask," Valerio said, "but I think I have made a choice regarding this. We will send a new task force to Manhattan to fight the Witch incursion there, and I will lead it myself. I will bring this Witch to justice."

"Um, sir, do you think that's wise?" Mary asked as a few gasps sounded around the table, along with a low muttering. She knew that Valerio supervised missions personally from time to time, but those seemed to be less and less common. She wondered what his angle on this was. Was he trying to protect her? Or did he see her as an incompetent female who needs to be shown how to do it?

"I know I don't go into the field much, but I'm more than capable of dealing with this little Witch, and I have more experience with this than most of you," he explained, his eyes resting on Mary for a couple of seconds.

"Of course, sir, my apologies, I did not mean to suggest…" Mary began.

"Duly noted," he said, dismissing her comment with a wave of his hand.

Mary sat back in her seat, confused about what had just happened. Why had he volunteered for this mission? Surely, she would have been the logical choice, this was her mission, and she was the one with a personal stake in it. Maybe that was why. Perhaps he feared she would make this personal and get too emotionally involved. She had to admit, it would have been a possibility. She wasn't the only one, either. Francesco also had a personal stake in it too, if her suspicions about Amanda having killed Vito were correct.

On the other hand, maybe Valerio had been trying to protect her. Her last big mission on the train in Paris had not gone terribly well. Was he trying to keep her from failing again? Or maybe it was plain old misogyny? He didn't want the frail little girl to head into battle.

The thought of men like that boiled her blood. She knew she sat in a room filled with men who held that opinion and who didn't think women were capable of the same things men were. The fact that she had swayed most of them when it came to her was something of an achievement. But they still held their outdated opinions when it came to the rest of her sex, and that rankled a bit. She should be grateful for small victories, she guessed. Views steadfastly held for generations would take time to sway.

The meeting came to an end and Mary made her way around the table and waited patiently for Valerio to finish speaking with those around him before she approached.

"General," she said after they were finally left alone.

"Valerio will do."

"Of course, Valerio. Please, you don't have to do this. I'm quite capable of handling the Witch in New York. I want to do it," she said, keen to take the glory for herself.

"I know, and you may yet have your wish, but I have made my choice. I'm not having any more Inquisitors killed by that Witch."

"Under my leadership," Mary protested, "I am confident we would prevail."

"Perhaps so. You are a skilled leader, Mary. But I have not forgotten the train."

Mary frowned. So, that was it. He was holding that mission against her.

Mary sighed in frustration. "I understand, sir."

"Have your secretary send over the details I will need," he ordered.

"Yes, sir," she answered and watched as he walked off, biting her lip in annoyance and thinking through what this meant, and how she could best take advantage of it. As she watched him hobble out of the meeting room, an idea formed in her mind.

She wouldn't make any more attempts to turn Valerio from this course. In fact, she would support him wholeheartedly, and make a fresh round of appeals to the Conclave members who mattered. There was an opportunity here that she did not want to miss. She rushed back to her office, her secretary struggling to keep up with her. She had a few phone calls to make.

- Nowhere

Alicia lay on the floor on her side, naked and in pain. This woman, who called herself Yasmin, had visited her every few hours, she guessed, and each time she either launched into a violent attack or comforted her and held her lovingly. She never knew which it was going to be, but sometimes, it was as if she were being rewarded for good behaviour.

The spirit inside her healed her slowly after each beating, but she frequently found herself in pain and discomfort.

She felt sick and helpless. She wanted to cry, but she'd shed so many tears these last few days she didn't know if she had more to give.

Why was Yasmin doing this to her? Why was she torturing her like this?

The minutes blended into hours and time lost all meaning. The dim light never changed, she had no idea of the time or where she might be.

Some indeterminate time later, the sound of a footstep close by made her open her eyes and look up.

Yasmin stood above her, and as she looked at her tormentor, fear grew within her, making her feel physically sick.

A smirk grew on Yasmin's lips as she showed her latest torture implement.

Alicia dry-retched at the thought of what was to come.

Orb

Antarctic

Angel stood in the control room of the Antarctic dig she had been helping to oversee for the past six months. The weather had improved, and although it wasn't too bright outside today, it did mean that the choppers could fly.

She stood not too far from Blake, an Initiated, who basically ran the dig for Mr Black, as they both watched the helicopter outside gently alight onto the camp's landing pad.

Angel had been assigned here to keep an eye on things from a Magical perspective. The Syndicate believed Angel to be little more than an Apprentice level Magi, just as she had planned, and they wanted her to make sure nothing Magical escaped their notice. She was to keep an eye out for traps and to make sure everything ran smoothly.

She hated it, living amongst the mortals and pretending to be a weak apprentice, but she knew she had little choice. Yasmin had sent her here to keep an eye on Mr Black's activities, so that's what she did. As it turned out, she'd only been here for three months before she had been rotated off and given a break that allowed her to get away and pursue her own interests before she was brought back two months later.

The time away had been put to good use, returning to her company in Milan and making sure everything was running as it should with her coven before she had to return to the snowy wastes.

The dig had progressed slowly, but without incident and now they were at their goal, and Mr Black had insisted that he should be here for it. He wanted to be the one to hold the artifact before anyone else.

So the dig had been halted while they waited for a clear day.

Angel wore a grey woollen hat, a thick grey jumper, grey gloves, insulated black leggings, and furry grey boots above layers of thermal clothing beneath. She saw no reason to not look good, even in the freezing cold here at the arse end of the world.

Outside, the helicopter door slid open, and several people climbed out, one of which needed help. They walked through the cold wind and up the steps to the control room entrance. They had to pass through an anteroom that kept the cold at bay before they entered the main room. They all wore dark extreme cold-weather gear and looked very official. Angel had a good view of their guests as they closed the outer door and shook the snow from their coats before opening the inner door. The computer system that controlled the building only allowed one door to be open at a time to preserve the heat.

Angel knew some of the people in the group. She'd either seen them around the Syndicate compound or she knew them by reputation. Mr Black had two prominent aids with him; one of them was a board member, the other she knew to be a Magus.

Two security guys entered the room first, double-checked it, and only when they were sure it was safe did they allow Mr Black through.

Mr Black looked old. He was about five feet tall due to his hunched back, had wispy silvery hair around the back and sides of his head, and walked with a walking stick. True to his name, he wore all black clothing, including a long black overcoat. He moved at a reasonably quick pace for a ninety-year-old man and came to a stop in front of Blake. Roxane Carter, board member and his most trusted aid stood behind him, as did Isha Darzi, who as far as Angel knew, was the most powerful Magus that Mr Black employed.

Blake performed a small bow and greeted Mr Black.

"Sir, it's a pleasure to have you here, finally," Blake said. He stood just in front of Angel, as she watched and took everything in. She concentrated hard on keeping her effect on the local Essentia under control, just in case Isha noticed anything to give away her true ability.

"I have been watching your progress closely, Mr Preston, and I have been most impressed. I believe you are ready to extract the artifact?"

"That is correct, sir. We have been waiting for your arrival before continuing any further."

"And you must be Angel," Mr Black said, speaking to her now. "I don't believe we've met in person before. I'm grateful for your efforts."

Angel smiled and nodded. "My pleasure, sir," she said.

"Your work and commitment has not gone unnoticed," he said, addressing both Blake and Angel. "Now, we have much to discuss. Do we have a place where I may sit?"

"Of course, sir. Through here. We have a meeting room ready," Blake said gesturing to an adjoining room they'd prepared earlier in the day.

"Come through, then, Blake. Thank you once again, Angel," Mr Black said and started to walk into the next room.

"Is Angel not allowed to come in as well?" Blake asked.

Angel watched as Mr Black turned and looked back at Blake, and then at her. She felt keen to be in the room and to listen to what was discussed as it would all be of interest to Yasmin, but she hadn't expected to be allowed into the meeting. Instead, she'd planned on enhancing her hearing and listening in from the outside, something she might have been able to get away with if she were careful to avoid Isha's notice. It would all depend on what countermeasures they put into place.

But Blake's unexpected question had given her a glimmer of hope that she might be allowed inside.

"Do you vouch for her, Mr Preston?" Mr Black asked.

Blake glanced at Angel, who remained neutral.

He turned back to Mr Black. "I do. I trust her."

Fool, she thought. Her face remained neutral, but inside, she smiled to herself.

"Very well, she may come in," he said as he led the way into the room and sat at the nearest end of the table.

Everyone else took their seats and waited for Mr Black to speak. Angel was always amazed at what a little money could buy you in terms of loyalty, although she suspected he had other tricks up his sleeve as most Magi were not swayed by offers of money. She wondered what secrets Mr Black knew about Isha that kept him loyal, or maybe Isha just owed a huge debt to Mr Black. She had no idea, but maybe one day she would find out.

Angel sat cross-legged at the table and waited with the others as Mr Black settled himself in.

"Thank you so much for all you have done for me down here in the cold. Today is a momentous day and will see the beginning of a long-planned idea, come to fruition. As you know, you have been digging here to reach a Magical artifact buried deep in the ice. I'm sure you're aware by now that this object is an Orb about the size of a tennis ball, but what you don't know is what this artifact is capable of."

Mr Black looked at Angel. "I'm sure you've seen the Magical signature that this Orb gives off and how powerful it is?"

Angel just nodded, listening closely.

"It is an ancient artifact. Its origins are, as far as I can determine, unknown, but the legends speak of it being used to kill an Archon in pre-history."

Angel kept a neutral face and glanced around the room, looking for reactions. Most people were blank-faced, but a few expressed their surprise upon hearing this.

Angel had heard the legends. That once, long ago, when the Archons ruled the Earth, one of their number was killed by a Magus using a powerful Magical artifact. The fate of both the Magus in question and the artifact had been debated for millennia. Could this really be the same artifact?

Mr Black had paused for effect, to let his words sink in, but Angel felt curious, so she raised her hand. Mr Black saw it and turned to her.

"Yes, Miss Alergeri, you have a question?"

"Apologies for my ignorance, but what's an Archon?" she asked. Angel knew exactly what an Archon was, she owed her allegiance to one of them, like most of the Nomads around the world. But did Mr Black know what they were?

"No apologies required, Miss," he said.

Angel noticed Isha looking at her, but ignored it and kept her Magic in check.

"The Archons, my dear," he continued, "are creatures of vast power. Millennia ago, before recorded history, they ruled the Earth with an iron grip. They created the creatures you call Scions—the Vampires, Were-creatures, and the other monsters of this world. They reside now within the Spirit World and control the Nomads while they plan their return to Earth. They may be ancient creatures, and they may reside within another dimension, but they are still causing pain and death today. I desire to stop this, to bring them down, and to kill them."

Angel nodded and was sure to listen to him with an expression of wonder and fear. It seemed to her that Mr Black had done his research well and perhaps knew as much as most Nomads did of their dread masters.

Much like most Nomads, Angel had aligned herself with one of the seven Archons. Each of these ancient and hoary creatures had a known personality and temperament. Most Nomads aligned themselves with the Archon who best suited their own outlook on life and the world, someone they would serve willingly and happily.

Angel swore her allegiance to Lilitu the Beautiful, the Night Demon and the mother of Succubi. She had created the Vampire-Scion bloodline.

The others, Tiamat the Dragon, Enkidu the Savage, Leviathan the Monstrous, Naga the Cunning, Oni the Demon, and finally, Samael the Reaper, did not suit Angel's seductive ways. She wondered how much Mr Black knew of these beings, these gods. Now wasn't the time to delve too deep, though. She didn't want to draw too much attention to herself.

"And this artifact will do this?" Blake asked, much to Angel's relief, taking Isha's attention off of her.

"This Orb is one part of my plan, yes. I desire to end the rule of these Archons, and this Orb is the first part of my plan, but things are coming together quickly now. The other elements are beginning to line up. Soon, my plan will come to fruition and I can finish the work which was started by that Magus a millennia ago."

"If I can be of service, I would be honoured to help you," Blake said.

"And I as well," Angel agreed, not wanting to miss out on what was going on.

"Very well, you both might come in quite useful. Now, enough about that. I wish to finally hold my destiny in my hand," Mr Black said standing up carefully. "Take me to the Orb."

Angel pulled on her extreme cold-weather gear and followed Mr Black out, over the snow and ice to the entrance of the ice citadel. Tents covered the start of the excavation, hiding it from view while members of the dig team stood outside and watched their employer hobble inside.

Once inside the tents, they could make out the large hole in the ice, easily big enough for anyone to walk through unimpeded. Mats covered the floor of the tunnel to stop workers from slipping as they descended through the ice at a slight downward angle. Isha and one of the security guards took point, while two aids helped Mr Black along over the uneven ground.

Angel had been into these caves many times now, and actually kind of enjoyed coming down here. The ice glistened in the artificial light of the lamps and torches they carried, creating beautiful glistening patterns over the walls. She'd done what she could to entertain herself during the long months she had to stay here, all the while trying to be careful not to draw any undue attention to herself.

She'd seduced a few of the guards, took long walks out in the ice fields where she could use her Magic to protect herself from the cold unnoticed, she'd even found a Russian base that she had taken to terrorising from time to time.

Wandering through these caves had been one such distraction she had indulged in as the dig team worked to locate the artifact. They had made a few wrong turns during the process, which left dead-end tunnels that snaked off into the darkness.

After walking through a few corridors, they entered into a large cavern that had only been partially filled with ice. Ahead, a mechanical lift had been installed, that dropped into the ice, leading to the artifact. They all squeezed into the elevator car and rode it down through the layers of ice.

At the bottom, they returned to walking the passages once more, the acoustics of the tunnels and the ice walls creating some curious echoes in the darkness until they saw light up ahead.

Approaching the glow, Angel saw several work lights were trained on the end of the tunnel and a man who Angel recognised to be the dig team's leader waited for them. She'd never gotten this far down before. The security was always tight and the power of the artifact, or a spell cast upon it always confused her attempts to scry down here.

"Welcome, sir. It's a pleasure to meet you. I'm Andreas, and I have been leading the dig here."

"Good to meet you, Andreas. I believe we are ready to extract the artifact?" Mr Black said.

"That is correct, sir. We will be using this robotic arm to reach in and pull out the artifact. But first, I wanted to show you something."

Before Mr Black could object, Andreas had reached down and flicked a switch. A light that had been embedded in the ice just above ground level turned on, illuminating the wall of ice in front of them from within.

Angel blinked at the thing she saw in the ice, illuminated by the light beneath it, and from the reactions all about her, she wasn't the only one who felt more than a little surprised by what they could see.

Within the ice, Angel could clearly make out the shape of a humanoid figure. It was at least a foot or two deep into the ice, which made details difficult to make out, but something was there, and it looked huge, maybe twice the height of a typical man.

"Is that...?" Blake asked, trailing off.

"My guess is that this is the Magus who used this artifact to destroy the first Archon, and he was buried here along with it," Mr Black said as he studied the creature. "Is it dead?" he asked as an afterthought.

"As far as I can tell, yes," Isha said in his Indian accent.

"Thank you, Isha, and you too Andreas for showing me this. This place is full of surprises. Now, let's move on, shall we?"

"Of course, sir," Andreas said and activated the robot arm. Using a remote control, he manoeuvred the arm into place and extended the grabbing hand down into a ten-inch wide shaft that extended deep into the ice.

"We didn't want to disturb the... thing in the ice, so we chose to retrieve the item with as little disruption to it as possible," Andreas explained over the low whine of the machine.

As they watched, Andreas performed some careful movements of the arm, and after several tense seconds, the sound of something being torn from the ice could be heard and the arm started to retract. Moments later, the hand came into view, and within it was the Orb.

A dull green in colour, it looked to be made from coiling snakes wrapped around each other to make the sphere. The carvings appeared incredibly intricate and detailed. Even as an art piece, it would have value.

Mr Black stepped forward and raised his hand, palm up. Andreas operated the arm and brought the Orb around, opened the metal hand, and dropped the Orb into his palm.

Angel watched all this in fascination and could feel the Magical energy that expanded out from the object and pressed in against her own Magic. This thing was powerful. As Mr Black held it in his hand, the Orb started to glow green, the light coming from within. He turned back to face the group, holding the Orb reverently in his hand, a look of rapture on his face.

"Finally, it's mine," he said to himself as he gazed at the tennis ball-sized item, his face cast eerily in green light.

"Well done, sir," Roxane offered. "That's a huge achievement; you should be proud."

"Thank you, Miss Carter, but our journey has only just begun. We have much to do."

"Of course, very good, sir. Shall we escort you out?"

"Yes, I wish to return to the surface. I need to check on the rest of my plans."

Angel watched them go. She walked after them, but slowly, keeping her distance. Things had kicked up a gear with Mr Black, and he now had a plan and supposedly the means to kill the Archons.

Could he do it? Could he kill the Archons? Angel didn't know. She was sceptical, but artifacts were a tricky business. One thing she did know was, she didn't like the idea. She needed to get in touch with Yasmin and tell her about this latest development.

- Nowhere

Alicia thought she might be going mad. What was real anymore? What had her life become? Every day was torture, pain, turmoil, and her mind felt like it might explode from the mess of rampant thoughts that tore through her brain at a rate that scared her.

Her tormentor, her torturer, held her lovingly in her arms and caressed her face like a mother holding a baby.

"You're mine, Alicia. You do know that, don't you? No one else's, you're mine to protect and love. Only I can do that for you. No one else."

Around them, scattered broken on the floor, were the bodies of three men. Three large men who had somehow found their way in here and had done horrific things to her until Yasmin had returned and saved her from them. She couldn't look at the lifeless bodies about her. She couldn't handle it. She just wanted it to end.

Maybe Yasmin would help her?

The L.A. Gambit

New York

Amanda looked up at the large black church that had been converted into a nightclub for as long as she could remember. Its gothic spires thrust into the midday sky like daggers. Known as *The Dark Side of the Moon*, or just *The Dark Side* for short, the building held many memories for Amanda. Not least of which were her recollections of Howie who had taken her in from the streets. He'd been working security here for as long as she'd known him. And then there was Georgina, who she first met here, and had become her best friend for those early years in the city.

Now, it belonged to new owners. Toni and Tabitha had recently bought it. This was the first time she'd visited since their acquisition of the business, and from the outside, nothing much had changed.

It was another cold day in New York. Winter approached, and it would only get colder before it got warmer again. Amanda, like most Magi, could use her Magic to keep herself warm and protected from the cold, but it was always a good idea to try and blend in with the crowds. Amanda wore her usual jeans and sneakers but wore a denim jacket buttoned up with her hands buried deep in its pockets.

She walked up to the club's side door and knocked. Within moments, locks turned, and the door opened to reveal Howie standing in the doorway.

Amanda smiled at him. She'd seen him a few months ago on her last social visit to the club, and after healing the slight rift that had formed between them, they were getting on well again.

"Mandy, great to see you! What are you doing here?"

"And you, ye big ejit," she said and went in for a hug, which he returned with gusto. "I'm meeting with Toni and Tabitha."

"Ah, so you're the guest they're expecting. I had no idea you knew them."

"Small world," she said with a smile and a wink.

"It certainly is. Come in," he answered, ushering her inside. He led her through the backroom and out from behind the bar into the club proper. Seeing the place quiet and well-lit seemed odd. It wasn't designed to be seen like this. It was a lot messier than it looked at night, and she watched the cleaners going about their jobs as she followed Howie towards the VIP area.

A set of circular stairs in the corner near the front entrance, cordoned off by barriers to keep the undesirables out, led upstairs. She had never visited the VIP lounge before. She'd only ever seen the people up there from the floor below as they watched the dance floor from the balcony.

Each floor in the club had a name. The basement, Amanda's usual haunt was called The Crypt and played heavy metal and darker music. The main level had the moniker The Tomb and played more popular music, while the VIP level had been named the Tower. The VIP Lounge was open to the floor below, as it was basically a large balcony above the ground floor, so the music from the Tomb served the VIPs too.

They walked through a seating area, past the pool tables and booths along the wall. Eventually, Howie led her to a door with a "Staff Only" sign on it. He knocked and waited for a beat before a voice called out from within.

"Come in," said a female voice Amanda recognised.

Howie opened the door to see Tabitha sorting some papers on the small desk that was obviously meant to be used by a secretary.

"Miss Tabitha, your guest is here," Howie said.

"Amanda, good to see you. Are you well?"

"Aye, I'm bang on, so I am."

Tabitha looked a little confused by Amanda's answer. "Good, I have no idea what you just said, but I take it you're well."

Amanda chuckled to herself. "I am, yes."

"Come in then, come in, take a seat in there," she said gesturing into the next room that looked like an office. Tabitha dismissed Howie and shut the door as Amanda took her seat. "So, you wanted to see us?" Tabitha said.

"That's right. Are the others around?"

"Let me see," Tabitha replied before she slipped from the room to hunt them down.

Moments later, Toni, Tabitha, and Melissa joined her in the office.

"So, I've spoken with Victoria this morning, and predictably she's run into problems trying to arrange an appropriate response to the Nomads in Los Angeles," Amanda began once the others were settled. "The Magi Legion is being their usual selves and are both blocking Victoria's suggestion that they should contact the Council for aid, and bogging Victoria down in negotiations about the force they should send into Los Angeles. Basically, they're throwing their weight around and being difficult."

"I'm not surprised," Tabitha said. "They never really liked us. They disliked that Liberty's Children and the Coven of Angels worked together on various projects. Between us, we could usually overrule the Legion and get things done. With the Angels gone, however, I'm really not surprised that the Legion is doing their best to make themselves heard. I'd wager that they'll try to get a more sympathetic coven to replace the Angels."

"So, what does this mean?" said Melissa.

"It means we're fucked," Toni said.

"Well, maybe not," Amanda said. "Despite the Legion not wanting to involve the Magi Council in this, they are quite aware of the situation in L.A. and feel a response of some kind is needed. So, Trevelyan has asked me to look into it. Victoria knows and has said that she would be happy to assign a few Magi to help us as long as we keep a low profile. Providing the Legion doesn't know about it, we'll be fine."

"So, are we going?" Toni said, with hope shining in her eyes.

Amanda sat forward, her tone serious. "I'm going. I'd like you to come as well, but I'm not forcing you. It could be dangerous. If you come, you do so at your own risk."

***

With a snap, four women appeared out of nowhere in the driveway to what was once an expensive-looking mansion in the Hollywood Hills. However, the police tape and the boarded-up windows took some of the sheen off the place.

Amanda looked up at the house, surrounded by bushes and trees. "Very nice."

"It used to be," Melissa answered.

Amanda used her Aetheric Sight and noted that the Magic that had once been in effect here had been almost entirely swept away.

"What's the plan?" Tabitha asked Amanda.

"Well, we have a few hours to kill before the Magi from D.C. get here, so I thought we could have a look around the house. I'll probably take in a little of the city as well, since I'm here."

"You're going in there?" Toni asked.

"You don't have to come with me. You know where to meet me later. I'll see you then, if you'd like to do your own thing."

Toni looked at the other two girls. "I don't really want to go in there again."

"Fair enough," Tabitha answered her. "I want to stay close, though, so how about we wait around back for you, Amanda?"

"Sounds good," she said as she sent a set of senses into the building to find a good place to Port to.

"That okay with you, Toni?" Tabitha asked.

Toni nodded her head. "Sure." She didn't look pleased to be here at all.

With that, Amanda willed herself into the house and appeared inside the main entrance hall.

The place had been ripped apart, burnt, and utterly ransacked. The fight that had happened here had been intense. The current stillness of the house felt a little creepy, probably due to the knowledge that there had been a lot of violent deaths here.

The house creaked and shifted as Amanda stepped on loose floorboards and other debris. It felt almost sacrilegious to make so much noise. Amanda's first line of investigation was to attempt to have a look back through the sands of time and see if she could see anything. Predictably, the period of the attack appeared hazy and indistinct, the powerful Magical forces that had been at work here and the protections and Aegises at play, threw off her scrying attempt enough that it was a lost cause.

Instead, she began to walk through the house. As she did, she opened up her mind to the Magic all around her, trying to get a feel for what had happened here.

As she moved, she could feel the residual, faint Magical signatures created by such powerful Magi and the Magic they'd used. It had been a while since the attack, but the last vestiges of the attackers' Magic were still here if you looked carefully enough.

She recognised the Magic and knew right away why the girls hadn't realised what it might be. It was rarely used, and for good reason.

The Nomads had been using Astral or Spirit Magic, and a lot of it. For thousands of years, Spirit Magic had been of limited use, to the point where some mentors didn't even teach their apprentices about it because they didn't see the point. Apart from a few very specific circumstances, it had limited use, and in some cases, was seen as dangerous.

But Gentle Water had taught Amanda quite a bit about Astral Magic, which meant she recognised the tell-tale signs of it right away.

Astral Magic allowed a Magus to access or control elements from the Aetheric Realm.

More commonly known as the Abyss, the Aetheric Realm had been barred from the Magi for millennia. When the Archons passed into that realm before recorded history, the Abyss was forever barred to the Magi. The Magi could no longer enter or affect it with their Magic. They could no longer summon Spirits to their aid, either.

The Aetheric Realm was also home to Sheol, the land of the Dead. But few Magi took an interest in that either, for fear of being branded a Necromancer.

Walking through the house, Amanda could feel the Astral Magic that had been at work here. These Nomads used it a lot, but there was little else to be found. Satisfied, she Ported outside and found the girls at the back of the garden, standing against the railing that looked down the hill and over the city in the distance.

"Anything?" Tabitha asked.

"Not much, they covered their tracks well, so they did. I did recognise the Magic they used though. It was Astral Magic," Amanda explained.

"Spirit Magic? Really? I thought that was useless?" asked Toni.

"Or dangerous," added Tabitha.

"It's both to be sure. But you said that one of them used that Magic to disappear and reappear, is that right?"

"I… yeah, I think so. That's what I saw, I'm sure of it," Toni said.

"Well, that could be an issue," Amanda said.

***

Amanda sat at an outside table of a coffee shop in downtown L.A. and watched the world pass her by. Even though it was approaching the middle of winter, it felt comfortably warm in California. It made a nice change from the cold of New York.

Thinking back to her walk around the coven house an hour ago, Amanda couldn't help but be troubled by her findings. If what the girls said about the Nomads using Astral Magic to Port was true, and if it had indeed been Spirit Magic the Nomads had used, then that meant only one thing. These Nomads had discovered the Holy Grail of the Magical world—how to pass into the Aetheric and bypass the barrier that had barred that Realm from the Magi for millennia.

Within Nomad circles this had become known as the Magnus Transitus, or the Great Crossing, and would mean the Nomads could travel through the Abyss to finally meet their masters—the Archons—in person, in the hope of limitless power. It was a quest that most Nomads dreamt about.

Had these Nomads actually achieved it? If so, it could be problematic for the Arcadians if they chose to share their wisdom with other Nomads.

Amanda took another sip of her coffee and nearly spat it out all over her legs when she suddenly recognised someone on the other side of the street.

She quickly placed her mug down and conjured a generous tip for the waitress before getting up.

Was it her?

Amanda peered at the woman using her Aetheric Sight and smiled. It was.

A second later, the young woman on the other side of the road stopped and turned, locking eyes with Amanda. It took another second or two for the girl to recognise Amanda and smile back at her.

"Celest! Wow, it's great to see you again, you look grand," Amanda said crossing the street and approaching the girl. Celest looked like she'd just been to the gym with her Lycra shorts and top. Only her biker boots seemed out of place. Celest dropped the gym bag she'd been carrying over her shoulder and hugged Amanda.

"You don't look so bad, either," Celest said.

"Thanks a million. How come you're in L.A.?"

"No reason, just passing through, really. I'm not sure where I'm headed. How about you? I thought you were in New York? You're a long way from home."

Amanda smiled. "I'm here on business."

"More Nomads?"

"Aren't there always?"

"You want some help? I could do with a workout," Celest offered.

Amanda paused and blinked. Did she want help? They were going to be going up against a powerful enemy who could potentially kill them. She gave it half a second's thought before she replied. "Sure. Yes, that would be grand."

***

The Liberty's Children delegation had come here quietly and covertly, only really Victoria and this group knew anything about this mission at all, and they wanted to keep it that way. The location of the safe house ended up being a currently disused old warehouse in one of the city's industrial centres, surrounded by other places of business that were presently shut for the night.

Several tables dotted the floor, some had papers on them, others had weapons, and one had a powerful computer. Amanda spoke with John Easton, the coven leader for the squad of Magi that Victoria had sent.

"Spirit Magic?" John asked.

"That's what it appears to be. The Angels Coven House felt like it was filled with it. These Nomads know how to use it and use it well. I also have reason to suspect that they can pass into the Abyss at will. You need to be careful; things could get pretty crazy if these guys show up."

"You think they will?"

"I've always been the optimist, John," Amanda said. John and his teams had contacted a local coven sympathetic to Victoria and the Liberty's Children and asked if they would put the word out that the three remaining members of the Coven of Angels were staying with them. The house would then be closely monitored while the coven itself had been moved to a nearby safe house to keep them out of harm's way.

That had been several hours ago. So far, nothing.

Suddenly, several of the Liberty's Children Black Ops Squad, including John, went quiet and seemed to internalise their thoughts.

Amanda recognised it right away and didn't need to look into the Magical spectrum to recognise when someone started to speak telepathically.

Without warning, John and the others in telepathic contact winced and held their heads in pain for a brief moment before Amanda sensed the Magical Link suddenly cut off.

"Trouble? Amanda asked.

"The Nomads, they're at the safe house," he said, before raising his voice. "Get ready. We're needed ASAP."

"The safe house? Where we hid the coven?"

John nodded meaningfully at her.

"Shite," Amanda cursed.

Everyone jumped into action, and within seconds, they stood together. As the most powerful Magus there, it fell to Amanda to Port everyone to the safe house, which she could do in two quick effects enacted by two parts of her Multi-tasking mind simultaneously.

They appeared outside the box-like building in a run down and quiet part of town. They'd erected several strong Aegises and instructed the coven members to create more once they were inside, in an effort to keep the Nomads out should the worst happen.

The worst had happened.

Amanda noted with more than a little worry that the Aegises were still up, protecting the building and yet according to the Mental Link John had received, the Nomads were already inside.

"This is feckin' banjaxed," Amanda spat as she quickly went to work pulling down the Aegises around the building. They'd hoped they would keep the Nomads out. Instead, they were protecting the Nomads that had somehow bypassed them and gotten inside. All the Magi present worked as quickly as they could to bring down the Magical Shields around the building, and when a window on the second floor of the building blew out, she knew they were wasting precious seconds.

Their Magic hammered against the remaining few Aegises until the final one fell. It felt like the air had been pulled taught and then suddenly snapped back like a rubber band breaking in two.

Amanda wasted no time and once more double-Ported the group into the main open-plan downstairs area of the building and appeared in what some might call Hell.

Just like in the Angel's Coven House, debris and chaos were everywhere. It looked like it had just been bombed. Piles of wood and fabric, which had once been furniture, were scattered about, while floorboards had been ripped up here and there, and small fires burnt merrily away.

In addition to the wood and plaster that littered the floor, dead bodies also lay all about them, broken and bloodied. Amanda heard a couple of people in the group gasp and cry out upon seeing the scene before them.

Farther into the room, three figures stood with their backs to Amanda and her friends. The figures stood in front of a kneeling Arcadian .

"That's enough," Amanda shouted at the trio.

The two figures—one male, one female—who flanked the man in the middle, wore somewhat similar shiny-black skin-tight garments and long flowing cloaks. As they turned to look at the new arrivals, their long black hair and similar facial features made Amanda wonder if they were twins.

Standing between them, the third man looked very different. Whereas the two in black looked neat and clean and clearly cared about their appearance, he wore old, dirty clothing, had dark, unkempt hair, and a full, messy beard. He appeared to be of Middle Eastern or Indian descent and looked somewhat unhinged with his wild eyes and gurning face.

"Let him go," Amanda called out.

The man in the middle laughed. "But of course," he said, as Magic flared and the body of the man they'd been interrogating ripped apart into messy sludge.

"Jaysus," Amanda cursed and finished fuelling her Aegis with Essentia.

Astral Magic flared out from this central figure and infused the dead bodies of the coven members at their feet. It all happened so quickly. Within a second, the dead bodies were suddenly no longer dead, or maybe that was being generous because they didn't look alive either, but they certainly moved.

The Nomads in black charged them, as a blood-caked hand grabbed Amanda's leg. It belonged to the corpse of a woman who she'd seen alive only a few hours before. Amanda recoiled from the Zombie, backing off in an involuntary reaction to something that should not be. Gasps, screams, and shouts of fear erupted all about her as the pile of bodies started to move and attack. The Zombies clawed and bit at them as Amanda's friends reacted in much the same way she did.

Gathering her wits, she kicked the Zombie woman, her superior strength breaking bones and sending the Zombie sprawling back, giving Amanda precious moments. Around her,

Celest transformed into her Were-form and tore into the Zombies while the two Nomads in black attacked.

Magic surged ahead of her, and where there had been only one man in rags, now suddenly there were three, then four, and five, and more.

Through her Magical sight, Amanda knew these weren't illusions or holograms, the man had used his Magic to clone himself, and they all seemed to be as powerful as he was.

"Feck me." She felt outclassed. She kept her eyes on the man she thought was the original, rather than a clone, and called on her Magic. She Ported across the room to stand directly in front of the man in rags.

"Aren't we the bold one?" the man said.

Amanda smiled and conjured a bolt of electricity and flung it at him.

The lightning played over the surface of the man's Aegis but did little to hurt him. Something brushed by her and raked at her with its claws. It passed right through her Aegis, ignoring it entirely and more followed. Insubstantial and nearly invisible things flew about, attacking her and they didn't seem to care that she had any kind of shield up.

"What the hell?" she yelped.

The man laughed and blasted her with Essentia, ripping at her Aegis.

Amanda staggered back and dropped to one knee as the man's Magic hammered on her Aegis again. Amanda noted her ripped t-shirt and the large gashes beneath. The pain burned through her mind like fire as she forced herself to ignore it.

Something roared behind her. She glanced back to see two massive humanoid beasts with deep maroon skin, horns, and enormous wings stepping from a Portal one of the Nomads had created.

"Demons?" she said incredulously as the two things attacked the Magi and Celest.

The ethereal things flew towards her again. She recognised the energy they were made of and adjusted her Aegis to repel Aetheric energy. The Shade screamed past her again, its claws flashing, but it did nothing to her. Her Aegis had protected her.

"Gotcha," she said to herself smugly and healed her injured body with a simple thought.

When Essentia began raining down on her from at least three of the man's clones, she gathered her thoughts and summoned all of her might to focus all of her minds on a single effect. Essentia strikes smashed into her Aegis, tearing lengths off it as she pulled as much energy in as she could. Another second passed. Her Aegis held and she released an intense wave of Essentia mixed with Kinetic and Spiritual energy. It blasted out of her as a rapidly expanding sphere, sending Nomads and Shades flying as it hit them like a battering ram.

Weakened, her defences low, she turned inward and used all but one of her extra minds to refortify her Aegis. She looked up, hunting for the man in rags. He'd been thrown against the back wall, his clones suffering similar fates. The one closest to Amanda rose up from the ground, laughing like a mad man.

"Give it up, this can't last. You will be stopped eventually," Amanda threatened.

Watching him, she stood her ground, not wanting to rush in as she brought her defences back up to full strength. His laugh subsided, and suddenly she watched his clones dissipate from view as he cancelled the Magic.

"That may be true, but this is too much fun!" he said, laughing maniacally.

Quicker than she could react, the other two Magi Ported next to him, and a powerful Aegis sprang up around them.

"No," Amanda called and watched as they disappeared in a flare of Spirit Magic. She'd just witnessed them complete the Magnus Transitus. It wasn't much to look at, not much different to someone Porting away, in fact, but the implications could be huge.

A yelp and the sounds of fighting behind her brought Amanda's attention back to the present, and she spun around to see the death that the Nomads had brought to bear upon her friends.

Celest, John, and Tabitha fought against two Abyssals, but they were the only friends she could still see. Amanda Ported instantly behind the Demon closest to John and Tabitha, grabbed the thing by the wing, and flung him across the room into the wall. She called on her Essentia and blasted its already weakened Aegis. The shield collapsed, leaving the Abyssal defenceless. Fractions of a second later, Amanda worked her Magic again and ripped at the creature's body, tearing it apart and killing it.

Beside her, Celest caught the other Abyssal by the neck and slammed it into the floor. She punched it with a fury Amanda had rarely seen. Over and over, Celest hit the thing, her huge furry fist crushing the thing's skull. Amanda stood and looked at the scene around her, breathing hard after the fight. To her right, Celest shifted from her huge nine-foot-tall, half-wolf/half-human form, shrinking back into her human form. She looked up at Amanda.

"You good?" Amanda asked.

Celest nodded and gave her a thumbs-up as she dropped into a sitting position, clearly drained from the fight.

A little further away in front of Amanda, John stood looking over the bodies of his dead coven mates. They'd been ripped apart. Nearby, Tabitha sank to a crouch next to Toni, who Amanda saw was also alive and was holding Melissa, who wasn't.

Amanda walked over to the girls, being careful not to step on the other bodies.

Toni looked up at Amanda as she approached. "Can you do anything?"

Amanda came up beside Melissa's body and concentrated, looking for her life force, her Anima. If it still remained in her body, as it should, then she could revive her. But there was no sign of it, she was empty. Looking closer, she could see spiritual wounds where her Anima Mundi had been ripped from her body. No doubt, the work of the Nomads.

Amanda hung her head. "I'm sorry, she's gone," she said and put her hand on Toni's back. Tabitha pulled Toni in close and the pair hugged.

Amanda stood up and left them to their grief. Using her Magical sight, she looked over the other dead Arcadians—the Nomads had done the same to each and every one of them, too. Their life force had been torn from their bodies and would doubtlessly be in Sheol by now.

She looked up at the coven leader. "I'm sorry, John. They're gone."

"I know. I saw the Magic they were using. There was no escaping that."

Amanda sighed and looked over the remains of the fight. The Demons had almost disintegrated now and would be gone entirely in a few more seconds, but she wondered if there might be any other clues they could find.

"So, what do we do now?" John asked, his face pale, his eyes nearly as lifeless as his dead coven mates who lay at his feet.

"Go back to the safe house. Take them with you," Amanda said, indicating the girls, "and wait for me. I'll be there soon."

John walked over to Tabitha and Toni, and within moments, they had Ported out. Amanda looked back at Celest who'd stood up again and was sniffing the air.

"What's the craic?" Amanda asked.

"There's something about their scent. I'm sure I recognise it, but I can't put my finger on it."

"A clue?"

"Maybe. If it's from a location, then they've spent a long time there."

"Find it. I've had enough of these guys, so I have. This needs to end."

Celest nodded. "I'll be in touch."

Amanda saw the Essentia within Celest surge as she shifted forms, dropping into a large, powerful-looking wolf. She barked once and moved from the building, sniffing at a couple of things as she went.

Feeling the fire of hope kindling deep inside her, she looked around again and then Ported back to the safe house. She materialized to find Toni and Tabitha standing next to a table with what she assumed was Melissa's sheet-covered body on it.

Amanda walked over to them, her face creased with empathy and concern.

"We want to have her buried in New York," Toni said absently as Amanda approached. "We've had it with L.A. I don't want anything more to do with it. There's nothing but death here now."

"I'm sure that can be arranged, don't worry. Try to get some rest, we'll get you home."

"Amanda," called John from a short distance away.

She left the girls and walked over to him. He looked a little worse for wear but seemed determined to carry on. "I'm going to bring all the bodies back here," He said. "Then we can contact Victoria and get things arranged."

"Of course. I'll help."

"Thanks," he said. "So where's Celest? That girl can fight."

"Yeah, she can. She's following a lead."

"A lead? You think you can find them?"

"I'm gonna give it a damn good try. These bleedin' ejits need teaching a lesson."

He nodded his agreement. "Well, best of luck to you. Shall we?"

It took them about an hour to hunt through the building to make sure they had all of the bodies, bag them up, and bring them back. Most of it was done with a judicious use of Magic and a great deal of care. Amanda watched John throughout their expedition. His face was resolute and his eyes were hollow as they worked, but she found his grim determination admirable.

They'd just finished up when Amanda felt the Mental Link she had with Celest flare to life. She opened her mind and let Celest's thoughts in.

"Found them," the Werewolf informed her.

- The Antarctic

Gil ran through the snow and over the ice as the wind blew. Shouts sounded behind him followed by gunshots and screams.

Might that have been another of his coven mates they'd just killed? How had their little trek gone so wrong?

They knew that something had been going on, but it had taken them some time to discover the location of this dig site. He still had no idea what they were doing, but they were being very secretive about it and it had turned out they were very protective of it, too.

They'd seen the site when they'd first Ported in. It sat before a temple carved into the rocky side of the mountain. They hadn't been there more than a few moments before a whole team of guys dressed in military fatigues Ported in with a Magus and started firing.

Gil's attempts to Port out had been foiled by the Magus, but he tried again now that he was a good distance away. It worked, and he collapsed in exhaustion inside their Antarctic base.

Someone needed to know about this.

Park Life

Griffith Park, Los Angeles

Amanda's Magic traced the Mental Link back to Celest, and she appeared out of thin air right next to her.

"Whoa, you gave me a fright!" Celest exclaimed, jumping as Amanda appeared.

They stood in the darkness a good walk into one of the valleys of Griffith Park. Trees and scrub bushes dotted the ground around them, while the two slopes of the valley rose up on either side, giving it a claustrophobic feeling.

The vast park encompassed an extensive network of hills that included the Griffith Observatory, several hills to their right, and the slope with the Hollywood sign a good way off to their left. There were also a few golf courses, well-to-do suburbs, some ranches, and plenty of roads and tracks snaking through it.

"They're here? In the park?" Amanda asked.

"That's the smell I picked up. I think we're close. The scents match, so keep an eye out."

Celest set off in a generally northern direction, stopping and sniffing the air occasionally as they wandered slowly up the valley, through trees and foliage.

The night felt cool and quiet in the secluded valley. To Amanda, this seemed a little too tranquil for a Nomad hideout, but she trusted Celest and followed her through the rural landscape.

Rounding a cluster of bushes, the trees thinned out and in the centre of a clearing up ahead stood a woman. She wore a long, simple, black halter-neck dress and a few pieces of fairly ostentatious gold jewellery. She had long, straight black hair and smooth swarthy skin that would have looked more at home in the northern deserts of Africa. Amanda's Magical sight confirmed she was a powerful Magus who was able to keep her ambient Magic contained, which explained why she hadn't sensed her from further away. This woman could be dangerous.

She smiled at Amanda and Celest. She seemed to be waiting for them. Amanda paused and glanced about, looking for a trap, but none seemed forthcoming.

Amanda sent a thought to Celest through their mental link, ~What do you think?~

~No idea,~ Celest replied.

"Welcome. Come, join me," the woman said in an accent that Amanda didn't recognise.

Leading the way, Amanda walked forward cautiously with Celest following close behind. "And who might you be?" Amanda asked.

"You may call me Nefertiti, and I am here to talk to you. I wish you no harm."

"Really? Well, we're a little busy right now…"

"You're looking for Shaitan."

"Shaitan?" Amanda asked.

"Indeed. You fought with him and his two charges, Lukas and Lucinda, mere hours ago, I believe."

Amanda shifted her weight to a more relaxed pose, her weight on one leg. She no doubt looked positively scruffy standing next to this gorgeous creature.

"Oh, that Shaitan? I get mixed up sometimes," Amanda quipped sarcastically.

"He is truly sorry for what he has done, and I am here to ask you to leave him be," the woman continued, ignoring Amanda's quip.

"He's sorry?" Amanda blurted out, incredulously. "Oh, that's all fine then, no problem at all. We'll just go and bury those bodies then, yeah? I mean, come on. Are you serious?" Amanda said, more than a little shocked by this woman's audacity.

"Shaitan is a troubled person with many demons. This occasionally means that he lashes out, attacks those he would otherwise mean no harm."

"This 'Shaitan', as you call him, is clearly a murderer and a bleedin' psycho. Putting him out of his misery would save lives. He doesn't deserve to live." All humour had drained from Amanda for the moment as she marvelled at this Nefertiti woman, who unbelievably, was trying to protect a murderous Nomad.

"Does he not? So you're saying that *you* should choose who lives and dies?" Nefertiti asked.

"Of course not, this is based on his continued killing of numerous Magi here in Los Angeles. This is based on facts—on what course of action will save the most lives."

"So, a few Arcadians have died. Friends of yours, were they? And when considered objectively, their lives are more valuable than the life of the one man in the whole world who can break the barrier into the Abyss? The one man who has invaluable knowledge of the Archons. Knowledge that might very well be the cause of these violent episodes. Knowledge that could stop the Nomads as a whole. In that light, would not the lives of a few Arcadians be a small price to pay?"

"That information would be valuable," Amanda conceded. There was no point denying such things. But valuable to whom, and who chooses what's more or less valuable? However, this Shaitan had killed people. Innocent people who did not deserve it and he needed to take responsibility for those deaths. "But my point remains, Shaitan murdered innocent people and that cannot go unpunished."

As she finished her sentence, Amanda felt a surge of Magic and wasn't surprised by the appearance of the three Nomads from earlier. Shaitan, Lukas, and Lucinda Ported in, appearing behind Nefertiti

"Ah, grand. The prodigal son returns," Amanda said.

Shaitan stepped out and stood to Nefertiti's right while Lukas and Lucinda moved off to the left. They went a good fifteen or twenty feet away and stood under the trees, looking sullen and annoyed. Amanda fed more Essentia into her Aegis. This had been a friendly meeting so far, but she knew it could potentially erupt at any moment.

"Amanda, is it?" he said, looking and sounding calm and serious with a curious accent that she couldn't place. "I must apologise for my actions. I... I don't know myself these days as much as I used to, and sometimes I just, well, I lose control. I don't mean to do the things I do. I just... I'm not sure. I don't really remember much from these episodes."

Amanda was at a loss for words. He'd seemed so crazy and unhinged before. Hearing him express remorse for his actions sounded almost strange. He didn't sound insincere, or like he was trying to deceive her. He sounded genuine. He seemed honestly sorry for what he'd done.

"Can you forgive me?" he added.

Amanda dropped her face to look at the ground. "Honestly, that's not for me to say," she said as she lifted her head to look at him. "I don't think you're lying, but the fact remains that you are dangerous, you've killed people. Heck, you tried to kill me!"

"I'm sorry. I just lose control."

"Does anyone have control over you during these episodes?" she asked, thinking that there should be a way to contain him.

"Um," he said as he glanced at Lukas and Lucinda. "That's difficult to say."

Celest roared, her voice shifting from human to animal as Amanda heard clothing tear and bones pop. Turning, Amanda saw Celest leap at the twins and land on Lukas, ripping at him with her claws.

Concentrating, Amanda worked her Magic and pulled Celest off the Magus with an invisible force. While Celest raged, Lukas backed off and looked at Nefertiti, who raised her hand, telling him to stay calm.

"Looks to me like you need to keep your lap dog under control," Nefertiti said.

Amanda cocked her head to the side. "Celest may be passionate, but she would never kill innocents. Those two feckers, however," she said as she pointed to the twins. "They seem to revel in the death and destruction they create."

Nefertiti looked over at the twins, who were scowling at Amanda. Nefertiti looked the pair over and then looked back at Amanda.

"So, hypothetically, what would you want from me?"

"That's easy. An end to the attacks, and assurances that it won't happen again," Amanda said.

Nefertiti dropped her chin to look at her from beneath her eyebrows. Amanda guessed she must be weighing up her options, wondering what the best course of action would be.

The woman lifted her head and nodded. "Very well, your demands are reasonable. Attacks like the one today will not happen again from this point onward."

"You expect me to take you at your word? What assurances can I get, what guarantee?" Amanda asked.

The Magic was quick and powerful, whipping out from Nefertiti like a coiled cobra striking its prey. It crashed into the twins with the force of a freight train at full speed and their Aegises dropped almost instantly while a second effect exploded their bodies into shreds.

Amanda stumbled back a step as she watched it happen. After a moment, she realised her mouth was hanging open, so she closed it.

"Well," she commented, "that does show commitment." She nodded to herself as she reined in her swirling thoughts. "That's... that's a good start, thank you," Amanda said. The whole thing had happened so fast and had been such a display of raw power that Amanda was shocked to her core. They might be Nomads, and their actions had made Amanda decide that they should be punished with death anyway, but Nefertiti had shown an utter disregard for their lives. For Amanda, this only served to reinforce how important Nefertiti thought Shaitan was. Not to mention, how powerful and ruthless Nefertiti was.

"Then, we're done here. Good day to you," Nefertiti said as she Ported away, taking Shaitan with her and leaving Amanda, Celest, and two patches of gore alone in the woods.

"Well, that didn't go as I thought it would," Amanda said, thinking out loud.

"You got the result you wanted, though, didn't you?" Celest asked.

"To be sure, I guess," Amanda nodded.

She still felt a little shell-shocked at the encounter. She'd thought she'd have to fight these Nomads, go toe-to-toe with them to get the results she wanted.

"So, shall we get back and let the girls know the good news?" Celest said.

"Yes, but let's not mention Nefertiti. I'd like to know a little more about her first. We can just say we took care of it and that they won't be bothering the city anymore."

"Understood," Celest replied.

***

It was early morning as Amanda and Celest sat in Central Park and watched the glow of the not-yet-visible rising sun light up the sky behind the towering buildings of Manhattan's Upper East Side. Celest had asked to return to New York with Amanda, having had enough of Los Angeles and wanting a change of scenery.

They'd Ported back and taken a walk up to the park, wandering through the greenery for a while before choosing to sit on a bench and watch the world pass by.

They talked about Lucian and New York, and what Celest's plans might be. Celest took an interest in Amanda, and she ended up asking if she had anyone special in her life.

"…so no, there's no one at the moment, and I think I might just give up on men for the time being," Amanda replied.

Celest nodded. "Men are too much trouble. Friends are fine, but anything beyond that and it gets too complicated, and if you knew what was best for you, you would be the same."

"So, you like women instead, then?" Amanda asked, curious.

"No, no. I'm not into women like that either. I'm no dyke. I mean, I just use men as and when I need them. I don't get attached. I don't want a relationship. A good shag from time to time is fun, but it never goes beyond that."

Amanda thought she might have offended Celest with her question, and the dyke comment made her wrinkle her nose. She didn't think she liked that word. "Okay, so, that's grand. Sorry, I didn't mean to…"

"Don't worry about it. I get that sometimes. People see the muscles and make assumptions."

"I didn't… that's not…"

"I know," Celest smiled. "Don't worry."

Amanda slumped back into the bench and sighed. She needed to learn to stop putting her foot in it sometimes.

A little later, the small misunderstanding long forgotten, Celest pledged to keep in touch and left Amanda to go and explore the city by herself. Amanda headed back home so she could get in touch with Victoria and deliver a report of what happened.

***

Tabitha walked up to Toni, where she stood looking out over the balcony to the club below. They were in the rafters of the building, on a purpose-built catwalk that gave the owners, or security, a bird's eye view of the whole club.

"Are you alright?" Tabitha asked, slipping her arm around Toni's waist.

Toni stood up straight and pulled Tabitha in for a hug. "I'm fine. As good as can be expected, I suppose."

"Yeah, I know."

"I've been thinking," Toni said, pulling away just enough so they could talk. "You know how Mandy couldn't bring Melissa back to life because her soul had left her body?"

Tabitha frowned. "Yes," she said cautiously.

"Do you think there's a way around that? Do you think she could be brought back?"

"I have no idea. I mean, what you're talking about, that's…"

"I know what it is. But we'd be doing this out of love, out of something pure. She was our friend, Tabby. I'm not sure I can just do nothing."

"Honestly, I don't know. Maybe it's something we can look into," Tabitha said.

"That's all I ask," Toni replied and pulled her lover in for another hug and held her tight.

- Nowhere.

One minute they were in the warehouse, the next they were in a small room, covered in white tiles. There was a raised area on one side with a bed, with a soft-looking blanket covering it. Her shackles had been removed, too.

"Alicia," Yasmin said. *She turned to see Yasmin with her arms out, so she went to her and Yasmin hugged her close.* "This is a gift to you, Alicia. You've come so far, so you deserve a reward. I'm so proud of you."

Alicia wasn't sure what she'd done to please her mistress so much that she would reward her like this. It seemed strange. Later, once she was alone, she lay on the bed, wrapped in the blanket to hide her nakedness and warm her against the chill air. She loved this small creature comfort so much. After days, weeks, months maybe, of the hard stone floor and the pillar she'd been chained to, this seemed like a luxury.

***

Hours later, her body bruised and abused once more, with pain filling her every thought, Yasmin, her mistress, her abuser, and her protector, hugged her close.

"You know you deserve this, don't you? You know you've been bad and you need me. I'm helping you, and one day soon, you'll understand and you'll be grateful. I know you will."

Curiosity

Greenwich Village, Manhattan

The day had been filled with conversations. Amanda had spoken to Victoria and Trevelyan about the events in Los Angeles. She'd been over the sequence of events out there several times and felt bored and exhausted by it all. How had this happened, she wondered? How had her life become bureaucracy, administration, and politics? She felt sure this wasn't what she'd signed up for.

Maybe this was what being an adult was like. At only twenty-one, she didn't feel like an adult. In fact, she didn't feel any different than she had just a couple of years ago.

She wondered when things might change. When would she suddenly feel like a grown-up? Maybe it never happened and she would feel like this for the rest of her life. Time would tell.

Celest had disappeared into the city, and she had no idea where she might be now. She hoped Celest stayed local as she'd proven herself to be a valuable ally. Someone she could trust and depend on, someone with a good moral compass, and someone who could kick some serious ass when needed. These were all qualities that made her a valuable friend to have.

The trip had not been without some losses though, and she really did feel for Toni, Tabitha, and John. She got the impression that John would fare better than the girls. She figured he'd been working these missions for Victoria for a while and had seen his fair share of soldiers killed action. No doubt, it never got easier, but she felt sure that John had coping mechanisms in place to help him through it.

Toni and Tabitha might not though, and it worried her that they could take things a little harder. She resolved to try and keep an eye on them and make sure they were alright.

But the day's stresses were over. Tonight she just wanted to relax and attempt to have a pleasant evening in good company.

So, she sat curled up on her softest sofa with Maria, who she'd invited over for a drink. Naturally, being Magus and living the lives they did, talk turned to recent events. She glossed over the less savoury elements, not wanting to dwell too much on death and destruction. But she did wonder if Maria knew anything about the woman she and Celest had met in Griffith Park. She'd mentioned her name to both Victoria and Trevelyan and from their reactions, they both seemed to know her, but neither had commented much and basically avoided the issue.

She hoped that Maria would be a little more forthcoming about this strange and powerful beauty she'd met and argued with.

"…so, do you know anything about this Nefertiti?"

"You mean you've not heard of her?" Maria asked, clearly surprised.

"No, should I have?"

"Did you take history at school?"

"I did," Amanda replied. "It wasn't my favourite lesson to be fair, though."

"I can tell. Well, Nefertiti was a queen from ancient Egypt, wife of the Pharaoh Akhenaten, and one of the most powerful and most well-known Egyptian queens."

"Wow, I had no idea. So, this Magus has taken her name?"

"No, Amanda. You met *the* Nefertiti."

"Oh, shite," she muttered, the full weight and the implications of what that meant washing over her. And she's lived all this time? She must be…"

"Over three thousand years old, yes."

"Jaysus, she didn't look bad for it, though. So, you know of her, I mean, as a Magus?"

"She's one of the few Arch Magi on Earth, and although she does keep to herself, she is one of the more well-known ones, yes. You don't get to be that powerful and live that long without people knowing about you."

Amanda sipped her wine, enjoying its fruity taste. "So, is she a Nomad or an Arcadian?"

"Neither. She stays out of all that; does her own thing. I suppose you could say she's an independent."

"I'm glad I didn't try to fight her, then."

"Me, too," Maria said and smiled at her over her glass. Amanda let her gaze linger, and they looked into each other's eyes for a long moment. A pleasant tingling feeling ran down her neck, and nebulous possibilities opened up to her, enticing her.

Amanda bit her lip behind her glass, feeling distinctly attracted to this beauty before her. Maria always looked gorgeous and well turned out. She had a smokiness to her twinkling eyes that promised pleasures and intimacy with her every look.

Maria ran the end of her tongue over her lips. Amanda didn't know if she'd done it on purpose or if it had been something involuntary, but Amanda felt a tingle, a pull in her pelvis that felt so good.

She looked away before she got utterly lost in those eyes, her mind filled with what might have happened if she had listened to her deepest desires.

"Any progress on the man front?" Maria asked. It was a leading question, Amanda knew that. Maria had one goal in mind, and Amanda wondered if she should let her score.

"Not really," she said, feeling just slightly short of breath, almost as if the amount of air she could hold inside her had diminished. Was it excitement, nervousness, or a mixture of the two? She paused after those first two words. She knew what she wanted to say next, but the connotations would be too obvious to miss. Should she be so bold, should she take a small step towards a leap of faith that could change everything?

Maria's legs shifted. They were tucked up beside her on the couch, and as she moved her leg, shifting one over the other, the movement drew Amanda's eyes. She couldn't help but stare at those shapely thighs and tapered calf muscles. She wanted to run her hand over them, to feel the smoothness of her skin and the warmth beneath her skirt.

"…I don't think about men that much, really," Amanda said, and looked up into those mischievous eyes once more. The words had just spilt out of her, almost beyond her control. She wanted to know what it would lead to, what would happen next. She took a breath as their gaze locked. Adrenaline surged through her body, making her heart pump at a furious rate, which made her exhale a little raggedly. Her skin felt incredibly sensitive and she could feel every movement of her clothes over her body, but she wanted to feel Maria's hands touching her instead.

But she felt frozen in place, like a deer in headlights, wanting to move, wanting to take the lead and that first step, but being terrified of what it might mean and where it might lead.

She'd put it out there with that last comment. Would Maria pick up on it? Would she see the invitation that Amanda had made and would she take it?

Amanda watched as Maria moved, and it was as if the world had suddenly dropped into slow motion. It almost felt like an out of body experience. Her senses were suddenly hypersensitive and she noticed everything as Maria took Amanda's wine glass from her and placed it on the coffee table next to her own before she returned and leant in, coming closer and closer to her.

She could smell her fragrant floral perfume as she approached. Maria's hand reached out and gently took hold of her jaw with the lightest of touches and guided her in.

Amanda followed the hand, leant in with it, going where it led and anticipating the meeting to come. Her face was so close to Maria's now, that she could feel her warmth as she tilted her head to one side while Maria did the same. She paused then, for a second, and let the anticipation of the moment grow just a fraction more. Neither of them took a breath. Amanda felt like she'd been holding hers for an age when Maria closed the gap and pressed her lips to Amanda's.

They were soft and warm, and they felt so good. Maria kissed her gently, once, and Amanda just let her do it. She revelled in the moment, soaking in the feelings that went with it. Maria started to pull away slightly. Was she trying to give her space? Time maybe to process what had just happened? But Amanda didn't want it to end, so she went in to kiss her back. Maria responded, and suddenly it wasn't just a peck on the lips. It became energised, passionate.

She went deeper, their tongues touched and danced with each other as they kissed.

Pushing Amanda back, Maria climbed on top of her and kissed her again as their legs entwined and their bodies pressed against each other. She'd wondered how it would feel, touching and holding the body of a woman, and she decided it felt great. The feeling of Maria's bust pushing into hers as she moved felt delicious. Maria seemed to sense her thoughts and ran her hands over her body.

Amanda explored Maria's body too, her hands enjoying the softness of her. Maria kissed her on her cheek and then down onto her neck while her hands moved over Amanda's body.

Maria pulled on her jeans' button and quickly undid it. Amanda's breaths came quickly. She wanted it so badly, she ached for it, for the feel of it. She wanted to know how it would feel to have another woman touch her. When the moment came, Amanda gasped, she'd never felt so aroused before. Maria's every caress and kiss felt like an electric fire. She needed Maria to take her to the very summit of pleasure like no one had done before.

Was it the taboo nature of their coupling that caused it? The long drawn out flirty relationship that just needed to explode and find some release for the pent up energy that had built up between them?

Amanda had never felt so connected with someone. Maria knew just what to do. She knew how to touch her and what she needed. Moving with Maria, Amanda rode the rising wave of intense pleasure until it finally tipped her over the edge into a body shaking orgasm that felt stronger than any she'd had before.

She clung on tight to her lover as the waves of pleasure rolled over her and carried her to new heights.

Her body writhed of its own accord, her hips rolling and moving to get the most out of the experience in a rhythm that did wonderful things for her.

As the last few waves of ecstasy faded, Amanda kissed Maria frantically.

"Oh, my God. I've never felt anything like that. Thank you."

Maria raised her hand and placed her wet fingers in her own mouth. Amanda could only watch as Maria tasted her and seemed to enjoy every moment of it.

"Let's go upstairs, I want to taste you for real," she said.

Amanda couldn't speak. She had no words to answer with, so she merely nodded.

Maria took her by the hand and led her upstairs. Their relationship had changed. Amanda had no idea what this meant, or where things would go from here, but for right now, she didn't care. She just wanted Maria in her bed as quickly as possible.

***

Amanda lay on the bed and looked over at Maria's sleeping form as the morning sun played over her naked body. Her skin looked so soft and inviting, the swell of her breasts rising and falling called to her.

She hadn't slept much all night, not least because they had spent most of the night until the early hours just enjoying each other. Touching, kissing, caressing, and taking a shower together, before returning to bed when the desire grew too strong. It had been the most fantastic night of lovemaking she'd ever had. She'd never felt so sexually gratified, and laying here looking at her lover now, made her want to wake Maria up and do it all again. She reached out and with the lightest of touches, ran the pad of her middle finger over Maria's skin.

Maria moaned and shifted in her sleep, making Amanda stop.

Not only had her relationship with Maria changed, but her life had changed too. She wondered what this meant, what did this make her? Was she a lesbian? She wasn't sure. She still liked men, she still found them attractive, so maybe she wanted a bit of both? Did this thing, did *she*, need a label? She just didn't know, but what she did know was that last night had been wonderous, and she felt a keen love and attraction towards the dark-haired beauty beside her.

She rolled herself out of bed and gently padded across her room and into the bathroom to use the facilities. Afterwards, she washed her hands and looked at herself in the mirror.

Is this what you wanted, she silently asked her reflection? Is this the right thing to be doing? She turned away and walked around the corner to look at her bed and Maria, still in a deep slumber.

She leant against the wall and just looked at her friend and now lover. She smiled, feeling content and happy. While she looked at her, everything felt right with the world.

She returned to the bed and pressed herself up against Maria's back, wrapping her arm around her and kissing the back of her neck. Maria stirred and moaned lovingly in her newly woken state.

"Mmmm, morning, Mandy. What a lovely way to be woken up," Maria said.

"My pleasure," Amanda answered as Maria pushed into her. Amanda used her fingers to trace gentle lines over Maria.

"Oooh, that feels good," Maria moaned.

Amanda kissed her neck some more and moved one hand down, caressing her ever so gently, moving her fingers in slow, deliberate movements that barely touched her skin at all. "And how about this?"

Maria rolled her pelvis around, clearly loving every second of it.

"Don't stop," Maria said. "Just don't stop."

***

A little while later, Amanda sat in Liz's room, on the edge of her bed while Liz busied herself putting her makeup on.

"You seem happy this morning, Mandy. Did things go well yesterday? You spent a long time in your office."

"Yesterday was a little stressful, dealing with the politics of the covens and the Council. It's all a bit of a nightmare, don't ye know. But I suppose things could be worse, the end result in Los Angeles was basically what I wanted."

"So, what's got you smiling like a hyena? Hang on," she said locking eyes with Amanda in the mirror. "Did you meet someone last night? I thought you had Maria over. Did you go out?"

Amanda chuckled. "We didn't go out, no, but I did have a grand night."

"Well, good, you deserve it. You've had to deal with some shitty things since moving here," Liz said turning her attention back to the makeup brush in her hand.

"We all have. We all deserve to have some fun from time to time."

"Ain't that the truth. So, what did you do?"

Amanda had come in here to see Liz while Maria got herself up. It felt like a few days since she'd really seen her and she needed to see someone she could speak to. Someone she could confide in.

Liz was still so young, though. She wondered what her views on same-sex relationships were. She had no idea, and poking around inside her head to find out would be rude. So, she'd just have to say it.

"Yeah, well. I did end up in bed with someone. With, um… Maria…" Amanda let it hang there and watched in the mirror for Liz's reaction.

Liz paused, but she then turned with a look of happiness on her face. "Heh, it's about time, isn't it?" Liz said. "She's been after you for months."

Amanda smiled. "Yeah, she has."

"And is that what you wanted? Are you happy?"

"I… I think so. I'm still kind of getting my head around it, but she does make me happy."

"Then that's all that matters. What about Maria?"

"I think so. We need to talk, though I think."

"I would say that's an excellent idea, and don't leave it too long."

***

Amanda returned to her room and found Maria sitting in a chair pulling on her boots.

"Can we talk?" Amanda said.

"Sure, what do you want to talk about?" Maria said.

"Us. I want to know what this is and how we move forward from here."

"Of course, sit down," Maria said. Amanda sat in the soft seat next to Maria. "I like you, Amanda. I think that's been clear to you for a long time. I've fancied you ever since I met you when you first arrived at the Legacy House. I think I've been quite open about that."

Amanda nodded. "You have. I have been in no doubt about that for a long time."

"But you also know that I am not a one-person girl. I can't and won't have just one lover. Girlfriend or boyfriend. That's not me, and it never will be. I like you, Amanda, I like you a lot. But I have other lovers who I am not prepared to end things with. No offence, but that's just not me. So, if you want this, if you want to be with me, you have to be open to that."

"I understand," Amanda said, staring at the floor. She'd known this was how Maria was. She knew she had several lovers on the go. But, it felt a little different hearing it put so plainly to her after such a passionate night. "That's pretty much how I thought it would be."

"Please, don't take offence. It's nothing personal and no reflection on you. And do feel free to have as many other lovers as you want, as well. Go wild, enjoy yourself."

Amanda smiled. She wasn't sure if that was what she wanted or not. Did she want other lovers? "Thanks, I'll bear that in mind."

"Are you alright?" Maria asked.

"I'm grand, it's just been a bit of a rollercoaster and, well, it's all a bit new to me, and I think I'm still getting my head around... this, around us, you know?"

"I get it, I understand. It's your first time with a woman, plus, with how this relationship is going to work, I get that will take a bit of getting used to. Take as much time as you need."

"Thank you. I do want to see you again, though."

"I want to see you again too. You're not getting away from me that easily if I have anything to say about it." Maria said with a mischievous smile.

"I won't be going anywhere. Last night was fierce fun, so it was. Oh yeah, how about the ball we're throwing at the World Trade Center? Will you come to that?"

"Just you try and keep me away. In fact, I'd like to get you an outfit for it, if you'll let me?"

"Oh, really? And what makes you think I don't already have an outfit?" she said in mock horror.

"You haven't got an outfit, Amanda, have you?" It was more of a statement than a question. Maria knew her better than she thought.

"No, I haven't," Amanda answered, the ball was still a few days out, and she just wasn't that organised.

"Then, would you mind if I got you something?"

"Go for it, go wild. I'll look forward to seeing what you get me."

- Bratislava, Slovakia.

Liz crouched behind the side of the car next to Xain and Orion as bullets slammed into the vehicle from the Initiated men they were facing off against.

Xain rose from his ducked position and fired before a fresh salvo of shots forced him to duck back down.

"Easy, my big black ass," Xain shouted to his partner in crime.

"Quit your complaining. You're enjoying this as much as I am," Orion shot back.

"Yeah, but I'm better at this than you are," Xain said.

"In your dreams, dude."

"Would they be wet dreams?" Liz piped up.

"Oooh, sick burn, man," Orion said, mirth in his voice.

"You'd best not be taking sides, blondie," Xain quipped as he popped up again for another shot. "Liz, one of the targets broke right, down there, you see?"

Liz watched the man run-off between two buildings. "Got him," she said and strengthening her Shield, ran in a wide arc that kept her clear of the fire team but brought her in behind the man who'd made a run for it.

She followed an intercept course and allowed her Magic to guide her. Knowing she'd meet him at the crossroads up ahead, she leapt at the last moment and delivered a savage knee to the side of the man's head before he even knew he was being attacked.

He dropped to the ground with a cry of pain, the Essentia in her attack having weakened his Aegis. With him down for a moment, she extended her hand towards him and blasted him with Magical energy. His Aegis sparked and spat with power as it tried to resist the Magic. But the Aegis was weak and with a shower of rolling blue energy, it dissipated, allowing Liz to deliver a knockout punch fuelled with more Essentia.

She stood above him, breathing hard, her heart pumping.

"Damn, girl, you got the moves," Xain said from behind her.

She turned to look at him. "Thanks," she said.

"Shit ain't over yet, come on."

Generals Gambit

New York

"...so then we head off and chase down the rest of the gang. They're hiding in one of the warehouses, so we sneak in and move through the building, taking them out one by one. Xain gets us to split up and I end up taking on two separate guys on my own."

"Wow, really? Sounds like you're doing well," Amanda said.

"She's doing great, Red," Xain said. They were in Amanda's kitchen, standing around the island in the middle of the room. Amanda sat on one of the stools nursing a steaming cup of hot chocolate as she listened to Liz's story, with the occasional interjection from Xain and Orion. Liz was full of energy and didn't seem capable of keeping still as she related the story of her latest mission with the boys.

Amanda brushed her loose hair back behind her ear as she smiled at Xain and Orion. Amanda admired Xain's physique and the way he filled out that tight black top of his rather nicely.

She pulled her eyes away and silently chastised herself. What had gotten into her? Ever since that first night with Maria, she'd had sex on the brain. She'd seen Maria a couple more times since then, the nights getting a little wilder with the addition of some Magic into the mix. Now she was eyeing up Xain? It was interesting to know that she still felt attracted to men, not that she would have been bothered either way, it was just interesting.

He stayed mostly quiet while Liz ran through the details of what she'd been doing with them, but he spoke more than his partner did.

Orion sat on one of the stools around the corner of the island from Amanda, playing with an apple from the fruit bowl that sat nearby. He wore black like Xain, but where Xain was all shiny leather, Orion sported softer fabrics.

Looking at them, Amanda couldn't help but associate the pair with two characters from a couple of action films. So much so, that on occasion she'd even called Xain, Blade and referred to Orion as Neo, especially when they wore their long coats.

"So, when's the next mission?" Amanda asked when Liz had finished relating her story.

"Nothing definite yet, but we'll have something soon."

"Will you be coming to the ball tomorrow night?" Amanda asked.

"Wouldn't miss it for the world," Xain said.

"We'll be there, so will grumpy," Orion said, referring to their companion Steven Loomis, who Amanda had met a couple of times.

"And Balor?" Amanda asked after their Scion friend.

"No idea, we'll ask him," Xain answered.

"Excellent," Amanda said.

They chatted some more, discussing recent events, and as they were saying their goodbyes, Amanda had a feeling in her head that someone wanted to speak with her. With the boys out the door, Amanda asked Liz to give her a moment before opening the link, knowing it was Shaun before she committed.

"Amanda, we have an issue, can you come down?"

"Be there in a jiffy," she sent before turning to Liz. "Alright, Wonder Woman, sounds like something's up. Want to tag along?"

Liz smiled. "Sure. Where are we headed?"

"We need to speak with Shaun," she answered and guided her apprentice into the basement.

Shaun stood behind Vanessa in his black outfit. What was it with people wearing black? There were so many other colours out there. At least Vanessa gave the room a splash of colour in her pink top as she worked the mouse.

"What's the craic, then, Shaunie my boy?" she said as she walked in with Liz at her heels.

Shaun looked around, blinking an incredulous look off of his face. He'd get used to Amanda's sarcastic manner one day. "We're not entirely sure. We've had a report come in from the Knights of Newark Coven. They said they were assaulting a building with a group of Inquisitors inside. We asked them to hold off, but I think they've gone in."

"Inquisitors? I thought we'd sent them packing?"

"We did, and we didn't have any reports that a new group was in the city."

"Could they get in without anyone knowing?" Amanda asked.

"Sure, that wouldn't be too difficult. Seems odd that the Knights knew of it, though."

"Have they been in touch since?"

"No, nothing. That was just a few minutes ago, so it's probably still going on."

"Where is it?" she asked. Vanessa pulled up a map on one of the screens, with a street marked on it, showing its position relative to Amanda's house. It was fairly close and if this really was the Inquisition, then this new safe house's proximity to her home did not feel good. It could easily be a coincidence, but the thought that they might know where she lived gave her shivers.

That could be dealt with later though, if it even became an issue at all. First things first, they needed to get to this new Inquisition safe house and see what the situation was.

"Do we know which building they're in?"

"No. I can try to find out. It's not far away, though," Shaun replied.

She nodded. "Come on," Amanda said to Liz, "it's only a couple of minutes away, we'll bike it. We'll figure out their exact location when we get there."

"Really?" Liz said in wonder as she followed her into the garage.

Amanda tossed her one of the helmets. "Pop your lid on and climb on," she said as she swung her leg over her Fireblade and pulled her own helmet on.

Liz climbed on behind her as she fired up the engine and the machine roared to life. The garage door had already opened most of the way having telekinetically flicked the switch to open it with her Magic. Pulling away, she swung out into traffic, her ambient Magic making sure she exited at just the right time into a gap between the cars.

Liz held on tight to Amanda's waist as she gave the bike some power and shot along the streets, weaving between cars, her Magical luck opening a gap up for her, keeping the lights green and the traffic cameras looking the other way.

Less than two minutes later, several blocks away from her house, and much closer to the Hudson River Amanda moved into a side street with just a few cars parked up and a handful of people wandering along the sidewalks. The road didn't have much down it, just a few boarded up shops and commercial units, a perfect place for a hideout.

Amanda pulled in behind a camper van that she recognised as the mobile home of the Knights of Newark. Looking around with her Magical senses, she could quickly pick out the fading remains of an Aegis around a nearby building. The local Essentia around the building was a mess of swirls and surges. The tell-tale signs of a fight between Magi.

Amanda jumped off the bike and banged on the back of the camper van with the base of her fist. After a brief pause, movement could be made out from within and then the back door opened and a face popped into view. He had messy hair and a jacket over a t-shirt that looked to have a *Star Wars* design on it.

"Amanda? Are you alright?"

Amanda raised her eyebrows in mild surprise. "Me? Are *you* alright, is more like it? You contacted us." This was Mike, a Knights of Newark Magus. He seemed most at home sat before a computer screen from what she knew of him. He'd be monitoring the rest of the coven as they went into the building.

"Only to let you know what was going on. I think it's mostly over now, though. We ruined them."

"You guys took on an Inquisitor squad?"

"Yeah! Don't look so surprised. I mean, we had a bit of help, but we took them on."

"Help?" Amanda asked.

"Well, yeah, but…" he said, never finishing the sentence as Amanda pulled the other door open and stepped into the back of the van. For such a small-looking van on the outside, it appeared deceptively big on the inside. No doubt, it had a bit of Magical enhancement. Ducking slightly to keep her head from banging into the ceiling, she looked at the bank of computer screens on the table and side of the van. There seemed to be a live video feed coming in from several body cams and she could see Magi from some of the other New York covens in there with them.

"What the hell…" she said, feeling a little bewildered. She turned back to Liz. "We're going in," she said, and moments later they Ported into the building.

They appeared in the centre of a huge room on the second floor that had been trashed by the fight. Furniture had been smashed, bullet holes peppered the walls, and in amongst it all, there were a number of bodies. Mostly, Crusader Knights. These guys were usually humans with Magical items like swords and such, but they were not to be underestimated.

On Amanda and Liz's appearance, a number of the Magi that were standing in the room raised weapons or readied Magic, only to recognise Amanda and relax, stifling their Magical attacks.

Amanda immediately recognised members of three covens in the room. All of them had recently moved to New York and had introduced themselves to Amanda on their arrival. The Knights of Newark she'd known were here, the other two covens though, were Tyranny Effect and Tiger's Claw.

They were all scattered about the room, giving the place a search, or talking amongst themselves. One of the Magi from the Tyranny Effect Coven sat tapping away on a laptop.

Amanda turned to Denton Klein, the leader of the Knights of Newark, dressed in a trench coat with jeans and messy brown hair. He had a rugged but not unattractive look, with a fierce personality, and eyes that twinkled with energy. He smiled at Amanda as she walked over. He'd been talking with one of his coven mates, Debra who was dressed similarly.

"What the bleedin' hell's going on here?" Amanda asked.

"Just fighting the good fight, Mandy," he said. She wasn't sure she knew him well enough for him to be calling her Mandy, but she let it slide.

"I can see that. You took on a group of Inquisitors?"

"Yeah, why, is there a problem?" he asked.

Amanda paused a moment and took a breath. She wasn't actually sure if there might be a problem or not. These Magi were only doing what she'd done countless times before; fighting those who would have them dead. So far, at least, they seemed to have handled it pretty well. So why did she feel a little affronted by this? She'd said before to several people that this wasn't her city. She wasn't the new Queen of New York, other covens could do as they pleased, and yet, something wasn't right.

"I'm not sure. This just seems strange."

"What? That we got the tip-off first?"

"Excuse me?" Amanda asked.

"The tip-off. We were given Intel that these guys were here and the information was good. We weren't the only ones, either," he finished, indicating the other covens.

"Who gave you this tip?" she asked. Something about this felt wrong.

"I'm not sure, Mike will know." He put his finger to his ear to listen more closely to the reply from his coven mate in the van outside. "Mike? How did this tip come through?" he asked before listening to the reply. "The Dark Web? You got a message? Ah, yes, I remember now. Thanks, Mike," he said and looked up. "One of Mike's informants on the Dark Web told him. I think these guys had the same tip," he said, indicating the other covens in the room.

"Any idea who these guys were, other than Inquisitors?" she asked.

"Sorry, no. I think the leader is over there somewhere, though," he indicated.

"Thanks, I'll check it out," she said and turned away to see Christina Lewis, one of the other members of the Knights, crouching beside a motionless body on the floor that Amanda recognised right away.

"Ah, shite," Amanda said. She walked over and stood next to Christina. The body on the floor was Jessie Maynard's, the same Jessie who'd escaped the Inquisition just a few days ago. She had a large, ragged, oozing wound in her chest and looked very dead.

"How long has she been like this?" Amanda asked Christina.

"I don't know, a little while. It happened right after we first came in. Jessie was too eager for revenge," Christina explained and stood up next to Amanda. Christina always looked quite striking in her Goth clothing and makeup. Her backcombed black hair looked pretty wild today. Amanda looked over Jessie with her Aetheric Sight and could see that her Anima Mundi was still inside her, but it had already started to pull away from her body.

"Damn it," Amanda muttered.

"Yeah, she's gone. The Council wouldn't like us bringing her back now." Christina stated solemnly.

"No, they wouldn't."

"I thought it took longer than that. It's only been a few minutes."

"A violent end always speeds it up," Amanda said, feeling somewhat helpless.

"Shame. She was nice, I liked her."

"I liked her, too. You'll sort her out, won't you?" Amanda asked.

"Of course, leave it with us," Christina said.

Amanda left her side and looked around for Liz. She'd wandered off and Amanda could see her picking her way through the debris.

Continuing on her way, she walked over the broken furniture and found three bodies on the floor in one corner of the room. Two were just Crusader Knights, but the other looked like an old man and had clearly been a Magus or Blessed as the Disciples referred to them. She walked over to his side and moved to get a better look at his face. She had to move one of the Crusader's legs, but a second later, she got a good look at him and stood there in a daze for a moment.

She recognised him.

She'd done enough research on the Inquisition to know who this was, but she couldn't quite believe that he would be here. Even harder to believe, was that he'd been killed by the Magi in the room. She stood up and looked over to Denton. He stood talking with Mercy, the leader of Tyranny Effect.

"Denton, Mercy, do you have a moment?" she asked.

They wandered over to Amanda and looked down at the man she stood over.

"What's up, chica?" Mercy asked. Amanda glanced at the striking woman beside her with her long wavy magenta hair, purple bomber jacket, and black Lycra leggings.

"Do you know this man?" she asked them both.

"Nah," Mercy replied.

Denton crouched down, flicking his coat out of the way as he went to get a better look. "I don't think so, should I?"

"His name is Valerio Rossi," she said, looking to see if either of them knew the name. Mercy frowned in thought, but Denton's eyes went wide with recognition.

"You mean…?" Denton asked in shock.

"Yes, you've just killed the Witch Finder General of the Inquisition," said Amanda.

Mercy whistled while Denton stood and put his hand on his forehead in shock.

"Shit!" Denton said. "I had no idea. He didn't go down easy. Took a bunch of us to do it. If there'd been any other Magi here and we hadn't caught them by surprise, things might have gone a little differently."

"Was it just you three covens?" Amanda asked.

"No, the Daughters of Shade were here, too, but they left just before you got here," Mercy said.

"What does this mean? Why did he come here and how come we all got the tip-off about him and you didn't?"

"I don't know," said Amanda, "but I don't like it one bit. You've been used somehow, manipulated into being here at just the right moment."

Movement out the corner of her eye drew her attention. She looked up to see Liz haul an injured Crusader off the floor by the scruff of his neck and slam him against the wall before punching him in the face.

"What the…" Amanda muttered as Liz hit him again and again. It didn't look like she'd stop anytime soon, and the others were staring at her.

"At a guess, I'd say she doesn't like Inquisitors," Denton said.

"No shit," Mercy said.

Amanda turned back to them. She'd deal with Liz in a moment. "Look, I don't like this. You've been manipulated somehow. I don't know how, but someone wanted this man dead, and now they have it. Get out of here, take your dead and wounded with you and forget about this. I'll look into it and if I have cause for concern, I'll be in touch."

"What are you thinking? Should we be worried?" Denton asked.

"I hope not. I suspect it's a power play in the Vatican, something internal, but I'll need to check things out to be sure."

With that, she turned from the two Magi and walked over to Liz. Using her superior strength, Liz held the man up with her left hand while her right fist slowly turned his face into a red mess, one punch at a time. The Inquisitor appeared to still be alive, just.

Amanda could see tears running down Liz's cheeks and a look of hatred was etched over her face.

On reaching her apprentice, Amanda caught her wrist as she wound up for another punch

"That's enough," she said.

Liz whipped her head around and looked at Amanda with fury in her eyes.

"No, it's not. I'm gonna punch his bloody head off!" she said and struggled to pull her arm free from Amanda's grasp. "Let go."

"Liz, you've made your point, you've just about killed him."

"Good, that's the least he deserves."

"Maybe, but you don't want to be the one to make that choice."

"Bull! You've killed people. You look alright to me," Liz scowled.

"Every day I wish I could have made a different choice. Every day I wish I didn't have to kill anybody," Amanda said.

"I'm a Magus, Amanda. I think it's fairly inevitable that I'll end up killing someone someday."

"That's probably true, but don't do it like this. Do it in self-defence or in defence of others, not out of revenge. You might be okay, that's true, but you have no way of knowing that for certain."

Liz stared at her, weighing up her options, before standing up straight and dropping the Crusader to the floor. Tears beaded in her eyes and fell over her cheeks as she blinked. "I'm sorry," she said, deflated.

Amanda pulled her in for a hug. "It's fine. Don't worry, let's get out of here."

- Tonopah, Arizona

Dust worked his Magic and the barbed wire fence split apart, allowing him to walk through unobstructed. He walked over the road with no regard for the car that nearly hit him as he focused on his destination and continued into the scrub bushes that barely reached his waist.

Up ahead, various buildings stood tall over the desert spread out before him. Some were square and blocky, others were domed, and they throbbed with a power that he could see with his Magical sight. He could see the intense radiation they contained and the electrical power they created in those buildings. But he didn't care about that. All he cared about was the confluence of ley lines that crossed here on the site of this nuclear power plant, and the powerful pooling of Essentia he could see up ahead.

This would be where he would enact his ritual. This is where he would summon the Demon, Horlack back from the Abyss.

He could also sense the hundreds of lifeforms within the buildings up ahead. He smiled. They would make a suitable sacrifice to his Archon master.

New Management

Harlem, New York

The alleyway had seen all kinds of things over the years—from the gross and ugly, to the heart-warming and wondrous. Its location opposite the Pit Club meant that revellers would use it as anything from a toilet to an ambush site, or as a quiet place for a midnight encounter. There had even been a couple of deaths in the shadows.

But most of these were not uncommon occurrences elsewhere in the city.

But the alleyway had also seen its fair share of Magic and Magi over the years as they passed through the area, visiting the previous owner, Lucian.

But for the past six months, no Magi had appeared in the alleyway and the nightclub had lain dormant.

Until tonight.

Magic flared and four people appeared in the alley out of thin air. Two women and two men stood in the darkness. Looking around, they peered into the night, searching for any hidden threats.

When none appeared, the lead woman, Eudoxia, made for the street, her long, straight, dyed-green hair catching the wind. She sported several piercings and tattoos on her light coffee-coloured skin. A pair of tattoos on the outside corners of each eye looked like the flourishes on the Eye of Horus symbol. Elsewhere, two huge tattoos of stylised tribal designs in the shape of snakes ran from the backs of her hands, up her arms, down her back, and along the sides of her legs to her feet. She wore a denim mini-skirt and a couple of layers of punk rock tops, over fishnets with Doc Martin-style boots that looked like they'd seen better days.

She paused at the end of the alleyway and looked over the road at the unlit nightclub sign and the set of stairs that led down to the first layer of the subterranean nightclub. Her coven mates followed and stood behind her, peering at the scene.

"That's it?" said the other girl, standing to her right. This woman also had long straight hair, but hers was black in colour with a harsh fringe just above her eyes. She wore a clean and pressed pants suit over a white blouse and stiletto heels.

"Yes, Ninette, that's the place."

"Looks like a dive to me."

"Then you'd better get used to it because that's going to be home for a while."

"I know, doesn't mean I have to like it."

"Looks like a great fixer-upper to me," said one of the men. He had short-cropped dark hair, chiselled features with fashionable stubble on his jaw. He wore simple practical clothing of jeans and t-shirt with well-worn sneakers. "What about you, Elba? What do you think?"

"I think if you girls are finished chatting and wasting time, we should get over there and check the place out," said Elba, a huge muscled man in a hoodie.

"Agreed, let's get in there," replied Eudoxia.

Moments later, they appeared inside the club on the top level, a short distance from the balcony that looked down through the various levels to the dancefloor far below.

Without lights or windows, everything was dark, but the Magi could see just fine. It had clearly been visited by some of the local delinquents as crude graffiti had been sprayed on the walls and the whole place had seen better days.

Eudoxia started to walk towards the balcony, curious to look down into the rest of the club.

"Careful," said the smaller man. "We have no idea how safe that floor is."

Eudoxia smiled and continued on to the balcony. "You worry too much, Tobias," she replied as she peered over the railing.

Whoever had been here had clearly had a great time throwing tables, chairs, and anything else not bolted down over the edge to the dance floor below, judging by the shattered furniture down there.

She turned back to Tobias. "Get some power on. Let's light it up. I'm going to check out the VIP area."

"I'll go with you," said Ninette, and the two Ported further into the club.

Eudoxia soon found the VIP area, and within it, the hidden doorway that led down into the former living quarters of Lucian and his coven.

"Looks like the Magi Council didn't want anyone coming down here by accident," Eudoxia said, pointing at the sealed up and invisible doorway which the Council had blocked off using Magic—a Mortal's eyes couldn't see it, but Magical eyes could.

Ninette stood a little way off, eyeing up the main VIP area with a critical eye. Eudoxia smiled. "See anything you like?" She knew that Ninette would like running an exclusive VIP lounge.

Ninette looked up. "There's potential here. I could do something with this, I think," she said.

"Good, consider this yours. Do with it as you wish."

Ninette grinned again and returned to giving the space an appraisal. "Excellent."

"I'll be back shortly. Just have to check something out," Eudoxia said and Ported one floor down into the first level of Lucian's private quarters.

She wandered the corridors and checked out the rooms on the top floor before heading to the next one down. Having been sealed off, these levels had fared much better than the club above, but the signs of the fight that had taken place here were still present, scattered throughout the rooms.

She found blood stains and even the remains of bodies, rotting and smelling like death.

She didn't find anyone that she thought might be Lucian, but she'd have a better hunt later. For now, they needed to set about cleaning up. They had a lot to do.

- Amarillo, Texas.

"Hey, what ya think about this, Waylon?" Reagan asked, holding up a white mini-dress in front of her body.

"That's great darlin'," he said from where he sat in the rocking chair, wearing only his underpants and socks with his guitar in his lap.

"You ain't even looked, you redneck!" she said, a small amount of outrage in her voice.

"Darlin', when you're as goddamn gorgeous as you, I don't need to look. You will be the best-looking girl at that there ball tonight."

Reagan nodded. "Ya, darn right," she said as she held a different dress up in front of herself and eyed it in the mirror.

"You lookin' forward to it, then, sugar?"

"You bet yer ass I am. I wanna see this girl that's come over here and taken over New York. Might give her a piece of my mind, too."

"That's my girl," Waylon said. "Now get that sweet ass over here, will ya? Let's have some fun."

Cold News

Paris, France

Amanda opened the door to the current leader of the Legacy Coven, Royston Kendrick standing on her doorstep. The balding man wore a long coat over his tan trousers and smiled warmly at Amanda.

"Royston, it's lovely to see ye," she said and welcomed him with a hug.

"And you, Amanda. You look well."

"Thank you, I'm grand. Come in, come in. Let's get you out of the cold, hey?"

Royston followed and removed his coat, revealing a garish Hawaiian shirt beneath.

"Another classic shirt, I see," Amanda commented.

"You like it?"

Amanda eyed him with a slight grin. "Very dapper," she said and invited him into the living room. He'd contacted her via a Mental Link a short time ago and asked if he could pay her a visit. "What can I do for you?" she asked, curious about what he hadn't been able to say over the Link.

"Are the others here?" he asked.

"Yeah, sure, you want me to get them?"

"If you wouldn't mind," he said.

It took a minute or so, but before long, Amanda sat in the living room with Maria, Liz, Gentle Water, Raven, Shaun, Vanessa, and Royston.

"Thanks for coming," Royston said, addressing the group. "Something has come to our attention and we need to check it out. We're stretched a bit thin in Paris at the moment, so I thought I'd ask for your help."

Amanda nodded from where she sat, holding Maria's hand. "Sure, how can we help?"

"We've had a report come in from a coven based in the Antarctic. They detected some strange activity near them and were monitoring it. The other day they chose to finally check it out. They Ported in and found a huge camp. A dig of some sort, outside the front of a temple or something built into the side of a mountain. They detected Magical workings all over the site and were about to look into it further when a team of men, including a Magus, surrounded them and started to attack. Two of the Magi escaped and made their way back to their base on their own. The other two have not been heard from since and we think they're dead. Whatever they discovered out there, the team have Magical support and seem keen to protect it. We need to know what's going on and why. So, I'm passing this one on to you, Amanda. You can deal with it however you like, but I need you to follow up on it for me, please."

"Of course, I'd be happy to," Amanda answered, feeling honoured that the Legacy came to her for this. She felt immediately keen to do her best for them.

"Today, if possible," Royston added.

"Ah, well, that might be an issue," Amanda replied. With the ball later tonight, taking on a mission like this could be problematic.

"I know you have your ball tonight. Is there anyone you can send?"

"I'll go," Gentle Water said.

"Aah, now, don't be an ejit, ye can't miss the ball," Amanda said.

"I have been to plenty of balls, Amanda. You do not need me there. You will be fine without me."

"To be sure. That's not the point, though. This is to celebrate the liberation of New York, and ye were a key part of that. I can't send you away while we all have a drink and relax."

"You are not sending me away. I am choosing to do this."

"Are ye sure?"

"Of course. Please, go enjoy yourself. I will be fine."

Amanda frowned. She wasn't thrilled with her mentor not being at the celebration, but she also knew the stubborn ejit well enough to know when it was pointless arguing with him. He was just trying to help so she could attend her own celebration. However, she was keen to make sure that this mission from the Legacy would be done correctly, and there was no one better than Gentle Water for her to send. She trusted him implicitly and Royston trusted him too. She didn't really see an alternative.

"Okay, then." She turned back to Royston, her mind filled with conflicting thoughts. She desperately wanted Gentle Water at the ball, but she also didn't want to say no to the mission. She knew he was the right choice, and there would be plenty of other people at the celebration. She knew this was the right way to go, and did her best to make her peace with it. "Gentle Water will go."

"Excellent. Thank you, Gentle Water. Let me send you the details of where you need to go," he said, and a brief flicker of Magic passed between them.

"Thank you, Royston. It is a pleasure to serve. I will be in touch the moment I have anything." Gentle Water said.

The rest of the day went fairly quickly after Royston left. Amanda tried to convince Gentle Water to go after the ball, claiming that Royston would never know, but he refused. Not long after Royston left, Gentle Water Ported away as well.

Most of the arranging of the ball had been left to the Arcanum. They'd booked the observation deck at the top of the World Trade Center and had carefully made sure that there wouldn't be anyone there who would freak out if they saw something Magical. All it usually took was a little money and a few favours, but sometimes a bit of Magic was needed to grease the wheels, as well. Although, the Arcanum always tried to do things without calling in one of their resident Magi.

Amanda had received regular updates about the progress of the arrangements, and everything seemed to be on track for a great night with plenty of guests. The only thing Amanda didn't know at this point was what she would be wearing because she'd left that up to Maria. As the time for her to get ready grew near, she started to feel a little nervous about what Maria might have procured for her. Maria had informed her that she had something, and would be bringing it from Paris shortly, so Amanda took the opportunity to freshen herself up.

She showered, wrapped herself up in her white robe, and stepped out into her room to find Maria waiting for her.

"Feeling refreshed?" Maria said.

"Much better, thank you."

"Would you like to see the dress?"

"To be sure. I have to say, though, I'm feeling a little nervous about this." What if she didn't like it? What would she wear and more importantly, how would Maria react? She didn't want to upset her.

"Don't be nervous. As a word of warning, it is a little daring, and it might show a little more than you're used to, but I know you'll look stunning in it," Maria said as she reached into a large flat box on the bed and lifted the dress out.

It was long and red with straps over the shoulders, and apart from a fairly high slit up her right leg and a plunging back, it would cover her up rather well.

But that wasn't the daring part. As Maria held it up and the dress swayed gently. Amanda could see that the dress was not only quite thin, it was sheer. When the dress was held before a window or light, you could see through it.

However, the dress also had some quite lovely lace sewn onto it in a few strategic places that would protect her modesty.

Amanda eyed the dress, feeling a little torn. She actually liked it, which was a huge relief. It was stunning and the delicate lace detailing was beautiful. She just wasn't sure about it being so sheer. She felt reasonably certain that she would need to be nude beneath it in order to really sell it.

"So, what do you think?" Maria asked.

"I like it, and you're right, it is a little more daring than I'm used to. But I think I need to try it on before I make my final decision."

"Then please," Maria said, holding it out to Amanda, "because I'd love to see you in it."

Amanda took the dress and changed into it, slipping it over her head. It felt surprisingly soft and very light like she wasn't wearing anything at all.

"Ooh, it does feel nice," she said as she turned to a mirror to look at herself, smoothing it out and making sure it fell just right. She turned from side to side and then looked at the back over her shoulder. Her confidence grew as she realised that you couldn't actually see anything through the dress at all. The detailing worked to cover her in all the right places and she really did feel great in it.

She turned back to Maria with a smile to find her holding up a pair of shoes and a clutch bag to go with the dress. The shoes were red and had straps that would wrap about her legs to just beneath her knees.

"And?" Maria said. "What's the verdict?"

"I love it. I'll wear it for you with pleasure, and I love those shoes! Wow. Thank you." She hugged Maria and gave her a lingering kiss before pulling on the heels and finishing getting ready, fixing her hair into a simple half-up hairdo. Nothing too fancy.

Satisfied with herself, she turned to Maria, who now stood in a long green satin dress that shimmered in the light. The top half was fitted to her body and showed off her curves, while the layered skirt had two slits up the front to show glimpses of her legs.

"Wow, you look stunning," Amanda said.

Maria smiled. "Thank you, we'll be the belles of the ball," she joked.

Amanda walked over to her and pulled her in for a kiss. Keeping their foreheads touching, they smiled at each other. "I'm excited for tonight. I want to have a really great time."

"You will, I'm sure. Shall we go and find the others?"

They went downstairs and found Liz, Raven, Shaun, and Vanessa all looking fantastic in their finery. Liz had a gorgeous slinky white dress on and Vanessa wore a black mini-dress showing off her legs in a pair of very high heels. Both of the guys wore suits with a tailored cut that did wonders for them. Shaun looked very prim and proper, his Magical item hiding his vampiric features and giving him perfect skin and slicked back, short, dark hair. Raven's hair had been tied back, while he chose to keep his suit more casual without a tie and the top couple of buttons of his shirt undone. Amanda still fancied him and enjoyed the glimpse of the top of his chest beneath his shirt.

He smiled at Amanda as she walked over to the group. "Looking great, Mandy," he said.

"Yeah, wow, that's a little daring," Liz commented. "You look great, though."

"Thank you. I love it."

"You should. You'll make quite the impression," she said as she gave Amanda a hug.

"Are we ready?" Maria asked. Everyone nodded or said yes and Maria worked her Magic, Porting them out of the house with a satisfying snap of air.

- Palo Verde Nuclear Generating Station, Tonopah, Arizona.

Dust stood on top of one of the structures inside the central containment building of the plant. The noise was a little deafening, but Dust didn't care. Around him, metal pipes and catwalks crisscrossed the room. They snaked around the reactor and other parts of the complicated building. The whole site had been put on lockdown shortly after his arrival, as he swept through the buildings, killing or capturing the workers on a whim.

Now, on a large flat metal section of the reactor core, he'd daubed a summoning circle on the floor using the dried blood of his victims, some of whom lay in a pile to his left. Before him, thirteen workers from around the site, chosen at random, kneeled inside the circle. Some of them were silent, others wept and begged for their lives, but none of them wanted to be there.

His Magic surged, pulling in energy from the Pooling created by the ley lines. The power strengthened the Aegis he'd erected around the circle. He pulled the Lazarus Scroll from his pocket and unrolled it, clearing his throat as he did so.

He found the passage he wanted and started to read it aloud in the language of the Archons. A glowing green mist began to appear and swirl about the circle, causing a few of the mortals within it to panic or hyperventilate.

Green lightning flashed within the circle, and suddenly the bodies of the thirteen people within were torn apart by an invisible force, covering the floor with their flesh and blood.

"Come to me, Horlack, return to our world once more," called Dust.

Ball of Destiny

One World Trade Center, New York

Amanda appeared in a smallish side room on the one hundred and second floor of One World Trade Center next to Maria, Liz, Raven, Shaun, and Vanessa. The room appeared empty and had been the one part of the observation deck not protected by a powerful Aegis. It had been created for tonight's event, to give any Magi who wanted to Port here a place to appear.

A door led out of the room and into the main observation deck of this level, which basically ran around the entire building. People were already here and they stood talking or looking out over the cityscape below, while waiters circulated with trays of canapés.

"Wow," Liz said.

Amanda watched as Liz skipped over to the windows to stare at the cityscape beyond.

"That's awesome. Amanda, come and have a look," Liz said, beckoning her over.

Smiling, she walked over, stood next to her apprentice, and looked out over the night-time view. Her apprentice's excitement gave Amanda a warm feeling of pride within her chest. Night had already fallen and the city was lit up by thousands of lights that shone like stars in the darkness. Buildings were lit up from within by an orange glow while the white and red lights of cars on the streets below moved through the caverns of the city like rivers, giving it life and energy. The vista was breathtaking and she could have easily stood and stared at the view for the whole night.

"It's beautiful," Amanda agreed. She felt a hand at her arm then and turned to see Maria smiling at her.

"I think there are people who want to see you," she said.

"Of course. Come and find me if you need me, Liz, and get yourself a drink," she said before walking with Maria towards the Magi already in attendance.

She recognised most of them, including members of the Legacy, Liberty's Children, and several covens who had moved to New York recently. She even spotted Celest in the crowd.

Victoria approached her first, smiling as she walked up. "Wow, look at you. Out to make an impression, I see," she said, greeting her with a kiss on either cheek.

"This is a great party, Amanda. Well done," Victoria said.

"Thank the Arcanum, not me."

"Of course. Well, just a word of warning, there are a few members of the Magi Legion here, most will leave you alone, but you might have a run-in with them if you give them a chance."

"That's fine. I'm a big girl. I think I can handle them," Amanda said.

Victoria smiled. "I have little doubt of that."

Amanda continued to circulate around the room and exchange pleasantries with the people she met. A representative of the Arcanum approached to ask if everything was as she wanted. While a little later, Celest gave her a big bear hug and told her she was very happy in New York.

Then a brown-haired girl approached and smiled at Amanda.

"Hi, I'm Louisa Hunt. I'm from the Ordo Obscura Coven, from Europe," she said.

Amanda recognised her name and the name of her coven. "Nice to meet you, I'm sure I've seen your name on a few Magi history books before."

"You probably have." She smiled. "Um, do you have a moment for some questions?" she asked.

"I have a moment, and if I can answer your questions, I will," Amanda answered.

"I'd like to know a little more about Lucian's death if you could shed any light on it for me. No one seems to know what really happened, but I've heard rumours that you might know something?"

Amanda smiled, the woman was fishing for answers, and maybe she hoped Amanda would bite, but Lucian's death was being kept a secret for the time being and Amanda had no desire to break that silence. She didn't want everyone to know that she'd been the one to kill him, not yet, at least. "Thank you for coming to me, I really appreciate that, but I'm afraid I know about as much as you."

"So, you weren't in the city at the time of his death?"

"Have you spoken with Trevelyan at all? He knows much more about this than I do, and I'm sure he'd answer your questions." Amanda hated not being honest, but she knew it was for the best. Best for her and best for the city. She didn't want to give Nymira, or any other Nomad, a reason to come here. She had enough on her plate.

"I haven't spoken to him about it, is he here?" she asked.

"I've not seen him yet. But he should be coming. When I see him, I'll send him over," she said before making her excuses and heading into the crowd.

Suddenly, a figure stepped in front of her. She didn't recognise the girl at all, but she eyed Amanda with an expression that did nothing to suggest that this would be a friendly chat.

"Um, hi, can I help you?" Amanda said.

"I doubt it, sugar tits. I jus' wanted to see what all the damn fuss was about, but I'm not impressed. You aren't all that," she said in a Texan drawl.

The girl's rudeness brought Amanda up short for a moment. She wasn't sure what she should say in return. The girl had big blonde hair and wore a tiny black dress that didn't leave much to the imagination. She spotted a skinny man with a scruffy suit and a mullet behind her, watching the confrontation.

She looked back at the girl and smiled, taking a breath. "Well, it's lovely to meet you, too, and that's such a cute outfit, very classy. You've left so much to the imagination, well done," she said, her sarcasm bubbling up to take control of her mouth again.

The girl looked a touch confused and glanced down at her dress before looking back up at Amanda. "Are you trying to be clever?"

"Ah, no. Not me. You look manky, so you do. That's Irish for gorgeous, by the way," she lied.

The girl opened her mouth to say something, but it seemed to escape her at the last moment. She gave a slight shake of her head as if to banish whatever train of thought she'd ventured down and looked back up at Amanda.

"Look, ya might have the power here in New York for the time being, but we'll be watching you."

"I don't want power. I'm not the queen of this city."

"Say whatcha like, I know your kind," she said, pointing at Amanda's face before she turned and walked away, past the man she'd been with, saying, "Come on, Waylon, let's find the others."

Waylon looked at Amanda as his girl walked off.

"You're a lucky man, she's pure haunty, that one," she said to him, again using Irish slang to confuse him. As he turned and walked away, Amanda couldn't help but giggle to herself. She'd already guessed they were members of the Magi Legion, no doubt wanting to look big and clever in front of their coven.

She'd spied the Legion across the room a few times already, occasionally catching one or two of them giving her a look of daggers from where they stood. She wasn't sure they were even enjoying themselves. They looked like they were just brooding in the corner for most of the time.

She spied Yoh standing by himself next to the windows and enjoying the view, so she wandered over to him. "How are ye?" she asked.

"Good evening. I'm well, Amanda-san," he said and put his arm around her for a hug. She returned the gesture and gave him a kiss on the cheek. "And you?"

"Very well. Thank you for coming."

"My pleasure. I wouldn't miss this."

They separated, and Amanda smiled as she looked over the view of the city. For every person who seemed to have a problem with her, there were always more who didn't, and she felt fortunate to have such great friends who would support her.

"I hope Reagan didn't just ruin your night," Yoh said.

"That's her name, is it? I wondered which member of the Legion I was speaking to," Amanda said.

"Hai, Reagan and her partner Waylon. Not the brightest of people and occasionally something of an embarrassment for Forest and Stella Ward, the leaders of that House."

"Ah, they're no bother. No harm done, really."

"Good. I'm glad to see you're in high spirits," he said.

"I am. I'm grand, thank you. Things are going well. New York is great."

"You seem really happy with Maria as well."

"She's lovely, yes. Very happy, thank you."

"I'm just happy you've found someone."

"You don't seem phased that she's a… well, a she," Amanda said.

"Why would I be? It's no comment on me, and frankly, who you sleep with is your business and is no reflection on any other part of your life. Providing you're happy, and it's what you both want, who cares? Anyone who judges you based on who you love has their priorities backwards as far as I'm concerned, Amanda-san."

Amanda hugged him again, grabbing him around his waist and pulling him to her. "Thank you."

"*Dō itashimashite*, you're welcome," he said.

She pulled away from him again and leant her hip against the railing next to the window.

"What about everything else? I heard you've had a bit of an issue with the Disciples of the Cross recently," he said.

"The Inquisition? A little, yeah, and there was an odd thing that happened the other day. The Witch Finder General came to New York His trip was leaked to a few of the covens in the city who attacked them and he ended up dead."

"The General? That is concerning. Any idea what happened?"

"I suspect it was a power play, something internal within the Inquisition. I think someone wanted him dead."

"Any idea who?" Yoh asked.

"Only my own speculation. I've only really dealt with one member of the Grand Inquisitors, but I wouldn't put it past her at all. I have no proof, of course."

"These things usually become clearer as time goes on."

Amanda smiled, he was right. She just hoped she'd find out sooner rather than later.

Circulating back through the party, Amanda exchanged more pleasantries with her guests as they congregated in groups or took in the view from different angles.

Amanda was walking around the floor once more when a side door opened and she saw Trevelyan standing just inside the Porting room. He stepped out and smiled at her.

"Good evening, Amanda. Thank you for the invitation. Sorry I'm a little late," he said. "I wanted to get here earlier, but Council business rarely fits around my social calendar."

"No bother, thanks for coming."

"My pleasure. I wanted to see you anyway, firstly to say thank you for your efforts in Los Angeles. I know it didn't go exactly to plan, but I think you did well, all things considered," he said.

Amanda flushed slightly at the compliment, but also felt a sense of sadness and regret at the loss of life on that mission. "It could have gone better," she said.

"Maybe. But you handled Nefertiti well and got the result you needed. The cost might have been higher than you anticipated, but to do nothing would have cost us much more. So, thank you."

Amanda smiled and nodded, keen to move on.

"So, I also need to speak to you for a short time. Do you have a few minutes?" Trevelyan asked.

"Sure, what can I do for you?" she asked, seeing no reason she couldn't take a few minutes away from the party. She'd already circulated through all the guests she'd wanted to speak with and had started to relax a little more and not feel quite like she was on parade so much.

"I'd like to show you something, and talk somewhere a little more private and protected, if that's alright with you?" he asked.

"By all means, where did you have in mind?"

"Have you ever been to the Council base before?"

"No, I've not yet had the pleasure," she said. She quickly Linked with Maria, Yoh, and Liz and sent them a quick message about what she was doing before she focussed on the here and now once more. "Lead the way," she said.

"Follow me, then," he said, indicating the Porting room. "I opened one of our Portals in here," he said as they walked into the room. There wasn't anything visible to the naked eye that any mortal could see, but to Amanda's Magical senses, some powerful Flux Magic burnt away in the corner, waiting for a Magus to step into it and call it to action.

"Walk with me," Trevelyan said, and Amanda moved in step with the Master Magus. She felt his Magic reach out and connect with the Portal's Essentia. As they touched it, the Portal flared into life and opened like a flower, its magical protections pulling away to allow them safe passage.

Stepping into the roiling energy, Amanda felt it surge over her like a wave, refreshing and exhilarating as the Magical power surged within her. Anyone watching would have just seen the two figures disappear with a shimmer in the air, like ripples on the surface of water.

With a brief flash of Magical energy, Amanda found herself standing in what appeared to be a stone room without windows or furnishings. Behind them, a circle of Essentia held the image of the Porting room in the World Trade Center, while ahead of them was a simple door.

Through her Aetheric Sight, Amanda could tell this wasn't stone at all, though. This room appeared to be made from Magical energy and Mana, the solidified form of Essentia that only really appeared in the Material Realm at Poolings, where ley lines crossed. She also had no idea where she was. Her Aetheric Senses that could usually pinpoint her location on Earth failed her utterly.

"Where are we?" Amanda asked.

Trevelyan smiled. "Don't worry. This is part of the security and defences that the Council has in place to protect against infiltration by Nomads and such. We're in a Null Realm."

"Null Realm? I've heard of those. Remind me what they are exactly?" Amanda asked.

"The Material World and the Spirit World are separated by a barrier we call Acheron that cannot be crossed and keeps the Archons in the Abyss. Although Acheron cannot be crossed, it can serve as a realm unto itself for those powerful enough to be able to carve out space within it. These Magical spaces are called Null Realms. They're not tied to any geographical place on Earth and can be accessed from anywhere around the globe. The Null Realm is expressly controlled by the creator of the Realm and those he links to it. They're often used as secret and very secure hideouts."

"That's right; I knew I'd heard of them before. I need to get one of those."

Trevelyan smiled. "In this case, rather than using it as a realm, the Council uses it as a security barrier. In a moment, we'll be asked to drop our Aegises to allow the Magi security team to check on us before they open that door and let us through."

Sure enough, a voice sounded in the room suddenly and asked them to remove their Aegises. Amanda obliged and felt Magic passing over her, identifying her. Moments later, security seemed satisfied and she heard the click of the lock on the door ahead of her.

"I guess they're happy?" she said.

"Apparently so," Trevelyan smiled.

"What was to stop me from just smashing through that door, though?"

Trevelyan smiled. "Because it's more than just a door, it's a Portal that's designed to look like a door which is controlled by the security team. You wouldn't get through if they didn't want you to."

"Oh, okay."

He walked forward, opened the door, and stepped aside so she could pass. She thanked him and walked into a large vaulted room. The whole place looked like something that had been built in the Middle Ages, only on a much grander scale. It appeared she stood within some kind of castle made from huge chunks of grey stone. The room they were in was roughly circular and over fifty meters across with a high domed ceiling. Before them, in the centre of the floor, a fountain burbled away with a short-walled pond surrounding an urn that water cascaded down the sides of.

Beyond the fountain, two sets of curved stairs led up to archways leading deeper into the building, while further arches on this level revealed corridors that snaked off into the depths of the complex.

Behind her, Trevelyan stepped through the door from the Null Realm and shut it behind him. It appeared to be one of several doors, all of the same type, although a few of them were bigger double doors.

"Welcome to Ultima Thule, the Council's Coven House," Trevelyan said. "Follow me."

Trevelyan walked to the left, over the beautiful mosaic floor, and headed towards one of the corridors. Amanda quickly caught him up and fell into step beside him.

"This is amazing. Where are we, where is this building based? It's huge," Amanda said. Her sense of location had snapped back into place, but she wasn't sure she believed what she was feeling.

"It is, and the answer to your question will become clear in just a moment. I don't want to ruin the surprise, and it's easier if I just show you," he said.

"Oh, okay." Amanda followed along beside him, getting the feeling that he wanted to talk once they'd reached their destination. The corridor they entered had a much lower ceiling than the room they'd been in, but the ceiling must still have been nearly ten meters high with its Gothic arches. Sconces burned on the walls at regular intervals, giving off plenty of soft light that illuminated the rugs and paintings that decorated the hallway. Some were portraits, others depicted scenes from history that Amanda didn't recognise.

The corridor had been bending gently to the right, and before long, Trevelyan walked up to a door on the left and stopped before it, his hands on the ring of steel that hung from the massive oak door and served as a handle.

"Shall we?" he said.

"Please." She nodded and watched as Trevelyan opened the bolt on the door and pushed the double doors open wide.

The room was another large one and seemed to be a kind of balcony. Massive Gothic arches acted as glassless windows encircling the crescent-shaped floor and giving a stunning view of the vista beyond.

Amanda thought that if Liz had been amazed by the view from the top of the World Trade Center, she would be stunned to silence by this one.

The castle sat within a freezing white landscape of ice and snow, of a kind that Amanda had never seen before. Huge chunks of ice jutted into the sky while deep ravines stretched off into the distance, creating an utterly wild and alien landscape.

Behind her, stretching up for hundreds of meters with its Gothic spires and flying buttresses, the castle appeared to have erupted from the ice.

But the true wonder of the view lie before her, hanging in the night sky, surrounded by a starfield so bright that she could clearly make out the misty Milky Way.

Saturn. The ringed planet hung in the sky, huge and imposing, but beautiful and awe-inspiring at the same time.

She had no idea how long she stood there staring at it, but it felt like forever. It was only when her tongue started to feel a bit dry because she had her mouth hanging open for so long, did she shake her head and come around a bit. She looked back at Trevelyan, who'd been admiring the view as well. But he smiled upon seeing her expression. Did she look that shocked?

"Is that…?" Amanda asked.

"Yes, that's Saturn. We're on one of its moons. Enceladus, to be precise."

Amanda tried to voice something, anything. Her mouth moved, but nothing came out. She just couldn't vocalise the thoughts she had in her head. The idea that they were this far from Earth seemed utterly insane.

"It's okay. It's a lot to take in. Come, there're a few seats over here. Let's just sit for a moment, shall we?"

Amanda just nodded and followed Trevelyan to the benches that stood close to the edge of the balcony and sat down.

For maybe five or ten minutes, she just sat there and marvelled at the view and slowly came to terms with where she was and what she was seeing. This close to the colossal gas giant, she could make out the clouds as they moved over the surface of Saturn, and even some detail in the rings.

"So, how long has this been here?" she asked.

"The Council has maintained a base of operations that has always been called Ultima Thule ever since the formation of the Council, but it's been located in various places until we built this over a thousand years ago."

"It's amazing. I had no idea… I mean, Gentle Water told me that there were Magi in space, but this is beyond anything I'd ever expected. Can Magi Port here?"

"It takes a powerful Magus to Port this far, but it is possible to do, as well as to travel in space. We don't have much contact with them, but there is a vast community of Magi spreading across the Orion Arm of the Galaxy. They're known as the Nexus and are made up of families of Magi called Dynasties. But they leave the Magi of Earth alone for the most part. So yes, there are Magi out here, but they usually travel around on Aether Ships because the distances are so vast."

Amanda turned to look at Trevelyan. "Why are you showing me this?"

Trevelyan smiled briefly. "How did things pan out in L.A., Amanda?"

His reply of a question to her question threw her for a moment, but she figured he would be going somewhere with this. "It went well. We found the Nomads who were targeting the covens there. The group was led by a man called Shaitan, and we were confronted by a Magus called Nefertiti, who seemed to want to protect him. She killed his coven mates and promised that it wouldn't happen again. I'm guessing she took Shaitan with her."

"You know, I met with Toni, Tabitha, and Melissa recently, before they went to L.A. with you. Their coven mate, Jonas, was a part of the Council, but he died that night during the attack on their House. Melissa died on the mission with you, didn't she?"

"She did. Toni and Tabitha aren't here… I mean, at the party tonight. It's a bit soon for them, I think."

"Of course, but you took on that Nomad, and you avenged their deaths, that's impressive. I applaud you for taking on such a powerful Nomad, but you should be careful, especially where Shaitan is concerned. Rumour is, he can pass into the Abyss at will."

"It's not a rumour. It's true, I've bleedin' seen it," she said.

"Then, maybe you can understand why I urge caution in dealing with him."

"Of course, without a spiritual component to an Aegis, he can ignore it and appear right inside of it. That's dangerous."

"It is. You should also know it is rumoured that he's set this knowledge down in a book known as the Libre Nox Noctis. We have no idea where this book is. We're hunting for it right now, because the power contained within its pages could be dangerous in the wrong hands."

"I understand," she replied.

Trevelyan looked at her then and seemed to be contemplating something. Then he looked away from her and stood up and walked over to the balcony.

Amanda looked out at the view of Saturn once more. It had already moved its position as Enceladus went about its orbit.

She shifted her senses into the Magical spectrum and observed the enormous Magical energies at work. She could feel the artificial gravity and air that the Magic produced as well as a colossal glamour effect that hid the structure from the sight of any passing space probes. There were many other effects at work here, all hugely powerful and all of them protecting the structure and its inhabitants from the harsh environment outside.

Trevelyan turned to her. "Come with me, Amanda. There's something I think you should see."

She stood up and followed Trevelyan out of the room and back into the corridor. He waited for her and spoke once she'd caught up.

"We should Port there. Are you ready?"

"Of course," she said, not resisting his Magic as the view of the huge vaulted corridor changed to a much smaller, homier one as they Ported. It was about three meters wide with carpet, tables with ornaments on them, and a few visible doors further along. They stood outside a door, which Trevelyan opened. It creaked as it moved on its hinges.

He walked inside, and Amanda followed him into a room fifteen meters across and less deep. A few electrical lights hung from the ceiling, giving off a dim illumination. The room had been carpeted and contained several glass-covered display cabinets and shelves, all of which looked like they belonged in a stately home.

Dotted about the room were glass-topped podiums and cases which contained books or scrolls or other written works. Trevelyan walked over to one and looked down at it.

Amanda had paused inside the door. It was tranquil in here and she felt the weight of history in the treasures on display. The books on the shelves and the delicate manuscripts within the cases all looked to be hundreds of years old.

"Wow, what are all these?" she asked.

"We've been gathering and preserving these documents for centuries. They're invaluable."

She walked over to the nearest one and looked inside. The document looked old and the writing, although in English, would take some deciphering. A modern, printed document beside it translated the original text and offered commentary, which Amanda read with interest.

This scroll formalised the naming of the Magi by the Magi Senate about two thousand years ago. When the Senate had been formed, and Magi from all over the globe joined, there came a need for a single word to refer to them, as every culture used their own term. So, a bastardised version of the word "Magi" was chosen. It was spelled the same but pronounced "Mah-Guy" rather than "Mei-Jai". This had been based on the hard G of the Greek word "goés", pronounced "Go-Ace", meaning sorcerer or conjurer, and also the hard G of the singular, Magus.

And so, the Magi had been born.

"Come, look at this one," Trevelyan suggested.

She walked over and stood next to him. She looked down at the old-looking scroll within the glass case. Again, she was unable to read the scroll itself. Instead, she focused on the plain English translation beside it.

THE PROPHECY OF HELENE

Many years from now, a time will come when the Archons will return.
Guided by the Red Witch, they will return to Earth.

You will know these times by the mark of the creator.
Placed upon the body of one of your own.

Mark her soul with colours of life and death.
See the body marked by the power of the creator.

Mark her passing into the Abyss
See the Weavers whose company she keeps.

She will be your guide in the dark times ahead.
Be ready to fight, for the time will soon be upon you.

All that I have prophesied will come to pass.
When Ishtar gives birth.

She finished reading and looked up at Trevelyan. "What's this?" she asked.

"It's a prophecy. Originally given by a woman called Helene in AD 42 to the Magi Senate, the organisation of Arcadian Magi that preceded the Magi Council. It talks about the return of the Archons, and of someone, a Magus, who might be a guide in these dark times. Amanda, your adventures and missions against the Nomads... they're getting noticed. Your name is starting to become known. I predict you will become quite a well-known Magus. It's my belief that this prophecy is talking about you, that you will be our guide through the dark times ahead."

Amanda looked up at Trevelyan, wondering if she'd heard him right and if he was just having a joke at her expense. But he stood there and looked at her with a sombre expression. "Me? Feck off. You're having me on, so ye are," she said incredulously.

"I assure you, I'm quite serious."

"Really? Are ye sure?"

"Quite sure."

"So... I'm some kind of, what, chosen one? Like Neo, or Anakin, or Harry Potter? And I'm what? Meant to save the world?"

"I have no idea who these people are. Some popular culture reference, I presume?"

"Well, yeah."

"Then you have me at a disadvantage, but to answer your question, honestly, we have no idea, it doesn't say what you must do."

"What *someone* will do, someone who might not be me," she protested.

Standing in that dusty old room, with no underwear on, in stupidly high heels, and wearing a see-through dress she did not, in any way, feel like some kind of 'chosen one'. Far from it.

Looking at Trevelyan, and seeing the conviction in his eyes as he looked back at her, she actually felt a little wary of him. This kind of faith in her was not something she wanted to deal with and she certainly did *not* want that kind of pressure, especially not from the Council.

"Who else knows of this?" Amanda asked.

"Of the prophecy? Many people. It's well known and I'm surprised you haven't heard of it before now."

"Well, I haven't," she said, feeling slightly affronted. "And who else knows of your belief that it's about me?"

"Very few, but it's not for me to say who they are. But what I can say is that I am not alone in this belief.."

"Gentle Water? Does he believe the same things as you? Does he think it's me?"

"He knows of the prophesy but you'd have to ask him what he believes. However, I think it would be wise not to mention this to anyone other than Gentle Water, for the time being."

"Oh, don't worry about that," she muttered. Amanda looked at the prophecy once more, shook her head slightly, and moved away from the cabinet. "Can we go, please?" she asked.

"Of course. I'm sorry. I know it's a lot to take in. My apologies."

She appreciated his apology and that he seemed to be reigning in this righteous fervour as she stepped out into the corridor. He locked the door behind them and then led her along the passageway. He spoke to her a few times as he guided her through the hallways, but she felt so confused and overwhelmed that she didn't really hear what he was saying.

Needing a moment to herself, she stopped at a series of windows that looked out over the white landscape while the huge gas giant and its rings of ice hung in the sky before her. She leant forward, rested her forearms on the window ledge, and just stared out at the view.

She'd only just gotten a handle on New York and was getting into the flow of things. She'd found someone she really quite liked, and who amazingly, seemed to like her back. Her life seemed like it was settling down a touch, and now Trevelyan had just completely thrown everything up in the air again.

She wondered who else knew of the prophecy and if they believed it might be talking about her. It sounded like Gentle Water knew, which felt odd since he'd always been so open with her. Had he been holding this back? Keeping it to himself? And if so, why?

Maybe he thought he was protecting her and keeping her safe from some of this craziness. But was it crazy? A few years ago she would have said that real Magic sounded crazy. And yet here she was, able to use Magic herself, able to do unbelievable feats, like teleport from place to place, conjure money from thin air, and manipulate energy and elements with a thought. Hell, look at where she stood now: On a feckin' moon of Saturn. Was a prophecy, whether it talked about her or not, that crazy?

"I'm sorry," she said, talking to Trevelyan, but not turning to look at him. "That was just…"

"Unexpected, I know. I'm sorry, too. That was a lot to dump on you without warning," he said.

She looked up at him and smiled. "That's no bother, I'm glad I know now, actually."

"I thought you'd want to know about it."

"You're right, I do," she sighed.

"Speaking of full disclosure," he said, coming to stand next to her and looking out over the view. "The Council has spoken with everyone we think knows about you killing Lucian, and they have been warned against making such information public."

"Who've you spoken to?"

"Your coven, the Legacy, the Legion, Victoria and her coven, everyone who we think knows for sure. It's been made clear to those who were most at risk of leaking the information that they're under threat of expulsion."

Amanda smiled. "That's good to know. Thank you."

"I have someone else who wants to meet you, if that's okay with you?" he said.

"Sure, why not, let's do it," she said. I've come this far, she thought, let's get this over with. "Lead the way."

They walked for several minutes, descending several flights of stairs as they went. Trevelyan had suggested Porting, but Amanda wanted to see more of the castle. Trevelyan acquiesced, playing tour guide and describing things as they went. The whole place felt wondrous and huge to Amanda. She'd never seen anything like it before in her life.

Soon enough, they reached a large oak double door with black metal hinges and fixtures, which Trevelyan knocked on using a steel ring held in the jaws of a titanium lion's face. When a voice invited them in, Trevelyan opened the door.

Following her guide into the room beyond, she took in the well-appointed room. It was filled with ornately-carved shelves and cabinets, expensive-looking rugs, and in the middle of the room, a large wooden desk that looked like it must be hundreds of years old.

A man in a dark, tailored suit sat in a wine-coloured, leather chair behind it. His face had an intense expression upon its harsh angles and handsome features. He looked to be in his thirties, although she knew appearances could be deceiving when it came to the Magi. His long raven-dark hair was tied back in a ponytail and he had a finely trimmed goatee.

The man stood as they walked in and smiled at them. "Amanda-Jane Page, I take it?" he said and offered his hand over the desk.

She stepped forward, took his hand in a firm grip, and shook it in greeting, "That's right, nice to meet ye, Mr…" she said, leaving the question of his name hanging in the air.

"Bathory. Stephen Bathory of the Order of the Dragon Coven."

"Bathory? As in…?"

"Elizabeth? Yes, she's a descendant of mine, unfortunately."

"Wow, that's crazy."

"Not as crazy as what you've been doing recently. Well done on your dealings with Lucian and the Harbingers of Darkness. They were something of an issue for the American covens for a while."

"It just seemed like the right thing to do," Amanda said with a shrug. "No big deal."

"I'd disagree, and I think many others would, too."

Amanda smiled, feeling a little self-conscious. "Well, thank you. I appreciate it."

"Stephen has only just joined the Council, taking the place of Jonas of the Coven of Angels who was killed by Shaitan. He wanted to see you," Trevelyan said.

"…To thank you for dealing with Shaitan," Stephen finished. "You're doing really rather well when it comes to the Nomads. Just be careful you don't make too many enemies."

Amanda nodded. "I'll try."

"Anyway, I just wanted to say hello as I'm a friend to the Legacy Coven and when I heard you were coming, I asked Trevelyan to drop by. I hope he's being a gracious host."

"He's been a true gentleman… so far," she said, winking at Trevelyan.

Trevelyan's eyebrows climbed up towards his hairline at her last comment.

Stephen laughed. "I'm sure. Well, I don't want to keep you. I know you have a party to get back to. But it's good to meet you. I'll see you soon."

They said their goodbyes before heading back through the castle. She noticed a flicker of Magic around Trevelyan's head, and after a brief moment of concentration, he turned to her. "I've just heard there's someone here from the party. They're waiting on one of the viewing towers. I'll Port you up there and they'll take you back."

"Oh, really? And who's that?"

***

Moments later, Amanda appeared on top of the highest turret in the castle. The circular stone platform with a waist-high parapet looked over the landscape of the moon and the castle below. A single, closed trapdoor sat recessed into the floor, and a cushioned bench stood in the middle of the space. In front of her, Maria sat on the wall at the edge of the turret looking up towards Saturn.

Amanda just stood there for a moment. The whole scene looked like a wondrous science-fiction painting, and she couldn't help but enjoy the view.

Maria turned around and smiled at Amanda. "Have you had fun?"

"It's been illuminating. How come you're here?"

"I served on the Council a couple of times, I know my way around. It's pretty amazing, isn't it?"

Amanda sat on the wall facing her lover and took her hand. "Honestly, I have no words. I've never seen anything like this, not even close."

"I come back here from time to time, just to sit up here and enjoy the view. Nothing humbles you quite like that," she said, gesturing at the vista before them.

Amanda slid closer to her. "And what's it feel like to share it with me?"

Maria looked up at Amanda and smiled. "Let me show you," she said and leaning closer, kissed her.

She wasn't sure what it was, but within moments, they were making love on the soft cushioned bench, under the sweeping misty glow of the Milky Way and the majesty of Saturn. Amanda put it down to the inherent romance of the moment. The mesmerising view, the presence of her lover, the sexy clothes, everything played its part.

Looking up at Saturn during the heights of ecstasy would not be something she'd soon forget.

- Haiti

Josette walked into the darkened room. Carefully picking her way through the tables covered with various dark Magic paraphernalia and the bodies that hung from the ceiling, she approached the cloaked figure of her master.

She waited, close enough to Nymira so they could speak comfortably when her master chose to address her. She waited for a few moments before Nymira hissed.

"Speak, child."

"My investigations in New York have gone as far as they can on a covert basis. I can only conclude that the truth of Lucian's death is being kept secret on purpose. The most likely candidates are Amanda-Jane Page and Yoh Takahashi."

Nymira turned and looked at Josette. The firelight caught the side of Nymira's face, illuminating the nest of dreadlocks that spilt from her scalp, and the trinkets, bones, and feathers knotted into them. Her dark skin was covered in white war paint, framing her eyes which burnt with energy and purpose. She wore a long cloak made from layers of fabric, hessian, and dried skins that fell from her shoulders to the floor and hid her lithe form beneath.

"Thank you, little one," she said and turned back to whatever she'd been doing.

"Would you like me to do more? I'd need to bring in some help and be a bit more public about it, but there might be more to learn," Josette said.

"You have done enough," her master said, dismissing Josette with a wave of her hand.

Josette doubted she was the only one that Nymira had sent to look into it. There would be others. Initiated like her, and Magi, who would be hunting for clues.

She left the room, wondering who would be unfortunate enough to be on the receiving end of Nymira's wrath.

New Lead

Antarctic

Angel stood back and watched as Isha held his hand above the glowing green Orb, his Magic pulsing from his palm over the Artifact.

The Orb had been placed in a metal holder on the boardroom table and Isha was trying to understand what they had in their possession. Mr Black, his wrinkled face lit by the Orb's glow, stood to one side, watching closely. He looked back and forth between Isha and the Orb, impatient curiosity etched on his wizened face.

"So, is it what we hoped for?" Mr Black asked.

Angel thought his desire for power was getting the better of him.

"I think so. It's difficult to get a read on it. If I could just hold it?" Isha said.

"No," Mr Black said emphatically as he stepped between Isha and the Orb. "No one holds it but me. You know the rules."

"Of course, I'm sorry, sir," Isha said, having stepped back at the abruptness of Mr Black's tone.

It had been a week since they'd found the item, but they'd been forced to stay at the Antarctic base due to poor weather. Mr Black had refused to be Ported out, preferring to wait for clearer conditions.

During that time, Mr Black had kept the Orb in his possession, never allowing anyone else touch or hold it. He clearly wanted to know more about it, but he seemed afraid that someone would take it. It had taken several days, and a lot of convincing, before he even let it be looked at by another person.

Today was that day, but he never stood out of arm's reach and he still refused to let anyone else touch it. Only a few key people were in attendance, including Angel, Blake, Isha, and Roxanne, Mr Black's personal aid.

Mr Black picked up the Orb and placed it back in the foam padding inside the briefcase on the table. He handcuffed the case to his wrist, all the while looking annoyed at Isha's request to hold it.

"We're done for today. Maybe, if you can abide by the rules, we'll do this again tomorrow. If the weather doesn't clear," he said, the implication that this might be the last time Isha was allowed to look at it being made strikingly clear.

Angel kept her face impassive, but inside she knew how Isha felt. The Orb had power—a power that drew Magi to it. Angel wanted nothing more than to have that item all to herself. She felt sure that having it in her possession would be a huge benefit. As it was, she had to purposefully look away and think of something unrelated to the Orb to shake off the feeling, lest it took control of her. It was an odd feeling, but when she wasn't caught up in the need to possess it, she knew that these feelings were being generated by the Orb itself. She could even see its Magic reaching out to the Magi in the room. And yet, when she stood in its presence, even with her Aegis protecting her, those feelings returned. The Orb's aura of attraction seemed to pass right through her Magical Shield, a sign of the ancient and powerful Magic it possessed.

This meeting seemed at an end, though, and everyone had started gathering their belongings when a sudden surge of powerful Magic flared and a figure appeared before them.

For a moment, Angel thought Yasmin had Ported in, as the woman who appeared had similar wavy raven-black hair, but there, the similarity ended.

The Magus had attractive features and wore a leather jacket over her black t-shirt with leather trousers and heavy boots.

She immediately scanned the room to pick out Mr Black. "Sir, I have news."

"Echo? What brings you here?" Mr Black asked. Clearly, they were familiar with each other. Angel had never seen her before, but she had a powerful presence and her Magic burnt wildly within her, but that wasn't all. Angel could tell she had no heartbeat and could see the tell-tale signs of her being a Vampire Scion.

This was news to Angel.

Isha saw her as well and offered a quick bow. "Master," he said.

Angel raised an eyebrow. This was Isha's master? So, he wasn't the most capable Magi in Mr Blacks employment? It seemed like she was learning all kinds of useful things today.

"Isha," she nodded in acknowledgement before looking back to Mr Black. "We have a development in Arizona that I think you'll want to know about."

"Go on," he said.

"We believe we've found the Lazarus Scroll. A Nomad has taken control of a nuclear power plant in the desert and he's just used the Scroll. We detected and confirmed the Magical signature of the Artifact."

"How long ago?"

"Not long, an hour or so maybe," Echo said.

"We're leaving now. Echo, you will Port us to the power station via the island. Isha, Roxanne, Angel, you're with me. Get the security team in here, Roxanne. Blake, get this dig broken down and out of here as fast as you can. We're done here. We have what we need. Let's go."

Angel was surprised. The fact that Mr Black had requested her presence on this mission marked something of a turning point in her relationship with the leader of the Syndicate. She'd always been outside the circle of power since she had infiltrated the group. She'd never expected to waltz right in and be privy to its most confidential meetings and missions, but she had hoped to rise through the ranks quicker than she had done. Of course, the fact that there were Magi in Mr Black's employ who could discover her true intentions much easier than a Riven mortal made things move much slower. But this mission to the Antarctic, as much as she hated it, had changed things. It suddenly seemed like Mr Black trusted her to a much higher degree.

Angel followed the others and moved in close to Mr Black, as Roxanne ushered in the security team guys from outside the room. With everyone ready, Echo drew on her powerful Magic and Ported them all off the continent.

- Antarctic

Gentle Water sat on the ridge in his extreme cold-weather gear and used his Magic to place his senses way up in the sky above the dig site and looked down. He used his Magic to zoom in and get a better look at the place. As he watched, powerful Magic flared in one of the portacabins, and suddenly there were several fewer life forms in the building, and from what he could tell, no Magi.

Moments later, he watched as men around the dig site started the long and arduous task of breaking down the camp. It looked like whatever this was, had come to an end. But he needed to know for sure, so he planned his next move and how he would approach the site.

Promotion

The Vatican

Mary pulled on the topmost layers of her robes, straightening the garments out as she looked at herself in the mirror. This could be a great day for her—the fruition of so much time, energy, hard work, and fighting against all the odds. Getting to the position of Grand Inquisitor had been a long slog, and had it not been for the support of Valerio Rossi, God rest his soul, and a number of others on the Conclave, such as Marcus, Nico, Claud, and Damion, she might have never made it. She'd worked as an Inquisitor out in the field, and proven herself to them time and again. She'd also made her ambition to be a Grand Inquisitor clear to anyone who would listen.

Simeon had been very vocal about his opposition to her appointment to the Conclave. However, even though he is the head of the organisation, its rules for voting in the Conclave members and the Witch Finder General were quite clear—his singular vote counted no more than any of the others' votes.

She felt like she got a kind of grudging respect from Simeon these days, that maybe she'd proven herself enough to be taken seriously by him now.

She didn't know him well enough to be sure though, and maybe he'd just given up trying to object at this point.

Whatever the case, she had served this organisation with a dedication that could not be questioned, much like her faith in the ever-loving God. And now, God had spoken to her, and she had heard him. She'd heard his will and knew she was on the right path.

She'd seen the decay and the apathy that had infected Valerio Rossi and how he had become paralysed by the Inquisition's continued defeats against the Witches. He'd even confided in her that he wasn't sure how effective they were any more, or how relevant they were.

She had prayed and asked for clarity on this from God and He had revealed His plan to her, and it was glorious. Apathy had infected Rossi. The Devil had dug his claws into him and sewed doubt in the man's mind. She had asked God for guidance, to know what she must do. She wanted to carry on the fight, reinvigorate the Disciples of the Cross, and show the world the righteous path.

The plan had been revealed to her a few nights ago, after the meeting when Rossi had declared his intention to go to New York. She'd prayed and asked God if her plan would be a just one, a blessed one, and He had said yes.

Mary had been cultivating leads and information in New York for a while now, after finding out that Amanda had chosen that city as her home. Mary had a special hatred for Amanda and her coven. They were clearly in league with the Devil, her red hair marked her as such.

Mary had the resources of the Vatican to monitor Amanda and send her all the information possible on the situation in that city, including the coven's that had just arrived. So getting a message to several of the more militant ones had not been terribly difficult.

She'd had to be careful, of course. She didn't want Amanda getting too much forewarning of what was happening. The Devil could smell a trap and would not want Rossi, one of the Serpent's own, being killed.

Purging the unclean from the Inquisition's leadership was a righteous cause, and Mary knew she would be granted her Kingdom in Heaven for expelling such a taint from the Warriors of God.

The plan had worked and word soon got back that Rossi had been killed in a surprise attack. That night, Mary had prayed for Valerio Rossi's soul, she prayed that God would take the taint away and grant Rossi eternal life in the Kingdom of Heaven.

She hoped to see him again one day when she walked through those pearly gates and to welcome him back into the loving arms of God.

From the day her plan had been formulated, Mary had been liaising with the other Grand Inquisitors, reminding them of some of their debts to her, debts she had purposefully not collected against for just this occasion. When the news of his death broke and had been announced to the Conclave, the need for a successor to Rossi had become apparent.

A new Witch Finder General needed to be found. They debated and were given time to deliberate before being brought back into the Conclave chamber. They were then asked who wanted to stand for the position. Mary put herself forward, as had Reynaldo De Sauveterre, making it a two-horse race.

The meeting had gone back into recess, and the candidates were allowed to mingle and talk until they were called to order once more, when they each had to speak before the group.

Having known this was coming, Mary had prepared well in advance, speaking with the Conclave members, preparing her speech, and getting ready for this moment. Her moment.

Then, after they'd each spoken, the meeting had ended. The vote would be cast and revealed this morning.

Mary couldn't help but feel nervous. Even though she knew her path to be the one true path, her fallible human soul and body felt weak at the thought of becoming the first female Witch Finder General.

But she pushed those thoughts to the side and locked them away because she needed to be strong. She needed to show she could be a leader for the Inquisition during this dark time.

Satisfied with her look, she left her quarters and made her way down to the Conclave chamber, lost in her thoughts of what she would do once she was voted into the position. There was so much she wanted to push for, including another female Grand Inquisitor to replace her on the Conclave.

She had someone in mind, but that would come later, after this much more important vote. Mary and Reynaldo were ushered into a separate side-room, where they would wait and also cast their own ballots, which weren't really in doubt.

Sitting in this room with her rival for the seat of the Witch Finder General felt uncomfortable, and she barely spoke. Mary had been sure to be cordial and exchange pleasantries, but beyond that, they both held their peace. Mary silently prayed, hoping that her path remained true and blessed in the eyes of the Lord, and that the other Conclave members would see that and vote for her to be the new Witch Finder General.

Mary found that waiting for others to choose your fate seemed to make time slow down as you thought about your campaign, who might support you, or who might support your opponent. It almost felt like a children's game when team captains chose from a line-up, and you were the last one to be picked.

She knew she'd played her cards well, though. She knew there was little else she could have done, but she also knew that her gender would be a constant issue for some high-ranking church members and maybe that would be enough to sway some of them to vote for Reynaldo.

She hoped not. She hoped they would see reason, see her blessed path, and want to follow her down it.

When the door suddenly opened, Mary jumped and then chided herself for having done so.

Walking back into the room, she could feel the eyes of the Grand Inquisitors following her progress across the room and no doubt, her opponent's as well. She did her best to ignore the pressure and walk tall and proud as a defender of the faith.

Mary stood beside the Conclave's aide, who opened a slip of paper and addressed the room.

"The votes have been cast and verified, and a clear winner has been chosen by the will of God Almighty. The new Witch Finder General and High Inquisitor is… Mary Damask."

Mary closed her eyes and smiled very slightly to herself, being careful not to look too pleased or too smug. Quickly, she offered thanks to God. She was now certain her path was the true one. God had smiled down on her and on the Disciples. A new era of strength was upon them, and she would make sure the Inquisition became a force to be feared once more.

- The Melchior Estate, Long Island, New York.

Maya felt the Magic flare and surge, announcing the arrival of the one Magus who knew the key to Porting into her private estate. It was the early hours and still dark outside. Maya's preferred time of day. But when she turned around, she could clearly make out the familiar features of the woman who stood nearby.

"To what do I owe the pleasure?" *Maya asked the figure.*

"It's time to head into the desert. Mr Black is making his move for the Lazarus Scroll, which means you need to take Amanda and capture the Scroll before they do."

"When, now?"

The figure nodded. "Right now."

"Yes, Mother."

Meltdown

Manhattan, New York

A buzzing in her head brought Amanda out from her restful sleep, waking her abruptly. She sat up and put a hand to her head. Groggily she wondering what on earth might be going on.

"Jaysus, what time is it?" she muttered, even though she didn't need to look at a clock. It was 3am, and she rubbed her eyes in protest at being woken up so early.

It took her a moment to realise that the buzzing sensation wasn't an alarm clock someone had set off in some spiteful prank, but instead, was because someone wanted to speak with her through a Mental Link.

She looked down at Maria's sleeping form lying next to her. Luckily, she hadn't disturbed her, so she concentrated on the presence behind the Link and recognised it as Maya.

That was odd. She'd not really had much contact with Maya and had never been contacted by her through their Mental Link before. She'd always found her to be friendly and pleasant, but Maya remained distant and had never asked her for help or contacted her in this manner.

So, curious as to what the fuss was about, she opened the Link.

~Maya, what's the craic? Do you know what time it is?~ she sent as she opened the Link.

~Sorry for disturbing you at this early hour, but I need your help,~ Maya replied.

Needed her help? Maya always seemed so independent, what would she need her help for? ~Sure, what can I do?~

~I've been following up on a few leads, and I believe I've found the location of a powerful Artifact called the Lazarus Scroll, but we need to leave now, just you and me. Can you help?~

~Just us two? Are ye sure?~ Amanda asked. That seemed a little odd. Why not bring the others?

~I'd normally ask Yoh, but he's no longer able to teleport,~ said Maya's voice in her head.

Amanda sighed. The mention of Yoh's transformation into a Scion instantly made Amanda feel guilty, even though she knew he didn't blame her. Despite that, she still felt somewhat at fault for his transformation.

She swung her bare legs over the side of the bed. ~Okay, sure, let me get dressed. Is this going to be a dangerous trip?~ Amanda asked as she grabbed her jeans from the nearby chair and pulled them on.

~Maybe, best be ready for all possibilities.~

~And where are we Porting to, might I ask?~

~Arizona,~ Maya sent.

Amanda looked at the pile of tops in her wardrobe and pulled out a cropped t-shirt which she pulled on and then slipped into her sneakers. ~I'll come to you, okay?~

~Sure, I'm waiting. Here's the key to the Aegis.~ A complex, abstract thought appeared in Amanda's head suddenly. She'd have to hold that thought in her mind to Port through the Aegis Maya was inside of.

Amanda walked round to Maria's side of the bed and gave her a gentle kiss, being careful not to wake her. Unsure if she would be back before morning, she conjured a brief note that she left on the bedside table, saying she'd been called out on an errand. Then, concentrating, she Ported to Maya, following their Link through space to appear beside her.

Amanda found herself standing outside on pea gravel that crunched underfoot as she moved. She'd appeared in the middle of a quadrangle with a building surrounding her on all sides. An ornate pillared arch behind her led out, while before her, a large set of shallow steps led up to an ornate entrance. Maya, dressed in black form-fitting clothing stood just a couple of metres away.

"Welcome to my home," she said.

Amanda admired the large mansion that surrounded her. "This is your house?"

"Yes, this is the Melchior Estate. It's on Long Island and has been my home for a long time," Maya explained.

"It's beautiful," Amanda said in awe.

"You should visit properly some time."

"That'd be grand, thank you."

"Another time, though, we need to move quickly," Maya said, a sense of urgency in her voice.

"Okay, so, where are we going?" Amanda asked.

"Here," Maya replied as a thought appeared in Amanda's head through their Link.

"Okay, grand. Let's be going, then," Amanda said and pulled on her Magic again.

***

From an upstairs window, the figure watched as Amanda talked with Maya in the courtyard below, before finally Porting away in a rush of Essentia.

"Good luck," she said, before Porting away herself.

***

With a quiet whip-crack of air, the pair appeared amongst the buildings of the Palo Verde nuclear power plant. In the darkness of the desert night, the lights of the plant itself illuminated the area with bright intensity as the plant hummed with power. A huge domed building stood nearby, and through her Magical senses, Amanda quickly picked up the traces of Magic coming from within. She could also see the tattered remains of an Aegis that had surrounded the building.

"We need to get in there," Amanda said, motioning to the building. She pulled on her Magic and sent a set of her senses just inside the building. With a little manoeuvring, she found a suitable catwalk they could appear on. With another quick working of Magic, they Ported inside and onto a raised walkway that threaded through the immense metal structures of the reactor core. They couldn't see anything from where they stood, so Amanda crept along the catwalk as she finished boosting hers and Maya's Aegises. The catwalk emerged from between two towering silos, branching left and right. Below them, two groups of people faced off against each other. On one side, a Magus in a tan-coloured duster stood beside a Scion that Amanda recognised all too well. The sight of it made Amanda reach out and grab the nearby railing to keep herself from stumbling.

Horlack, the enormous Scion-beast that had attacked her in the alleyway in New York several years ago, which had triggered her Epiphany and transformation into one of the Magi, stood alive and well next to this Magus. Things had just become much more dangerous.

"Holy fecking shit," Amanda whispered under her breath.

"Horlack," Maya muttered.

"You know him?" Amanda asked in surprise.

"I've had problems with him in the past," she said. "I can deal with him."

Amanda glanced over at Maya, her face having taken on a much darker and more severe expression. Amanda looked back at the confrontation below, and couldn't help but stare at Horlack. She felt sure she had killed this creature with her Magic, blasted him into nothing. Had she been wrong? Well, the answer stood just a few hundred feet away, alive, and seemingly not very inconvenienced by his apparent death.

Approaching them, a much larger group of people filed out of a doorway onto the huge flat platform that had a summoning circle painted on it in blood. Numerous dead bodies were scattered around the area, some of them whole, some of them in bits and pieces.

The group that confronted the Nomad Magus and Horlack seemed mostly made up of Riven. They wore black tactical gear and carried silenced submachine guns which they pointed towards the Magi and the Scion.

As she watched, Magi joined the Riven soldiers and were being led by an old man with a walking stick who seemed to be in charge.

Behind him, the three Magi consisted of a dark-haired woman in leather, an Indian man with a handsome face in a shirt and trousers, and finally a blonde woman in a mini-skirt, jacket, and heels.

Suddenly, Amanda realised she recognised the last Magus. It was Angel, the Magi who had attacked her on the train in France and nearly killed her. What had Maya brought her into?

"What do you want to do?" Amanda asked. "There're some powerful people down there."

"Let's see how it pans out. This is much more dangerous than I thought it would be. We might not get the Scroll today."

"No shit," she replied, watching the confrontation below unfold and trying to hear what they were saying over the noise of the reactor.

"Horlack," the old man said, his voice ringing with authority.

"Do I know you?" rumbled Horlack.

"No, but I know you," he said, before addressing the Nomad. "Dust, is it?" the old man asked. "Give me the Scroll and we can avoid any trouble."

Magic suddenly flared from Dust as he tried to Port away. The dark-haired woman's Magic washed over him and disintegrated Dust's effect before it could do anything.

Horlack looked down at the man next to him, clearly sensing his attempt at Magic and escape.

"What are you doing, weakling?" Horlack demanded. With his massive left hand, Horlack shoved Dust towards the old man.

Dust shouted in protest, but Horlack had been too quick and too strong.

All hell broke loose as the men with guns opened fire. Essentia flared as Magic was called on in response to Horlack's movement. Angel, however, just watched. In fact, Amanda noticed the Magical signature which surrounded her seemed much weaker than when Angel had attacked her on the train. What was she up to?

Horlack leapt away, bounding over the side of the platform and disappearing from view as Dust died quickly and painfully under the onslaught of Magic and gunfire.

"I'm going after Horlack," Maya called to Amanda. "Don't let them cause any more trouble, and if you can get the Scroll, go for it, but don't get yourself killed," Maya said as she sped off, running down the catwalk towards where Horlack had disappeared.

Amanda looked back to the scene below and watched as the old man walked up to the body of the now-dead Magus and bent to pick something up. It looked like a rolled-up piece of paper, but it throbbed with Magical power that Amanda could feel from her perch on the catwalk.

The Lazarus Scroll. Amanda rose from her crouched position, looked right and knew what she must do. She ran silently along the catwalk and then jumped into mid-air, further and higher than any normal human could ever do. She used one foot to bound from a pipe to the top of a huge tank, and then leapt into the air, dropping down between the old man's group and the door they had appeared through.

She landed in a crouch with a loud echoing bang which dented the metal beneath her feet. Rising up to a standing position, she looked at the surprised faces of the group before her.

***

Maya ran around more machinery and suddenly found herself standing before Horlack, who skidded to a stop and looked down at Maya, his huge dark eyes wide in surprise.

Horlack's transformation into a Scion had permanently changed his body into a massive beast. He was easily over twelve feet tall, covered in patchy black hair, with massive talons on his hands and at the end of his dog-shaped legs.

His head, although huge in its own right, looked tiny on his massive shoulders and didn't look remotely human anymore. He sported a bat-like nose and ears, while huge tusks spouted from his mouth, dripping with saliva. The horrific look was finished off by a long, cancerous-looking horn which erupted from his forehead and ended in a wicked point.

"Maya!" he boomed. "What a pleasure. Is your mother here?"

"Horlack," Maya said, ignoring the question. "You're back."

The thing stood tall before her. "Was there any doubt?"

"I thought maybe your encounter in New York…"

"Never. I was merely thrown into the Abyss. Reports of my death have been greatly exaggerated," he boomed, his voice loud and powerful.

"Indeed."

He lowered himself down, bringing his face closer to her level. "But now that I'm back, and a little more like my old self, maybe you would consider…"

"This again?"

"It's always been you, Maya, you know that," he said, his voice suddenly softer and filled with emotion.

Maya placed her hands on her hips, looking up at the monster before her. "A lot would need to change before I could ever consider you as anything other than a savage killer. Your vendetta against Amanda, for instance, would need to end."

Horlack's eyes narrowed as he glared at Maya. "I'm listening."

***

Half a second after turning their heads in surprise at the sound of Amanda's landing, the men all came to their senses and spun round to point their guns at her.

Simultaneously, the woman in leather stepped in front of the old man, pulling on the local Essentia as she moved.

Amanda drew Essentia to her, strengthening her Aegis, and getting ready to deflect bullets and the woman's Magic. Her split Multitasking mind raced, getting ready for the fight that was about to erupt.

"Wait," called the old man from behind the Magi woman, his hand pulling on her sleeve as he stepped forward. His gaze locked onto Amanda, his eyes wide, mouth open, and a look of utter incredulity on his face.

"Sir?" the woman asked.

"Stand down," he said, as he stepped forward. "Continue with the plan. Echo, you wait there," he said, speaking to the woman and pointing to a spot behind him. Echo stayed put, but everyone else began filing out, including Angel, who shot her a knowing look as she left.

The old man looked back at Amanda and paused for a moment.

"Give me the Scroll," Amanda said, feeling weirded out by the old guy. She wasn't sure what was going on or what else she should say.

"My god. You look just like her. It's uncanny," he said, his voice full of wonder. "I mean, I always thought... I always kind of knew, but... it's you, isn't it?"

"Excuse me?" Amanda answered. He spoke like he knew her, but she felt sure she'd never met him before.

"You're what? Twenty-one years old now? Yes, that fits. What's your name, child?"

"I'm not sure that's any of your business."

"Of course, you don't know, do you? Did you know your mother?"

"What the hell?" Amanda said, surprised and shocked by the strangeness and rudeness of his question. "Who are you?"

"If I'm right, I'm your father," he said as he looked at her in fascination.

The world around her nearly fell apart as she took in those words. Everything else seemed a secondary concern as she tried to process what he'd just said. Could this true? She looked at the man again and felt disbelief wash over her. "My arse ye are," she said in an almost automatic response, denying his accusation.

"You look just like your mother, the resemblance is uncanny. Your hair, your eyes, your nose, even your Irish accent is similar. If I didn't know better, I'd think you were her."

"I can assure you, I'm not," she said. "I think I'd remember you."

"But of course, and that was more than twenty years ago. Shortly before you were born. It all fits."

Doubt filled her mind. Was he telling the truth? Did this man know her mother, and could he really be her father? There was something about him, something compelling. "You... you're saying you knew my mother?"

"And you don't?" he asked.

"I'm an orphan," she said. It almost felt like her heart had stopped. She felt short of breath and had a desperate need to know more, to know who she was and who her parents were.

The man considered that for a moment, surprise quickly ceding to acceptance. "I suppose that makes sense," he said. "What's your name?"

"A... Amanda, Amanda-Jane. Who... who was she? What was her name?" she asked, suddenly desperate for answers.

"Mr Black!" shouted a voice from the nearby doorway that led onto the platform. Amanda looked around, following the gaze of the old man to the mercenary who had shouted for him. "Everything's in place, we're ready," the man barked.

"Time's up, Amanda. Let's do this again sometime," Mr Black said, his voice all business now as Echo's Magic whipped about them and Ported them away before Amanda could bring herself to react.

"W... wait," she said. The brief revelations from the old man, Mr Black, had disarmed her completely, giving her no chance to counter Echo's Magic and stop them from Porting away.

Amanda stood on the platform amongst bodies and spilt blood, feeling like she had been given half an answer and then had been left hanging. She desperately wanted those answers.

He'd said he was her father. He looked in his eighties or nineties, so he must have been in his sixties when he'd gotten her mother pregnant, which seemed a little old. Who was this man, and what kind of name was Mr Black, anyway? It all felt so strange, and yet, something about him, the way he spoke and the little details he knew about her age, could it be? Could he be her father?

A claxon shrieked with an ear-splitting siren that made her clamp her hands to her ears. She swore and used her Magic to take the edge off the noise as she looked about her. The siren had snapped her out of her reverie. She needed to find Maya.

PLEASE EVACUATE THE BUILDING, THIS IS NOT A DRILL.

The voice boomed over the speakers installed in the containment building. What had Mr Black's men done? She used her Magical sight and quickly picked out the sudden and fast build-up of heat in the core. She got a strong sinking feeling in her gut. This was not good. She needed to try and stop whatever was happening to cause the alert. Amanda knew nothing of nuclear power, though. She had no idea how reactor cores worked. The best thing would be for her to find Maya and get out of the building as fast as they could.

"MAYA!" she shouted, but heard nothing back. She concentrated and sent a Link request to her telepathically. It was quickly accepted.

~I'm here, I'm fine. I'm coming to you,~ Amanda heard in her head. She felt a rush of relief at Maya's reply. She was alive. Magic flared behind her and she whipped around to see a man in a strange dark outfit that looked like a mix of Japanese ninja and American Special Forces, but without the weapons. He also wore a mask that left only his eyes visible.

"What now?" Amanda said as she eyed the man. She recognised the fading Spiritual Magic he used and felt reasonably sure he'd just crossed from the Abyss into the material world.

Up until this month, she, like everyone else in the Magi community, believed that crossing into the Abyss was impossible. Now she'd met a total of four people in one month who could do it, including apparently, this mysterious man. It didn't look like Shaitan. Could it be another of his apprentices?

The man dropped into a fighting stance. Amanda clenched her fists and readied her Magic, as a powerful blast of Kinetic energy hit her like a speeding train. She flew back into a large metal pipe, causing it to dent from the impact.

Amanda grunted. That had hurt. Bracing herself, she leapt towards the man as steam blasted from the ruptured pipe behind her.

In mid-air, her Magic flared. Lightning, fire, and an invisible force smashed into him and his Aegis fluoresced.

She landed, rolled, and in a blur of motion attacked with a kick. His head snapped sideways as the kick hit his Aegis like a Magical hammer blow.

She followed it with a punch, which he blocked. But still, her attack threw more Essentia against his Aegis, weakening it further while her extra minds did the same with Essentia Strikes.

As they traded punches and kicks, Amanda noticed a series of small explosions as steam burst from nearby pipes.

Was this a meltdown? If only she knew more about how power plants like this worked and if only she didn't have to fight this stranger.

"Do we have to do this?" she shouted as she ducked his next strike and blocked his kick before delivering one of her own to his sternum. "We have to get out of here and stop the meltdown."

As she watched, the man got his balance and merely frowned before rushing her again and continuing his attack.

"God damn it, listen to me," she shouted. He ignored her and kept up the assault. Suddenly, she saw Maya rushing up behind him, unnoticed for the moment. Amanda pressed her attack, keeping his attention on her while she gathered her Magic.

Maya held her hands out wide, her fingers splayed with her keen-looking talons extended from her fingers. She leapt and landed behind him, slashing across his back, making his body arch in pain. Amanda unleashed another powerful Kinetic and

Essentia filled attack that hammered him to the floor, dropping his Aegis, and knocking him out in one fell swoop.

Around her, the whole place seemed to be descending into chaos. Steam blasted from pipes, klaxons sounded, and fires flared into life amidst the loud and ominous sounding noises that echoed from within the machinery around her.

"We're leaving," Amanda cried and gathered her Magic, Porting herself, Maya, and her mysterious attacker outside the domed containment building.

Maya looked over at Amanda. "You have to stop the meltdown," she said.

"To be sure, happy to, but how do I do that?" she answered.

"It's overheating, it needs to be cooled down," Maya said.

Amanda looked back at the building a few hundred feet away with her Aetheric Sight. She could see the heat building inside, so she concentrated, pulled on the Essentia around her, and focused her power on the core, lowering the temperature inside it.

It didn't take her long, but the concentration required was intense. Minutes later, she slowly eased off her Magic as she felt the reactor stabilize as its natural cooling processes took over.

Happy that the immediate danger had been averted, she stumbled back and dropped to the ground, sitting next to the unconscious body of her attacker, close to where Maya crouched down, looking at the clothing of the man.

"Jaysus, that was intense," she gasped. She looked at Maya in the darkness of the desert night. Maya seemed a little confused by the man before them. "Any ideas?" Amanda asked.

"Nothing I'd bet my estate on. Well done, by the way, that was impressive."

"Thanks." Amanda blushed. "We could do with getting an Arcanum clean-up team out here, so we could. There's way too much evidence of Magic."

"We can do that at your house. Are we taking tall, dark, and unconscious with us?"

"Sure, sure, let's find out who ye man is. What do you say, shall we go?"

"Go for it," Maya said.

Amanda looked Maya in the eyes then. "Thank you," she said.

"That's okay, happy to jump in and help," Maya replied.

Maya probably thought she was only talking about the fight, but Amanda actually meant it about way more than that. If Maya hadn't chosen to take her, she might have never met Mr Black nor would she have had the chance to find out who her birthparents were.

She realised she actually quite liked Maya, she got on really well and easily with her, and they seemed to just slot together as if they'd known each other for years.

Amanda smiled and pulled on the threads of Essentia again, Porting them home.

The inward rush of air kicked up the dusty sands of the desert in a small cloud as they disappeared.

- Nowhere

Alicia fell to the floor of her room, blood leaking from uncountable cuts all over her body. Pain filled her mind, but she felt at peace for she knew she deserved it. Above her, Nate, Yasmin's apprentice, spat at her. He stood there topless, his entire well-muscled body covered in blasphemous tattoos depicting the Gods, Prophets, and Saints of Christianity, Islam, Judaism, Hinduism, Buddhism, and more being raped and tortured by demons.

Earlier today, she'd spoken out of turn, asking something of her mistress without having been given permission to speak first. She'd known it was wrong the minute she'd done it, but she sometimes forgot herself, reverting to her old and incorrect ways. She knew she would be punished. Sometimes Yasmin did it, sometimes Nate, sometimes Kez, or someone else.

She'd improved, though, and the punishments were less frequent now, making Yasmin happier.

Later on, with her injuries nearly healed, Yasmin came to visit and hugged her close, kissing her and whispering words of love into her ears.

Home again

Greenwich Village, New York

In the basement of her house, Amanda stood next to a long table with her mysterious attacker laid out on it, unconscious. To Amanda's left, Maya leant on the edge of the table and looked down at the man.

"Sorry you didn't get your Scroll," Amanda said.

"It's not a problem. There will be other times, other opportunities. Just be glad we got out of there with our lives," Maya said, without looking up. "Anyway, it should be me apologising to you for dragging you out there and nearly getting you killed."

"Heh," Amanda said. "It's no bother, nothing like a bit of a clatter from time to time to get the blood pumping." She looked down at the man on the table and took a breath. She was keeping him subdued with her Magic, so he wouldn't wake up until they wanted him too. But her mind wasn't focused on who this man was. Her mind was elsewhere, thinking about Mr Black's words to her.

She needed some time to think.

"Look, I just need a moment, I'll be back soon," she said and left Maya in the garage just as Shaun stepped out of his office and looked over at the body.

"What's that doing in here?" he asked her.

"Maya will fill you in, and don't forget to inform the Arcanum," she said as she ascended the stairs.

Without really thinking about where she was heading, she walked through the house, heading up through the levels, and eventually stepping out onto the roof of the building.

Whenever she needed time to think or just to get away, she usually came out here. As the morning sun started to peek above the horizon, splashing an orange glow over the glass of the surrounding buildings, she sat on the edge of the roof and let the wind catch her hair, enjoying the feel of the cool winter air.

She'd never thought much about her parents. They had never been there for any part of her life, and although she occasionally wondered who they might be, it had never been a large part of her time growing up. She knew that some of the other orphans had thought about it a lot. It had been a huge missing part of their lives like they were an unfinished jigsaw puzzle that would never be complete until they found that one missing piece.

Amanda had never felt like that. She'd just accepted her situation and never questioned it. The nuns were her parents, the other children were her siblings, and the orphanage had been her home.

Even as an adult she hadn't wondered about them, especially not since becoming a Magus. She had way too many other things going on for her to be worrying about something so obscure.

But today, something had changed. Meeting Mr Black and the tantalising glimpse he'd given her of her parentage and her origins had ignited something inside of her. Suddenly, she'd discovered that she *did* have a part of her puzzle unfinished. She wasn't as complete as she'd thought she was, and now she had a chance to learn more about her past, who her parents were, and why they left her at the orphanage. Whoever this Mr Black was, he seemed to be involved in the supernatural somehow, with at least three Magi working for him. Had her mother been involved as well? Might she have been a Magus? She found she suddenly needed to know more. She needed to know where she came from.

Mr Black had wanted the Lazarus Scroll for himself. She had nothing else to go on, but that name had connotations if you knew the Bible. Lazarus had been the man that Jesus had raised from the dead. So, did that mean that the Scroll could do that, too?

Why would Mr Black want such an Artifact? Who did he want to raise from the dead?

Could it be her mother? Was she dead? Her stomach ached and her head pounded from the possibilities.

She suddenly remembered the knowing look that Angel had given her as she'd walked out of the reactor core. What had she been doing there? Angel was a powerful Magi, as Amanda knew all too well. She was also clearly masking her Magical signature to present a much weaker Magi profile to infiltrate and deceive. She couldn't fool Amanda, though. She knew how strong Angel was, which meant the ruse must be for Mr Black's benefit.

Did Angel want the Scroll or could there be a bigger plan at work there?

One thing was for sure, she didn't have all the facts or all the pieces, so she would need to dig deeper.

But that wasn't all. Horlack, the monster who wanted to kill her, had returned from the dead. Every time she thought she got a handle on things, they got flipped upside down and she had to start all over again.

Amanda heard movement and saw Maria step out onto the rooftop. She stopped when she saw that Amanda had noticed her.

"Hey, are you okay? Everything all right?"

Amanda sniffed and suddenly felt quite emotional as tears welled up in her eyes. She blinked, and they fell down her cheeks.

A moment later, Maria was beside her. She took Amanda's hands in hers. "Hey, it's okay. It's alright. What's happened?"

"I went with Maya on a mission to find an Artifact, but we weren't the first ones there." She went on to explain the confrontation she'd witnessed. Horlack's appearance, the group of Magi who'd confronted the Nomad, and eventually, the conversation she'd had with Mr Black. "He said he was my father. He knew how old I was, said he recognised my mother in me and that we looked very much alike."

"Anyone could say that Amanda, anyone, and it doesn't take a rocket scientist to guess your age," Maria said.

"But he knew I didn't know my father, he knew that. He was speaking the truth, I just… I know it. I just know it," she said.

"You're sure?"

"As sure as I can be. I need to find him. I need to know who he is."

"Then that's what we'll do. We can get Shaun on it; get him to see what he can find out about this Mr Black."

Amanda smiled. "Thank you for understanding."

"If it's important to you, it's important to me," Maria said, smiling up at her.

Maria kissed her then, before pulling her in for a hug.

"Hey, girls?" Vanessa said from the doorway. "Royston's here. They're looking at the man you brought in. You might wanna…"

"We'll be right down," Amanda answered, separating from Maria, wiping her eyes, and sniffing back more tears.

Moments later, they appeared in the basement, having Ported down to save time. Shaun, Liz, Vanessa, and Maya stood with Royston close to the table, with Maya telling him what had happened at the power plant. Amanda listened and waited for Maya to finish. She spoke rather vaguely about her encounter with Horlack, saying only that he got away.

"Horlack?" Liz asked. "Wasn't that the one who attacked you and..?"

"The same," Amanda replied. She'd have to ask Maya more about that later. Royston turned to her then.

"So, this guy appeared out of nowhere?" he said.

"Using the same Spirit Magic that I saw Shaitan using," Amanda said.

"Meaning, he came through from the Abyss," he finished, frowning and considering this. He turned then and looked at the motionless figure and removed the glove from the man's right hand. "As I thought," he said as he turned the man's hand over so his palm faced up.

Amanda stepped forward. "What did you think?" Amanda looked down and saw a black brand of a single dot, surrounded by seven tiny flames in a circle tattooed on the man's palm. "What's that mark mean?"

"It means he's a Sentinel."

"A Sentinel? What the bleedin' hell's a Sentinel?" Amanda asked. It sounded like it would be just one more enemy to add to the ever-growing list

"Honestly, we're not really sure. They're a group of Magi that seem unrelated to the Arcadians, Nomads, or the Inquisition. They're outside our little war and take no part in it. What we do know, is that they occasionally show up when things get a little too public and do their best to protect humanity. They're on the right side of things, but they take a very hard line and have frequently killed Arcadians as well as Nomads," Royston explained.

"So, we're on the same side, then?" Amanda extrapolated.

"Technically, but they would insist otherwise, I believe."

"So, how's he passing through Acheron into the Abyss?" Maria asked.

"I'm not exactly sure, but you can see that his tattoo seems to have a Spirit Magic aspect to it," Royston said.

Amanda shifted her vision into the Magical spectrum and looked closer at the mark. Royston appeared to be right as she noted the subtle Astral Magic that seemed to emanate from it.

"Hmm, well, I'd quite like to talk to him then," she said and loosened her Magical grip on the Sentinel.

The man leapt up and off the table, making Amanda and those closest to him jump in shock. Aegises flared into life around the room as the man came to his feet behind the table and looked around, saving a special scowl for Amanda, no doubt due to the fight they'd been in at the power plant.

Astral Magic flared out from him and from his tattoo as he tried to slip into the Abyss, but Amanda had added an Astral Magic element to the building's Aegis, and it stopped the Sentinel from Porting away.

"Hey, hey," Amanda called out. "No need to panic, we don't want to hurt you."

The man took no notice of her and looked around the room. He seemed like he might be considering fighting his way out.

"No, no, no. Calm down, we don't want to hurt you, please," she pleaded.

He didn't seem to be listening to her, though, and after a moment of indecision, he bit something.

The moment he did, a small shockwave of Magical energy flooded his body, passing over him as he suddenly dropped to the floor. With her Magical sight still on, she could clearly see that he'd literally just dropped dead. His life force had been ripped from his body as his physical form became abruptly inert.

His heart stopped, his synapses and nerves stopped firing, everything just died and he hit for floor hard.

"Brutal," Amanda said in shock and awe.

Liz gasped while a few others offered their own expletives on seeing the man take his life so suddenly.

Royston walked over to him and crouched down, checking his vitals and looking once more at his palm. "His tattoo's gone," he remarked.

Amanda walked over and looked for herself. Royston was right; the black brand on the palm of his hand had disappeared as if it had never been there.

"He killed himself?" Amanda said. "Why'd he do that?"

"From the few encounters I've read about, the group seems highly ritualised, very strict, and very secretive. We think they've been instructed to kill themselves rather than risk capture, and I think what we've seen here today pretty much confirms that theory."

The sound of footsteps from the back of the room caught Amanda's attention, making her and the others turn and look.

Gentle Water stood halfway down the stairs, looking over the scene before him.

"Did I interrupt something?" he asked.

- The Sentinels, a discussion. By Louisa Hunt

There have been reports of the Sentinels throughout the recorded history of the Magi. They always appear out of nowhere using Astral Magic, possibly meaning they can pass into the Abyss. They're highly trained and often very powerful Magi. They appear to have no loyalty to the Arcadians or the Nomads or anyone else, fighting and killing any Magi or Scion regardless of affiliation. The one motivating factor we can gather from their actions is that they wish to protect humanity from anything Magical.

They clash more often with the Nomads than with us, as we're essentially on the same side. But when the actions of Arcadians get too public or involve too many Riven, they have no issues with killing us, also.

Within this book, we will examine some of the most well-known and most infamous encounters with the Sentinels to see what light can be shed on this mysterious and secretive organisation.

Cold Trail

New York

"Sounds like you've been busy. Shame we not discover more about this Sentinel. We be more careful next time," Gentle Water said.

"It was stupid of me. I'd heard the stories of them killing themselves, I should have checked more thoroughly," Royston admitted.

"Knowing of stories or rumours is one thing, it's a very different thing when they're right in front of you, so it is," Amanda said.

They'd all retreated across the garage and into Shaun's Ops room where a large conference table had been set up. Amanda felt tired from the mission to the desert, but she wanted to hear what Gentle Water had to say about his mission to the South Pole. Also, she wanted to speak to him anyway about Trevelyan's revelation about the Prophecy.

She eyed him from across the table, wondering what he knew. Had he kept it from her? She looked back down to her lap where she'd been absentmindedly playing with the threads on the edge of one of the holes in her skinny jeans. What was she thinking, she chastised herself? Gentle Water was the most loyal and kindest person she'd ever known in her entire life, why was she thinking horrible things about him now?

Life as a Magus seemed to be a constant struggle against those who wanted to do her harm. It was like being in a warzone or being undercover in enemy territory. The only difference being that her hostile environment just so happened to be everywhere and hidden from plain view. It's not paranoia if they're really out to kill you, she supposed. Still, she needed to remember who her friends were and not allow anything to come between them.

"Don't keep us in suspense any longer, Gentle Water. Did you find anything in the Antarctic?" Royston asked.

"Yes. The leads you gave, led to camp hidden well away from Riven base, with what must have been very tight security," he said.

"Must have been?" Royston asked.

"Yes. The base was still there, but they starting to dismantle it," Gentle Water replied.

"Okay, go on," Royston said.

"I observed, before infiltrating base and asking questions of security man. The base is part of large dig. They hunt for powerful Magic Artifact in ice."

Amanda enjoyed listening to Gentle Water's soft Chinese accent and the way he left out the occasional joining word. Her mentor had always been laconic at the best of times; only speaking when he needed to, but that just meant that what he did say always mattered. He went on to explain the site and its location before what looked like a temple entrance and the strange Magic that lay scattered about the site.

"So, did the guard you interrogated give you any further information? Like who this dig was for and what they found there?" Royston asked.

"They found Magic Artifact, the guard not sure what it was, just heard rumours. But dig funded by man called Mr Black…"

"What?" Amanda blurted out, her head snapping up. "Did you say Mr Black?"

"Yes, why?"

Amanda let out a laboured breath and looked into the middle distance. This couldn't be a coincidence. Meeting Mr Black mere hours ago in Arizona and then this report from Gentle Water.

She'd left out the part about meeting Mr Black at the power plant. Despite her certainty that this Mr Black was being truthful, she still had her doubts, and it was all just a little too close to home for her liking. But between the plant and this dig in the Antarctic, it was clear that something was going on. She needed to be honest with her friends.

She looked up at Maria who sat next to her. She nodded, encouraging Amanda to let everyone know what had happened.

She looked up at the expectant faces around the table and took a breath before speaking again. "The group of people at the power plant, who were after the Lazarus Scroll and who confronted Horlack and the Nomad, Dust were led by a man called Mr Black," she said. This set her friends around the table muttering and looking at one another.

"Mr Black? You're sure," Royston asked.

"And...?" Maria said to Amanda, urging her to go on. Maria's single word silenced everyone and they looked back to Amanda.

"And... And he claimed he was my father."

"Your father? Your real father?" Liz asked looking shocked.

"That's what he said."

"And you believed him?" Liz asked, incredulous.

"I did. I mean, I do. I believe he was telling the truth, or at least, he believed he was telling the truth."

"You're an orphan, though, right?" Vanessa asked.

"That's right, abandoned at an Irish orphanage as a baby. I never knew my parents," Amanda answered.

"This is concerning," Royston spoke up. "So, you say he has apparently acquired a Magical item from the dig in the Antarctic," Royston said to Gentle Water, who nodded. "And he also got hold of the Lazarus Scroll in Arizona?" he asked Amanda and Maya.

Amanda glanced at Maya, and they both nodded.

"Tell me more of what you saw, Amanda," Royston asked.

"A group of maybe fifteen well-trained and well-armed men, along with at least three Magi accompanied Mr Black."

"And Mr Black himself was not a Magus?" Royston asked.

"From what I could tell, no, but he did seem to carry plenty of Magical items on him."

"The three Magi, what about them?" Royston asked.

"Oh, yes, I forgot to mention. I knew one of the Magi with Mr Black, so I did. It was Angel, ye blonde one who attacked me on the train in France." She could see that this sparked Gentle Water and Liz's interest, since they'd been on the train with her. "I didn't recognise the other two. The brunette woman was bleedin' powerful, though."

"Rank?" Royston asked.

"Easily a Sage, or Master maybe, based on what I experienced."

"So Angel is working for Mr Black?" Liz asked, her tone curious.

"That's the strange thing, she must have been hiding her Magical signature because she appeared much weaker to my Magical sight," Amanda said.

"She's infiltrating them," Royston concluded. "So, she wants the item for herself, then."

"Who knows, she's a sneaky one," Amanda said.

"Agreed. We can't make assumptions about Angel's motives, but she's clearly working her own angle on this. Suffice it to say, I don't like this at all. This Initiated mortal, who we know nothing about, but who seems to know a hell of a lot about Magic and about us, is collecting up Magical items from around the world very quickly. I don't know about all of you, but I have a bad feeling about this."

Amanda had to agree. This all sounded very, very bad, and her link to this made things just that little bit more personal. Was this really her father doing this, and what did he want with these items, other than more power? He'd successfully kept himself hidden away from the Magi world, gathered loyal Magi and who knows what else to his banner, and hunted down some of the most potent Magical items in the world. He clearly wanted something, but what was it?

One thing was for sure, she wanted to know, and she wanted to find him as quickly as she could.

"Did you go down into the dig? Did you see anything in there of interest?" Amanda asked.

"I did not go into the tunnels, no," Gentle Water answered her.

"Then, I want to go back there. I want to see for myself what ye man dug up from that poxy ice."

"Are you sure you want to do this, Amanda? You're not too close to it, are you?" Royston asked.

"Are ye questioning my judgement because Mr Black might be my father?"

"I have to ask the question, Amanda," he said.

She knew he had to. If this man turned out to be killing Arcadians for whatever reason, she needed to keep her head clear and not let her emotions cloud her judgement so she could do what must be done. She desperately wanted to know who this man was and the truth about her parentage, but if worst came to the worst she would be expected to do whatever it took to stop him. Could she do it? Honestly, she didn't know, and until the moment came to make such a choice, she doubted she could answer that question with any honesty.

"I want to do it. I need to know more about who he is. But don't worry, I'll do my job if it comes to it," she said.

Could she, though? Could she actually kill him if it came to that, knowing that he could potentially be her father? That was the critical thing, though, wasn't it? It was all maybes and possibilities, just his word and nothing else to go on. He could be lying, he could have found out enough about her to throw her off the scent.

Unlikely, though, as he had no idea that she would be there, and even she didn't know about the power plant crisis until Maya invited her on the mission.

No, everything pointed to him being truthful. Otherwise, how would he have recognised her?

"If you're sure, then great, go. I hope you find what you need," Royston said.

"Thank you," she said before turning to Gentle Water. "Shall we?"

"Of course, is it just you?" he asked her.

Amanda looked around the table.

"Ooh, can I go?" Liz asked, bouncing up and down in her chair in excitement.

"Of course," Amanda said.

"Awesome," Liz said and jumped up, moving around the table to Amanda and Gentle Water.

Amanda looked at Maria, who simply said, "You go. I'll be here when you get back." Amanda nodded and smiled affectionately at her.

"We'll monitor you from here," Shaun said. "Keep a Link open so I can hear what's going on."

"Can do," Amanda said, and immediately opened the Mental Link to Shaun and Vanessa. She turned back around to face Gentle Water and smiled. "Ready," she said.

"It will take two jumps to get there, and it will be cold," Gentle Water said.

"Good point, well made." Amanda smiled and pulled on the local Essentia to fix the ambient temperature of her body and the air closest to it. She also cast the same effect on Liz, warning her before she worked her Magic.

Essentia suddenly flared around Gentle Water and wrapped about Amanda and Liz, folding in on itself and pulling them into it. With a rush of air and a flash of light, Amanda had a brief moment of seeing a lush landscape of dense jungle undergrowth, perhaps the Amazon Basin, before the scene changed once more and suddenly everything turned white.

Amanda found herself standing on a snow-covered ridge next to Liz and Gentle Water. The wind whipped about them, blowing Amanda and Liz's long hair wildly about their heads, forcing them to tie it back to keep it out of their eyes.

The environment was freezing cold. They were standing in snow halfway up to their knees in a very bleak, almost entirely white landscape. Amanda, still in the ripped jeans and short-sleeved top she'd worn in Arizona watched as Gentle Water pulled out a woollen beanie hat from his coat pocket and pulled it over his bald head.

Mountains rose up into the misty sky, and in a depression that cut into the side of the range, she could see various prefab buildings with some of them linked together to create a complex of rooms. She could see the last dying remains of a now ineffectual Aegis that had been left to fade to nothing. Within the camp, there were several hot spots of Magic in front of the vast temple that had been cut into the rock face, no doubt the Magical traps that Gentle Water had told them about.

"We walk in. Less risk," Gentle Water said darkly, peering at the view ahead of them.

Amanda nodded. She agreed. They could Port in, but there could still be a few alarm effects in there, which they had a better chance of spotting if they moved cautiously.

From what she could make out, maybe a dozen people moved about the camp, working machinery as they dismantled the buildings and packed things away. The large size of the base meant that moving through the area would not be difficult and even without Magic, they could most likely go undetected. Always better to be safe than sorry, though.

"Let's do this quietly," Amanda said, and with a working of Magic, bent light around them, rendering them invisible to the Riven mortals in the camp. They set off, trudging through the snow, their Magic keeping them at a pleasant Goldilocks-temperature. Not too warm and not too cold. Amanda also took the time to bolster her Aegis, making sure her defences were in place and ready for any surprises they might find.

Before long, they were walking into the camp, through the outlying buildings, some of which were partially dismantled, exposing their insides to the environment.

Wandering through the remaining buildings, not getting too close to the workers, Amanda looked for anything that might shed any light on Mr Black's operation. As they went, she sent her senses into the buildings and looked through the rooms inside. She discovered nothing at first, but when she found what she believed to be the operations centre of the site, she paused and brought her Magic to bear once more, sending her mind's eye back through time to see if she might see Mr Black himself. But her efforts were hampered when she found some kind of Magical interference preventing her from scrying back to certain times and places within the building and the camp in general.

She pushed further back and before long, caught sight of Mr Black as he was about to move into the tunnels within the temple itself, probably before he found the Artifact. Amanda frowned. Whatever the item was, it preferred to remain hidden from casual view. Like the Golden Book.

She looked further back and saw visions of Mr Black speaking with people in the control rooms and his arrival into the site. She also saw Angel, still hiding her true power. Angel seemed to be rather good at this, and if Amanda hadn't known better from previous experience, she would have assumed her Magi rank to be an Apprentice or an Adept at best. Eventually, she found herself watching a meeting between Mr Black and his team where he spoke about an Orb and his plan to use it to kill the Archons.

Replaying the meeting, this time she focused on Angel's face in particular. Amanda couldn't help but be impressed by Angel's self-control when Mr Black spoke about his plan to kill her masters—never once had she let her façade drop, or her emotions show.

"Hey, guys, let me share this with you," Amanda said, allowing her two companions to watch the conversation as well. Once it was over she asked, "What do you think?"

"Good find," Gentle Water said.

"Kill an Archon? How's he going to do that?" Liz asked.

"That's a very good question. I don't know enough about these items to say if that's even possible. G.W.?"

"I could not say for sure," he said.

"That looked like a closed meeting, I doubt anyone here will know more," Amanda said, indicating the workers nearby.

"Agreed," Gentle Water said.

"Didn't you look back through time when you were here before?" Amanda asked Gentle Water.

"I dislike using Time Magic. I have mentioned the Weavers to you before," he said.

"Aah, yes," Amanda said, suddenly remembering one of her lessons back in the Irish countryside. All Magic carried an element of risk. It didn't happen often, but if you lost control of an effect, it could cause damage to yourself and others, but one of the riskiest forms of Magic was Time Magic. Messing about with the timeline was a sure-fire way to gain the Weaver's attention. They were shadowy creatures that policed the timeline and dealt harshly with those who abused it. Few had met them and survived, but the stories of them were numerous. Some said that the worst offenders were simply erased from history as if they'd never existed.

The threat of the Weavers could often be enough to put even the most powerful Magi off of Time Magic entirely, preferring to avoid using it at all rather than tempt fate.

To the best of Amanda's knowledge, looking back through time, speeding up or slowing time down, or travelling forward in time didn't attract such deadly attention from the Weavers. It usually happened when someone travelled back through time or changed something in history that would affect things going forward. Basically, if you caused a paradox, then you could expect a visit from a Weaver.

Amanda hadn't done any such thing. But just the mention of the Weavers made her stomach flip as she suddenly doubted herself. Deep down, she knew she'd done nothing to attract their attention, but she went through what she'd just done in her mind anyway, just to be sure.

She totally understood if someone didn't want to take such risks, though. Better safe than sorry when it came to the Weavers.

"Right then, shall we check out the tunnels?" Amanda suggested, refocusing on their mission at hand.

"Lead on," Liz said.

Heading towards the back of the camp and the temple carved into the mountainside, they found a tent just in front of the entrance, placed there to help keep the elements at bay from those who had once worked inside.

Feeling intensely curious, Amanda walked into the tent and saw a roughly circular tunnel bored into the ice that had long ago filled the temple. Mats had been placed on the floor to prevent anyone from slipping, and cables snaked down into the semi-darkness to lights and other machinery.

Not wanting to hang around, Amanda walked ahead, dropping her invisibility effect as she went and started to descend into the depths. The wall-mounted lights had been spaced well apart from each other and cast a dim light into the tunnels. Their shadows played across the walls, causing her to startle a couple of times from the strange movements. The path seemed quite clear, and after what seemed like a very long time, they came to a short stretch of tunnel that had been made much wider and was also better lit than the others. Work lights lit up the dead-end of ice up ahead, while silent machines stood about the space like strange monoliths of an alien culture.

Amanda stepped forward slowly, looking about her, heading towards the well-lit back wall.

"Careful," Liz said, her voice creating strange echoes that danced with the sound of their footsteps through the ancient complex.

"Sure, sure," Amanda said and continued forward.

She stopped just before the back wall, standing amongst the machines, tools, and work lights, looking at the ice-wall before her. It looked like two things had been removed from the ice. At about waist height, a tennis-ball-sized, clean-cut borehole had been cut into the ice. Nearby, a robot arm that looked like it might be able to reach inside the hole stood immobile. Amanda guessed that had been where the Artifact that Mr Black had referred to as the Orb had been resting. But below that, a huge hole had been created, or blasted into the ice, with chunks of it all about the floor around her, as if something had burst out of the ice itself.

A quick look through time proved to be fruitless. Liz stood next to her, with Gentle Water close behind.

"Is that where…?" Liz asked.

"Looks that way," Amanda answered. "Whatever yoke was in there is gone now, I can't see us finding much else here," Amanda said.

Suddenly, a small monitor on a trolley popped into life with static on the screen, causing Amanda and her friends to spin and look at it.

"What the bleedin' hell?" Amanda said.

"Ah, crap," Liz exclaimed in surprise, but Gentle Water remained quiet.

Amanda eyed the monitor for a moment and stepped forward, sensing only electricity rather than Magic at work here.

Then, just as suddenly as it had turned on, a signal came through, and a picture of a wrinkled old face appeared on the screen. She recognised Mr Black right away.

"Amanda, you found my dig site. Well done. I'm afraid you're too late, though, we have what we need from there," said Mr Black, his voice scratchy and worn.

"Mr Black, what are you up to?" Amanda asked.

"You seem to be a clever girl, I'm sure you can work it out. I'm afraid I cannot divulge the rest of my plans to you. I'm sure you understand. You might be my daughter, but I'm just not able to trust you with that information yet."

"I only have your word on that, though. What proof do you have that I'm your child?"

"Did I lie? I think you know better than that," he answered.

She did. She couldn't explain it, like so much in her life these days, but it didn't seem logical. She just knew he'd told her the truth. "You didn't lie," she admitted.

"Then know that I am sincere when I say that I would love to spend some time with you and get to know you better, but my plans are too important, and I cannot let anything jeopardise them. I'm hoping we can catch up later, once all this is over with."

"You mean your plans to kill the Archons?" she asked.

Mr Black frowned. "Good day to you, Amanda," he said before the screen went dead.

"Well, that went well," Liz quipped.

***

On a nearby rock face overlooking the camp, the dark figure squatted on a ledge and shivered. She'd been asleep in the ice for so long that she felt like she herself had been made of ice on first waking up. Although, after breaking out of the ice, her movement and feeling soon returned and she felt a little more normal. Draining two of the men she found in the tunnels of their blood had also proved to be very helpful. As she looked down, she saw three figures exit the tunnels, each of them Magi, and all three keeping out of sight of the Riven mortals.

She felt like she had much to do. It had been so long for her, trapped in that ice. But finally, she'd been set free. She could feel her power and connection to Essentia returning, although her mind still felt a little foggy on some of the details of her life and her ability with Magic.

She hadn't forgotten the Orb, though. That item would be forever dear to her, and waking to find it stolen had been troubling, to say the least. Although, it could be that its absence from her vicinity could have been the trigger for her waking up. Whatever the reason, one thing remained clear in her mind: she wanted it back, and she would make the thief pay for their actions.

Luckily for her, the workers she'd eaten had also given her some rather useful information on just who it was who had taken the item, and where she might find him.

- Nowhere

She had been through this same ritual the past two days, but today would be different. Today she would not hesitate, she would not be afraid, and she would do as her mistress asked of her. Then she wouldn't be beaten or kicked or cut or hurt again. She would receive praise and love from her beloved mistress. She hated it when Yasmin was displeased with her. She loved her mistress and only wanted to please her.

Yasmin walked ahead of her, and Alicia found she couldn't help but stare at her mistress. She wanted to look like that. She wanted to be perfect in every way, too.

Finally, they entered a room, and again the same woman sat on the floor before her, her face filled with tears and fear as Yasmin handed Alicia her huge kukri dagger, its curved blade feeling heavy in her hand.

"Cut off her arm," Yasmin said, her voice calm and measured as if she'd just asked her to pass the sugar.

Alicia took the dagger and walked forward. She looked at what was left of the woman's left arm; the one Yasmin had cut off yesterday when she had hesitated for the second time. She also remembered being dragged off by Nate, who had punished her once again back in her room.

She didn't blame Nate. She had displeased her mistress, so the punishment had been warranted.

This time though, she didn't hesitate. She just acted. Pulling out the woman's right arm, she brought the heavy dagger down on it as hard as she could, burying the blade deep into the bone of the woman's upper arm.

Blood sprayed across the dagger and into her face as she levered the blade free and swung it again to the sound of the woman's screams. It took her four hits before the arm dropped away from the woman's torso and hung limply in her hand. She felt surprised at the weight of it.

"Don't stop there, she has two more limbs," Yasmin said in an offhanded manner.

Under the Sea

Over the Pacific Ocean

The last time she'd been on a huge cargo plane like this, Angel had been on her way to the South Pole and the dig that had led to this moment. Things had progressed so far now that she actually felt somewhat surprised at how well it had gone.

The huge cavernous body of the plane stood empty apart from the people standing within it. Angel felt a little out of place, her skirt suit probably wasn't really suited to what she was about to be involved in, but she didn't really care. She liked looking good. As she stood listening to Mr Black, she kept her feet a shoulder-width apart to keep from falling over as the plane flew through the night sky.

Around her were twenty highly trained and very well-equipped men and women in black combat gear, complete with helmets and masks and high-powered weaponry strapped to their bodies. Through her Aetheric Sight, she could make out a range of Magical items upon them, including powerful Force Shields and enhanced armour. She knew they would be faster and more deadly than anyone they came up against.

To her right, stood Isha in similar clothing to the troops, but without the guns, headgear, and Magical items. Beyond him, Mr Black leant on his walking stick, a focused frown on his forehead as he glanced up at Echo, who Angel had come to learn was Mr Black's other daughter, and a powerful Magus.

This had been a week for revelations, it seemed. Seeing Amanda again at the power plant had been a surprise, and as much as she hated the red-headed bimbo, she couldn't deny feeling slightly grateful that Amanda hadn't said anything that might have given her away. If she ever got her chance, she'd quite like to silence Amanda for good.

She knew Yasmin would be unhappy with her if she did, though. She'd already expressed to Angel that Amanda was not to be harmed. For now, Angel would play along. While, going along with Yasmin's plans had allowed her to finally reach the upper echelons of the Syndicate organisation, Angel had decided that her loyalty to Yasmin would soon come to an end. She just wanted to see how Mr Black's plan played out first.

Of course, walking away from Yasmin was never easy, but she'd resolved to make it work, one way or another.

Angel doubted that Mr Black would be too happy with her either if she killed Amanda, given the news that she might also be his daughter. She had no idea if that was true, but he seemed to believe it, so maybe it was.

"Today will be another momentous day," Mr Black said, addressing the troops. "Today, we take our first steps toward freeing ourselves from the bondage of the Archons. What I am going to ask of you over the next few days will not be easy. You are going to have to do some difficult things, but you must understand that we do this for the greater good. You have all worked with me for a long time. You have all seen things that are not easily explained, and you know the true and very real dangers that lurk out there in the shadows. They want to enslave humanity, they want to bring back their masters and conquer the world, but we will stop them. We will stand in their way and say, 'No!' We have some of the tools now. We have the two items that will allow us to take the fight to these so-called Archons, these dark gods worshipped by some of the Magi out there. I have dedicated my life to fighting them and have built this organisation to do just that. I have brought in Magi like these standing next to me who are sympathetic to our cause and will help us finish this great work. You have already served me with distinction, but these will be some of the toughest days of your lives. Not because you will be fighting against Magi, but because you will have to fight against your own kind, against mortals like you and me. In order to serve the greater good and to end the threat of the Archons and the supernatural, we need tools that are in the hands of governments like the United States of America and which are guarded by their highly-trained men. But I trust you, I have faith in you, and I know you will not let me down."

Angel blinked. That had been a powerful and rousing speech, aimed perfectly at the people who stood before her, and she could see the dedication in their eyes to Mr Black and his cause.

Echo stepped forward now to address the troops, nodding to Mr Black as she did so.

"I'm sorry we have had to keep things from you until the last moment, the nature of this mission is such that the utmost secrecy was required. We're currently over the Pacific Ocean, and somewhere ahead of us and below us is an Ohio Class nuclear submarine, owned by the United States. Inside that sub is our target—the warheads it contains. Our mission is to storm the sub and take control of those warheads. Our fight is not with the Riven men and women aboard that sub, your job is to capture, not kill. Of course, should you be under threat, use your best judgement and do what you need to do. I have here a file for each of you giving you your individual missions, as well as all the details you will need on the submarine itself and its occupants. You have two hours before we Port down to the sub, use them well," she said.

She then handed a folder to each soldier and left them to organise themselves. Mr Black, Echo, and Isha then moved away from the men, with Angel following suit. Echo then turned to them, handing them a folder each. "You're to give support throughout, use your gifts and help us secure the payload," she said. Angel nodded.

"What's the plan once we have the warheads?" Angel asked. She had no idea if Echo would fill in the gaps, but it felt like the kind of question she should ask.

"We'll be headed to an island that we own, where we will unload the warheads we need and enact the ritual. We will infuse the warheads with Essentia, creating Essentia nukes. It will take all three of us to do this. The Scroll has the ability to weaken the Null Realm and pull things through from the Abyss. With the Orb's ability to enhance the strength and power of the Magi who possess it and the Scroll, we plan to push the Essentia nukes into the Abyss and destroy the Archons."

Outwardly, Angel kept her face neutral and nodded, but so much of what Echo said didn't really add up. The Orb's main power did seem to be that it enhanced the Magic of whoever possessed it, whether it would enhance the Magic of the Scroll, however, was another question. The Lazarus Scroll seemed to be a more diverse item, with a range of effects attributed to it. But passing into the Abyss did not seem to be one of them. It could pull things out, under the right conditions, as had been evidenced by Dust bringing Horlack back from the Abyss, but given the desperation of many Nomads to make the Magnus Transitus, the Great Crossing into the Abyss to meet their masters, if the Scroll could do that, she felt sure more would know about it. Things didn't add up. It seemed to her that Mr Black and Echo were looking at the known effects, and then, almost randomly, trying to put things together to try and make them work as they wanted them to. Also, the Abyss was known to be at least as vast as the Earth, and most likely bigger by at least double. How could they guarantee to get the nukes to dread Tartarus where the Archons slept?

This plan stunk of desperation, and Angel had significate reservations about it. Who knew, maybe Mr Black and Echo were right, but she doubted it.

She couldn't voice these opinions, though, it would give her away, and she needed to remain close, but she just had to prod at this a bit.

"Are you sure this will work?" Angel asked.

"It's a long shot, we know that, but we feel it's a worthwhile risk, and we're taking safeguards," Echo explained.

"What kind of safeguards?" Isha asked. Angel felt a sense of relief that Isha had asked the question, she didn't want to be the only one questioning things.

"That, I cannot divulge at this point, but you will see soon enough," Echo said.

Angel sat back and nodded her satisfaction at Echo's answers, although she felt anything but, and opened her folder. Isha sat next to her and did the same.

"This is exciting, right?" Isha whispered to her.

"It certainly is," she answered, feigning interest. That was one word for it, she thought, another would be idiotic or maybe suicidal.

Angel spent most of the next two hours in silence, looking through the documents, swapping the occasional comment with Isha, but mostly she sat waiting, itching to see how this would play out.

She also knew she needed to contact Yasmin the first chance she got, but she needed to be away from Echo and Isha to do that, so it would need to wait for now.

At the end of the two hours, Angel stood with the team in the centre of the plane as Echo concentrated, working her Magic and looking at the submarine beneath them. The aircraft flew in a circle, banking around the location of the sub as directed by Echo, and as Angel watched, Echo's Magic unfurled.

"Now," she said. With a series of snaps, small groups of their strike force disappeared over the next three seconds until Angel found herself wrapped in Echo's Magic and being Ported to the sub, as well. She appeared in a corridor between two groups of Mr Black's forces, who were shouting at the submarine's crew. Remembering her directions and the map, she set off down the corridor. There wasn't much for her to do. They thought she was an Apprentice-level Magus, so her mission was of little consequence, which suited her just fine. She walked along the cramped corridor, ducking through bulkheads and passing empty rooms already cleared by the group ahead of her.

As she moved, she could hear gunfire in other parts of the sub where the resistance appeared to be more concentrated, but as Mr Black's forces swept the boat, the opposition died away and the crew were steadily herded into a handful of rooms away from vital areas, such as the officers' berthing and dry storage.

Eventually, Angel found herself standing on the sub's bridge with Mr Black, Echo, and Isha. Nearby, a couple of Mr Black's troops flanked the captain of the ship.

"I don't care who you are, you won't get away with this," the captain spat with hate and bile in his voice.

"Captain Reed, I appreciate your viewpoint and how stressful this must be for you, but I assure you, I will get away with it. In fact, I already have. The boat is mine and you are powerless to do anything."

As the others focused on the captain, Angel's keen senses picked up on the approach of an armed sailor in the corridor behind her. Casually, she positioned herself where she needed to be, and as he burst into the room, roaring his defiance at the invaders, she moved like lightning. Disarming the man, she brought him to his knees with his arm locked behind him.

Angel looked up to see Mr Black, Echo, and Isha staring at her, looking somewhat surprised.

"Thank you, Angel," Mr Black said, nodding his approval before returning his attention to the captain. It had been a calculated move. No Magic had been involved and she had potentially just saved Mr Black from injury. She hoped it would engender a little more trust in her. Echo's gaze lingered on her a touch longer than everyone else's, though. Did she suspect something? Angel smiled at Echo, who nodded back to her and returned to the matter at hand.

The sub was theirs now, and they were soon underway to the island, wherever that might be. Angel wasn't privy to any further events on the bridge. Instead, she and Isha were tasked with infusing seven of the warheads with as much Essentia as possible in the time allotted. The work soon became boring and she found herself counting the hours until something interesting happened.

***

Angel stood on the hot tropical beach of an isolated atoll somewhere in the middle of the Pacific. Keeping such a place private and off the maps created by corporations such as Google would be one hell of a task, but it seemed like Mr Black had done the impossible.

The circle of sandy islands surrounding the bright blue lagoon were a mini-paradise with palm trees, endless sapphire seas, and azure skies. Angel thought they must be near the equator, given the intense heat of the noonday sun and the burning sand beneath her bare feet. Anchored in the lagoon, creating a black eyesore in the middle of this heavenly setting, sat the submarine. Half-submerged, with several of its missile tubes open, Mr Black's soldiers were extracting the warheads they needed for the ritual.

Nearby, Mr Black had his coat off and his shirt-sleeves rolled halfway up his liver-spotted arms, watching Echo and Isha supervise the operation.

More of Mr Black's forces had been waiting on the Island, including more Magi, Scions, and Mr Black's personal assistant, Roxanne.

Ideally, it would have been easier to Port the warheads over to the beach from the sub, but that had proved to be impossible due to an energy field that emanated from this island in the atoll. She'd only seen this kind of effect once before in person, and that had been around the Golden Book on the train where she'd encountered Amanda.

Something must be generating the field, so as Mr Black and Echo walked along with the first of the nukes, Angel followed, heading towards the huge rock that jutted out of the center of the island like a mini mountain. Upon reaching the base of the rock, the bulk of it towering above her, she watched as Echo brushed away the vines and undergrowth, revealing an intricate chrome door that shimmered in the light. There was a hint of something Magical beyond this door, but it was difficult to make out. Angel watched as Mr Black lifted a key on a chain from around his neck and used it to unlock the door.

With the press of a button and a hiss of air, the door sank back into the rock before sliding up and out of the way. As it opened, Angel could physically feel the powerful Magic that crashed out of the doorway and washed over her.

Angel recognised that Magic right away and instantly felt nervous.

Time Magic.

As everyone else stepped through the doorway, carrying the warhead, Angel paused. Angel wasn't keen on anything to do with Temporal Magic. The Weavers were the ultimate source of her fear. They were merciless in their hunt for those who violated the timeline, with a particular hate for Nomads.

Through the door, Angel could see hidden lights had come on and filled the space with a diffuse glow while Mr Black, Echo, Isha, and Roxanne looked around. Gingerly, feeling more nervous than she had in a long time, Angel stepped through the doorway, the metal feeling cool and refreshing against her feet. She found herself in a large room shaped like a cheese wheel. In the centre of the room, a circular raised dais about four meters across dominated the space. The room itself must have been maybe eight or nine meters wide and made entirely out of polished metal. The walls, floor, and ceiling were covered in holes and apertures cut into the metal that displayed some of the inner workings of the device. The incredibly powerful Time Magic she could feel emanated from it.

Mr Black stood at the far side of the raised dais and watched everyone as they entered. He seemed mildly amused by their reactions but waited for everyone to take it all in. As everyone's attention drifted back to him, he smiled.

"As some of you have no doubt guessed, this is a Magical item we now stand within. A very specific one. This is my Time Device. A Time Machine, if you will. But a very special one."

Angel had thought as much when she'd first felt that wash of Magic pass over her. If Mr Black's madness had ever been in doubt, this must surely cement it for most Magi. He might as well have called it a Weaver Magnet, Angel thought. What was this man thinking using such a thing, and why on earth would he risk everything for a way to travel through time? Beyond that, were the questions of who built it for him and why?

"You don't need to know the details of how it works or what it does," Mr Black said. "The important thing for us today is that the Magical shielding in here is so powerful, you could detonate a full complement of Nukes from that sub in here, stand right outside the closed door, and it wouldn't affect you in the least. Because of this, and because I have no desire to harm anyone other than the Archons, we will enact the ritual inside this device, so that, should the ritual fail, we will be protected."

"So, we're not using the Time Device to travel in time?" Isha asked. He also looked a little wide-eyed and worried by the device he stood within.

"No. The device has only been used once before, and it will not be used again after this."

He'd already used it? Angel thought, incredulous. Angel wanted nothing more than to reach inside Mr Black's mind to discover the secret of this device and why he'd used it before, but she couldn't. At least, not yet. Maybe another time.

"So, we're just using it for protection?" Isha asked.

"Correct," Mr Black replied.

Angel felt relieved.

"Now, if there are no further questions, we must move quickly to get the remaining nukes inside."

***

Hours had passed, but finally, Angel found a moment to slip away. She managed to get outside the Magic dampening effect that the Time Device created and instantly Ported away in as discrete a manner as possible, preferring to be as far away from Echo and Isha as she could realistically be in order to speak with Yasmin. She appeared on the deserted beach of another island and opened the Link to Yasmin. Moments passed, but eventually, Yasmin opened the connection in her mind.

~My Baal, I have news for you,~ Angel sent.

- An Overview of the Archons, by Louisa Hunt.

The Archons. No one is really sure what they are or who they once were, and very few, if any, are alive today who have actually encountered one. Millennia ago, they left the material world that they had ruled over as gods, disappeared into the Aetheric Realm, and a barrier was put in place to bar entry into the Spirit World.

No one knows if they went willingly, or if they were forced or tricked into their imprisonment within the fortress known as Tartarus deep within the Aetheric Realm.

Before they left, the area of the Aetheric Realm that Tartarus is in had been known as Arcadia, but the corrupting influence of the Archons has twisted the once beautiful Spirit World into a hellish landscape filled with monstrous creatures.

Most scholars of Nomadic history believe the evidence points to the Archons being forced or tricked into their imprisonment, as they seem to want to continue their corruption of humanity and direct their followers, the Nomads, to corrupt and kill as many Riven mortals as possible.

The Prophecy of Helene also seems to confirm that they wish to return to the world of man one day.

Here's a brief rundown of the seven known Archons:

Lilitu - the Beautiful, the Night Demon, the Mother of Succubi. She spawned the Vampire bloodline of Scions.

Tiamat - the Dragon, the Shaper of Life, the Dweller in the Deep. She spawned the bloodline of Scions we know as Chthonic Old Ones.

Enkidu - the Savage, the Beast of the Wastes. He spawned the Were-creature bloodline of Scions.

Leviathan - the Monstrous, the Twisted, the Coiled. She spawned a bloodline of Sea Monsters and Merfolk.

Naga - the Cunning, the Snake, the Hidden Death. He spawned a bloodline of Ethereal Creatures, similar to ghosts.

Oni - the Demon, the Fallen Angel. He spawned a bloodline of Demonic Creatures.

Samael - the Reaper, Charon, the Angel of Death. He spawned a bloodline of Zombies, Liches, and other undead creatures.

Dark Information

The Jade Palace, New York

Amanda sat at the table with her mentor, Gentle Water inside the bar area of The Jade Palace. It was early morning and she held her hot chocolate in both hands, enjoying the heat of the mug as it warmed her fingers. The steam from the chocolaty beverage wafted up to her nose, filling her senses with the lovely sweet smell of cocoa.

She sat sideways to the table with her knees crossed. Across from her, Gentle Water sat facing the table, his back straight, a cup of green tea on the table before him.

"I still not know what Mr Black wants with the Orb and Lazarus Scroll," Gentle Water said. "The whole situation is very concerning. Has Shaun found anything yet?"

"No, he's scouring the Dark Web for information, but this man seems to be a ghost, so he is. There's no record of him anywhere. It's as if he's never existed. Did you or Royston discover anything through your contacts?"

"I am afraid not. Everyone we ask know nothing. It is as you say, he is ghost. And he also say, he your father?"

"He did. Crazy, eh?" Amanda replied, the weight of her unanswered questions pulling her shoulders forward. "It's… incredibly frustrating. I mean, who is he, why did he abandon me, and what is he trying to do now? Have I got a Nomad sympathiser as a father? I just want to know what the hell is going on, so I do."

"I understand. Sorry you feel like this," Gentle Water said.

"It's no bother. There's nothing you can do, not really."

"I wish I could help more."

"I don't think there's anything anyone can do, really. Only this Mr Black can answer my questions. But… as you want to help, I do have something I want to ask you about," she said, uncrossing her legs and turning to the table to face her mentor.

"Of course, Amanda, anything," Gentle Water said, looking hopeful.

"At the ball, I spoke with Trevelyan, he told me about the Prophecy of Helene, and how he thinks it's about me," she said. She watched her mentor for his reaction, noticing his silent "Aah" head movement and slight deflation from the hope that had filled his face a moment before.

"Did he?" he said.

"He did. He said not to tell anyone but you."

"I understand."

"Did you know about it? Did you know people believe it refers to me?" she asked, her voice cracking a touch as her emotions rose to the surface.

"Okay, the Prophecy of Helene is quite well known within Magi community. But, there are other prophecies and passages from Magi history. They difficult to decipher and often lead to many interpretation. A few do think it refer to you. Others do not."

"And you didn't think to tell me about it?"

"I debate it many times, but I think that other things more important. How people interpret old prophecy did not seem important. You did not need extra worry. You have enough in your life, without this."

She could see his point of view. Telling her something that might make her worry about what others might think of her would not be a productive way to teach a young Magi. After all, it's just how a few people interpret a pretty obscure passage from two thousand years ago. Its relevance was somewhat limited. "And what do you think?" she asked.

"I am not scholar, and prophecy not my area of expertise. I know of prophecy. Does it speak of you? It may, it may not. I not know. My focus, always you, Amanda, not what others think of you and not ancient scrolls. I just want to teach you, help you. That is my goal."

Amanda felt bad. She felt like she'd questioned his friendship and his intentions, something that she really should never have done with the man who has stood by her side throughout her introduction to the Magi world. "I'm sorry G, I didn't mean to…"

"It okay. You have nothing to apologise for. Trevelyan's comments were not good, raised questions in your mind. I sure he meant nothing by it, however," he said.

"I know he didn't," she said.

Suddenly, the chair between them, just to Amanda's right, was pulled out from beneath the table, the noise it made as it dragged its feet over the floor caught both of them by surprise.

Just next to the chair, looking tall and imposing stood Yasmin, wearing black wet-look leggings and an over-bust corset that pulled her waist in. Her alabaster face, framed with a mane of raven-black hair looked down at Amanda. Her expression seemed blank at first, unreadable, although her features had a cruelty to them that would send a charging rhino running for its mother.

"Ooh, I'm sorry, might I have been interrupting something?" she asked, her blank face suddenly coming to life in mock apology.

Amanda blinked in surprise at the sudden appearance of the Nomad, but she recovered quickly "It's no bother, nothing for me to give out to you about," she answered, her Irish slang filtering through.

Yasmin smiled, her expression saying, "touché." She walked around the chair, her heels clicking, before she lowered herself into it and crossed her legs. "Please, don't stop on my account, I'll wait."

Adjusting her position, Amanda turned more fully to the newcomer, frowning at her in curiosity. The last time Amanda had seen Yasmin, she'd turned up on her doorstep to tell her about Liz's kidnapping, helping her for some unknown reason.

Yasmin could possibly be the most powerful Nomad on the planet. The rumours about her were plentiful and were used to scare young Magi into compliance. And yet, she'd always been somewhat friendly with Amanda, even helping her at times.

She felt sure that she must be up to something, although she was at a loss as to what that might be. She wondered how much of these rumours about Yasmin were true and how much might be propaganda or the result of things being blown out of proportion.

The rumours Amanda had heard about herself, such as how she'd killed Lucian's entire coven singlehandedly, to Trevelyan's personal views of her connection to a prophecy had already illustrated to her how things could be exaggerated.

Yasmin might be a Nomad, but how bad was she, really, given how much she'd helped?

"No, no. We'd finished our conversation anyway. So, what brings you here?" Amanda asked. "This is becoming something of a regularity."

"Yet again, straight down to business, Mandy. We should chat more, I'm sure we would have a lot to talk about," Yasmin said.

"Feck off, Yasmin," she said, raising one eyebrow as she said it.

Yasmin barely moved or shifted her position, but the brief look of daggers that Yasmin gave in reaction to Amanda's comment would have killed most people.

Amanda looked at Gentle Water and could see the Aegis he had been slowly powering up as he listened to them talk. She widened her eyes for a moment, knowing she'd strayed over a line for a second.

"I am here on business," Yasmin said. "Yet again, I have some information for you."

"Well, unless you can tell me where Mr Black is, it can wait," Amanda said.

"How fortuitous, I seem to have arrived at just the right moment, then."

Amanda sat forward, suddenly interested. "You know where he is?"

Yasmin sat back in her chair and ran her hand through her sable locks. "Indeed, I do. Do you want to know what he's up to?"

"Of course."

"Mr Black is on an island, an atoll to be precise, in the Pacific and he's acquired an American nuclear submarine."

"What? Feck, are you sure?"

"Quite sure. He's planning on using the nukes in a very poorly-conceived plan to try to destroy the Archons. It sounds doomed to failure, so who knows what will happen?" she said.

"Where is the atoll? Amanda asked.

With a flick of her fingers, a small slip of paper appeared. "Here. Use this information with care, and be prepared for a fight, little one," she said.

Amanda snatched up the paper and looked at the two strings of numbers and letters on the paper. Coordinates.

She looked up at Yasmin again, feeling confused. "Why do you help me? What's your angle?"

"Me? I'm just a Good Samaritan. Good day to you," she said as she stood and turned to leave the building.

"Yasmin," Amanda called after her, making Yasmin pause and looked back at her. "Should I want to… contact you, how would I go about that?"

Yasmin's eyes narrowed as she looked back at Amanda, thinking things through. After a moment, Amanda felt Yasmin's Magic reach out to her and wait just outside her Aegis. Amanda knew this was an the offer of a Mental Link so that she could effectively call Yasmin at any time. Amanda hesitantly accepted the Link, reaching out with her own Magic to cement the connection between them.

Amanda watched Yasmin turn and leave. She admired Yasmin's body as she strolled out the door. She looked great, and Amanda found she had to tear her eyes away from Yasmin's shapely behind.

Nope, she did not want to get involved with a Nomad. That would be a very, very bad idea.

She looked up at Gentle Water. "Do you believe her?"

"She was right last time. I doubt her motives are entirely altruistic, but we need to look into this," he said.

"Agreed, let's go."

- The American Wilderness

Horlack roared in frustration and slammed his fists into the cave wall, causing rocks to break and tumble to the ground. Turning to the entrance, he roared again, the sound echoing throughout the mountainous landscape beyond.

He got a grip on his emotions and breathed deeply, calming himself down. His imprisonment in Egypt had made him a little crazy, but seeing Maya in that strange building in the desert had brought old feelings flooding back. He remembered how he felt about her. How he wanted her. But not as a conquest, he didn't want to just take her, have his way with her, like he used to do. This was different, this was something he'd not felt for millennia. He wanted her to want him back. He wanted Maya to love him, and to want to be with him.

But he wanted revenge as well, but to take it would alienate him from Maya for good.

He needed to make a choice.

Black Dawn

The Atoll, the Pacific Ocean

After a flash of light and the fleeting feeling of acute dislocation, Amanda's first impression was that she'd Ported into an oven. The extreme heat hit her hard as her feet sank into the sand of the tropical beach. A quick working of Magic cooled her down a fraction as she looked around.

To her left morning approached, splashing crimson and fire across the heavens, as the waters of the atoll's lagoon lapped gently onto the sand. Amanda wore her usual jeans and tank top, but briefly considered a quick working of Magic to transform her jeans into denim shorts but dismissed it.

To her right, Gentle Water and Liz stood closest to her. Liz pulled her hair into a ponytail as she looked ahead, boosting her Shields with Essentia. Her apprentice's growing confidence made her smile.

Maria stood next to them, and just beyond her, Orion and Xain looked ready for action in head-to-toe black combat gear. And finally, Maya and Yoh stood furthest away.

Everyone looked at each other, they all knew the plan.

Amanda and Gentle Water had returned to the house as quickly as they could, bringing Yoh and Maya with them from The Palace and calling Orion and Xain over from Paris.

With everyone there, they quickly discovered that the island didn't exist on any conventional maps found online or in print, but a quick scrying of the area confirmed there to be an atoll at those coordinates, along with a submarine, and lots of activity on the beach.

Everyone had been briefed on the basics and were under instructions to capture and subdue whenever possible and secure the nukes. Amanda had no idea if Mr Black was truly on their side or if he might actually be insane. Either way, nuclear bombs were not to be trifled with.

Ahead, further along the beach and well inside the Aegis that stopped them from Porting too close, Amanda could make out work lights lighting a path from the shoreline to the enormous rock in the middle of the island and figures milling about on the sands.

Amanda nodded at her friends. "Shall we?" she said.

With nods of agreement, the group started to jog over the sand, quickly but silently approaching Mr Black's team.

Amanda watched the figures ahead of her, and it soon became clear they'd been spotted. Magical energy started to build, and dark silhouettes moved into position, ready to fight.

The men with guns opened fire, lighting up the beach with their muzzle flashes.

The Essentia rounds skimmed across the sands and slammed into the Aegises of the group. In her Aetheric Sight, bursts of light peppered their shields with pops, bangs, and the whine of the occasional ricochet.

The weak Essentia rounds did little to Amanda's Aegis other than light it up as the bullets tried to find their targets. Amanda just pushed more Essentia into her Aegis to compensate, using one of her Multitasking minds to do the job.

Taking a wider arc in her approach, Amanda tried to draw some of the gunfire away from Liz, and ran through the edge of the water, soaking her trainers and the legs of her jeans.

Ahead and to her left, the sea erupted in a massive surge of water. A lizard-like head, a good six feet from its nose to the back of its skull, rose from the sea on a serpentine neck and swung towards Amanda. It held its fang-filled maw wide as it snapped at her.

"What the bleedin' hell is that?" she said to herself.

It moved quickly, but Amanda saw it coming and jumped away. Landing in a roll, she came to her feet and looked back. The creature's massive arms heaved its body from the sea with surprising speed and it came in for another bite. Essentia surged as her Magic flared, smashing its head sideways with a powerful Kinetic attack. It howled, but only looked angrier.

Amanda could see the thing's Aegis. Was it a Scion of some form? This creature was entirely different from the Vampire and Werewolves she'd seen before.

Amanda turned and ran up the beach towards her friends. They'd already started to fight with the other members of Mr Black's supernatural forces. She could see Magic being thrown around and bullets flying everywhere.

Just ahead, Gentle Water and Liz had taken on a Magus and a freaky-looking thing that looked like it had stepped straight from the pages of H.P Lovecraft. Its top half was mostly human, apart from its head being one large fang-filled mouth. It wore a long-sleeved red robe embroidered with gold runes. From beneath the hem of the garment extended a mass of huge tentacles that whipped about, trying to attack them.

Hearing the sea creature roar from behind her, Amanda turned. She'd have to deal with this thing first before helping her friends.

"Come on, then, slimy, let's be havin' ye," she said as the enormous mouth lunged for her. Amanda dodged to her right, out of the way, as the creature hit nothing the sand.

"Ooh, good try, Nessie," Amanda quipped. She threw a punch at the thing's head, putting as much of her strength and Essentia into it as she could muster, causing the head to whip away as the creature roared in pain. Gunfire sounded nearby and Essentia-filled bullets hit her Aegis, damaging it.

"Jaysus, gimme a break," she yelped.

One of her Multitasking minds sent out a wave of force at the three troops which hit them like a speeding car, knocking them into the air. The serpent's head swung back with a howl, clearly wanting to bite her in half. She'd been ready for it, though, and delivered a powerful spinning kick to the thing's jaw with a grunt of effort and a snap of Magical energy.

The head veered away as the Essentia Strikes from her Multitasking minds pummelled the Aegis of the thing, breaking it down quicker than the Scion could repair it. The creature backed up for a moment, coiling its neck like a snake ready to strike. .

Amanda faced it and lowered herself into a crouch "Come on, then, ye wee beastie, I'm ready for ye."

The thing's head whipped out, but its jaws snapped on empty air as Amanda sprang up and over the serpent's head. She landed just behind its skull, straddling its neck like a horse ride. Unleashing an Essentia strike as she landed, she finally shattered the thing's Aegis. Clinging on for dear life, she followed it up with a powerful Kinetic blast to its head while another of her minds reached into the serpent's brain and with a tiny tweak, sent the beast to sleep. Its body suddenly went limp and Amanda rode it down onto the sandy beach.

"That's beauty one, beast zero," she quipped to no one, before jumping off and patting it on its head. "Night, night."

Turning, she strode towards the fight ahead of her. The three troops who'd opened fire on her were scrambling to their feet as she approached. Half a second before the fastest of the trio brought his weapon to bear, she shot forward and knocked the gun to one side. A punch to the face knocked him unconscious.

Next to her, the female of the three lifted her gun. Grabbing it, Amanda twisted the weapon and the woman's arm with a jerk. A bone cracked. She screamed as Amanda swept her leg through where the woman stood, dropping her to the sand. The soldier let go of her gun. Still holding its barrel, Amanda swung it like a club, hitting the third man's face and spinning him like a top as he fell to the ground unconscious.

Satisfied these three weren't going to be anymore trouble, she dropped the gun and ran. She sprinted towards Liz, who'd ended up facing the tentacled thing alone as Gentle Water dealt with the Magus.

As she closed the gap, the Old One, as she believed they were known, pressed its attack on Liz and managed to wrap one of its long, fast-moving tentacles around Liz's ankle and swiftly lifted her off the ground. The Old One brought Liz to its mouth, gaping wide with rows of shark-like teeth, only for Liz to kick out with her free foot and deliver a powerful Essentia strike against the thing's head, knocking a few teeth flying in the process.

Amanda smiled in pride at her apprentice's action. As she got closer, she jumped and hit the tentacle holding Liz with an Essentia-infused kick. It spasmed and dropped Liz.

"Lovecraft called, he wants you back in Arkham," Amanda called as she landed. The thing backed off for a second momentarily unsure and hissed.

"Sarcastic little bitch, are we?" the thing growled at her.

"I bet it's an awful tough job doing your makeup in the morning with no eyes," Amanda said. "The lipstick must go everywhere."

"I see well enough," it roared as it lunged. Its tentacles swept around as it wound up its taloned right arm. With a spinning jump, Amanda kicked the thing in the face. It staggered and flailed about to keep its balance.

"Oooh, my bad, I think I clipped you there," Amanda joked as she reached out and pulled on Essentia. A powerful Kinetic

Ram smashed down on top of the thing. The Old One howled in pain as it was crushed beneath Amanda's Magic.

She glanced at Liz behind her. "Go help Gentle Water, I'll finish this one," she said. Liz nodded and sprinted off. Amanda looked back at the Old One, who rose up from the ground.

"Finish me, will you?" it rumbled.

Amanda just smiled and released a wave of Essentia in a focused blast at the Scion. It fell backwards in a mass of flailing tentacles and crashed into one of the work lights behind it. Another of Amanda's minds took hold of the electricity in the light and amplified its power. The other lights connected to it glowed brightly before exploding in a shower of sparks while electrocuting the Old One. The thing went into a violent fit from the shock as the electricity coursed through its body while the rest of Amanda's Multitasking effects hammered the Scion's Aegis, breaking it down.

Somehow, the thing managed to heave itself off the broken light, backing away from Amanda. Its Aegis destroyed, it looked at Amanda with fear, and after a moment of thought, it turned and moved away, quickly heading off down the beach and away from the fight before Porting away altogether.

Satisfied, Amanda turned back to the fight to see Liz holding her own against several gun-wielding Initiated. Close by, Orion and Xain were fighting four Scions and were only just holding them off. Since Liz appeared to be okay, Amanda turned to the Scion fight and ran at a huge Weretiger who was fighting the boys. Walking on two digitigrade paws, it looked like a massive, powerfully-built man covered in tiger fur with human arms, but animalistic legs and feet. The Scion's head looked entirely tiger-like, though, and it roared at Orion.

Flanking the Weretiger, her flashy flying spin-kick took the Scion by surprise. Her foot slammed into its face, spinning the creature back with a cat-like yelp.

Amanda landed, focusing on the Weretiger. "Let's get it on, fluffy," she said.

The tiger smiled, which looked very disconcerting. Seeing a human level of intelligence behind those predatory eyes was damn freaky.

Feeling slightly more concerned, Amanda fed a little more Essentia into her Aegis, just to be sure.

The Scion leapt forward, slashing at her with its wicked black claws. Amanda blocked the Scion's attacks as best she could. Her superior strength held off the beast despite the Were-creature being twice her size Keeping her primary mind focused on not being hit by those claws, her Multitasking minds worked overtime to send daggers of Essentia against the Scion's Aegis.

Getting nowhere fast, she used one of her minds to throw a blast of Kinetic energy at the Scion, hitting it hard. Forced back and away from her, it dug into the sand with its massive paws, its Aegis resisting the worst of the hit, spitting and flaring from the Magic.

A heartbeat later, the Scion rose back up and attacked. It was a feint, and the creature shoulder-barged her. Catching Amanda off guard it knocked her over and onto her back. The tiger leapt on top of her with a roar, claws out and ready to cut her in half.

She caught the wrists of the Scion before he touched her, grunting with the effort of holding him off.

"Not so flippant now, are we?" the Scion taunted as it lunged in for a bite. Amanda dodged to the side as the Weretiger's maw snapped shut just beside her head.

"I don't go to second base on a first date," she said, pulling her leg up and under the Scion. With a blast of Telekinetic energy, she flipped the Scion over her head.

Amanda spun sideways into a crouch to face the Scion as it similarly righted itself, growling at her.

"And I'm not a fan of threesomes…" it said.

Amanda had just enough time to frown, before something large and powerful slammed into her side like a freight train, sending her flying. She landed in the sand, rolling several times before coming to a stop on her back. No sooner had the world stopped spinning when a huge Werespider pounced on top of her.

"…but in this case, I'll make an exception," the Weretiger finished.

Amanda looked up in shock at the hideous thing above her. The main body of the creature looked like a giant hairy spider, two or three meters long with eight large, powerful legs. But from where the spider's head should be, a human woman's legless body grew. The coarse hair that covered the spider extended up onto her feminine hips, before thinning to nothing below her navel. The woman's body was otherwise naked and human, apart from the huge black claws on her fingers and her curiously mutated head framed by a mane of black hair.

She had two human eyes and six inky black ones, extending up over her forehead, pushing her hairline way back on her scalp. The Scion's mouth was filled with needle-like teeth. Two large fang housings, normally found on the front of a spider's face, sat on either side of the woman's mouth with huge black fangs dripping with venom, extending from the bottom of them. They clawed the air, looking for something to stab.

One of the spider's legs knocked Amanda's blocking hand away, while the woman's human hand slashed at her face. The Essentia laced claws momentarily broke through Amanda's Aegis and cut her cheek open. Amanda yelped and punched up at the Scion, hitting her square in the face. The spider-woman hissed and went in for another attack. Amanda was ready and caught one, then the other of her human arms before they could hurt her. The creature's two front spider legs went crazy and started scratching and tearing at Amanda's chest and stomach. The Scion ripped her shirt and skin, drawing more blood.

Glancing behind her, Amanda saw the Weretiger approaching. She needed to get out from under the spider, or the tiger would tear her head off. Lifting her legs, she kicked out. Essentia flared from her feet, knocking the spider-woman away.

Amanda got one leg under her before the spider was back. Amanda exploited a careless opening and punched the thing hard in the chest and she felt a rib or two crack beneath her fist.

The spider-woman jumped back and squealed in pain. "You bitch, you'll pay for that."

Amanda turned just in time for the Weretiger to slash at her. Breaking through her Aegis, the claws cut her upper arm leaving deep gashes. Amanda winched.

Pulling her arm away, she spun and kicked the Weretiger's face. He staggered as the spider-woman charged in, screaming at her. Feeling a little more in control, Amanda continued the spin. She dodged out of the way and grasped two of the woman's spider legs. Heaving the Werespider off the sand, she spun once and threw the thing at the tiger. The huge spider-woman hit the dazed Weretiger full in the chest and both went down in a mess of limbs, screams, and roars as they kicked up sand all about them in their confusion.

As she watched, Orion and Xain finished off their Werewolf opponents and turned to look at Amanda and the remaining two Scions.

"Kicking ass and taking names, Amanda?" Xain said as he drew his sword from his back and walked towards the spider and the tiger. Orion nodded to her and followed his partner in crime, reloading his guns.

Amanda put her hands on her knees and took a few seconds to catch her breath before she noticed the pain from the cuts on her body and face. Her arm stung the most. The tiger's claws had bitten deep into her arm and it was bleeding profusely. But the fight wasn't over yet, and she still hadn't seen Mr Black or the other Magi-woman, Echo.

A wall of Kinetic force and explosive fire hit Amanda out of nowhere. It drove her into the sand with a power that frightened her. Her Aegis held, keeping her from the worst of it, but she could feel her Shield buckle slightly from the attack. She looked up in time to see Echo step from a large doorway in the side of the huge rock in the middle of the island. Behind her, standing in that doorway, Mr Black watched with a stony expression.

Barely a fraction of a second after opening her eyes Magic flared from Echo again. It smashed into Amanda like a wrecking ball, knocking the wind out of her. As she tried to breathe she focused all of her minds on bolstering her defences. An invisible force lifted her into the air and then pounded her down again, closer to Echo.

"No quips?" Echo asked.

A series of Magical strikes hit her about the head and bells rang in her skull as her neck twisted in painful ways.

"No jokes, Amanda?" Echo added as a lightning bolt flew from her hand and struck Amanda in the chest. It slammed her into the ground again. Her body spasmed in shock while her Aegis tried in vain to keep it at bay.

"I'm disappointed in you. I thought you'd be a more worthy opponent," Echo said as more Magic crashed into her.

Amanda needed to fight back, she needed to defend herself. The next Magical strike rolled her over the ground. Quickly, she stopped herself and sent a blast of energy at Echo. But with a casual flick of her hand, the attack flew to Echo's side missing its target entirely.

"Hah, is that all you've got?" Echo taunted. Amanda jumped up to run at her, only to have another of Echo's attacks get through her counter effects, sweeping her legs from under her, and throwing her to the ground. "You're not worthy to have Mr Black as your father or me as your sister."

Sister? Had she said sister? Amanda's mind reeled through the haze of pain that clouded her mind.

"I'm sorry, Amanda," Mr Black said from maybe ten meters away. "But I simply cannot let you ruin my plans. I have invested too much in this to see it fail now."

Amanda started to get up, but her legs felt like jello. She had aches and pains in every part of her body. Her mind swam with it as she struggled to get a grip on reality and what was happening to her. Echo's Magic and power had turned out to be way beyond hers. This was a powerful and dangerous woman and Amanda had no idea if she could go the distance with her on a good day, let alone after she'd been injured. Her Aegis remained intact, so she could defend herself for a little while longer, but something needed to change, otherwise… well, Amanda didn't want to think about what the consequences might be.

A powerful Magical strike from Echo collided with Amanda's Aegis.

Amanda leant into it, resisting its relentless force as their Magic fought, flaring and sparking with Magical fire in her Aetheric Sight.

Nearby, Amanda watched as Gentle Water, Liz, and Maria struggled against Mr Black's forces. Liz hung back nursing a limp arm. Maria defended her while Gentle Water held off two skilled Magi, who were causing him some problems.

This did not look good. Amanda could feel her Aegis slipping away beneath the raging torrent of Magic that hammered against it. She couldn't hold this for much longer. She locked eyes with Liz, saw the look of desperation in her eyes, and knew she had to do better.

Amanda closed her eyes and focused on resisting this torrent of power and energy. She held her Aegis against it, forcing as much Essentia into her shield as she could. She felt the inevitable cracks forming as the Aegis started to weaken and disintegrate.

She didn't want to die like this. She couldn't let it end like this. She'd only just discovered her father, even if he was an old, psychopathic, and seemingly insane man with a daughter who Amanda sensed hostility from. She had started to question whether she would invite Echo to any family gatherings.

She laughed a little to herself, finding humour in the darkest of moments.

Then something changed. The attacks from the Magi her friends were fighting faltered. After a moment of confusion, Maria and Gentle Water were winning. Looking up, Amanda saw Angel backing off. Then, she attacked Mr Black's forces. Angel flanked Mr Black's Magi enforcers and destroyed their Aegises.

Gentle Water and Maria took the upper hand as Angel turned and ran into the trees.

Magic flared from somewhere behind Echo. Powerful and dangerous, it ripped into Echo's Aegis.

Echo's Magic faltered seconds before Amanda's Aegis failed. Amanda dropped to her knees and did her best not to collapse entirely. She looked up to see Yasmin's familiar silhouette standing on a rocky ridge, as hideously powerful Magic brought Echo to her knees.

For a moment, Amanda sat in stunned silence as she watched a Nomad fight on the same side of the Arcadians. Yasmin had likely saved her life and the lives of her friends.

She didn't know how she felt about that. News of this could easily be twisted into something less favourable for her and her friends if it got out.

She'd wanted to do this herself. She didn't want to be saved by someone more powerful. Not that she wasn't grateful, though. Quite the contrary, but she didn't like that she and her friends couldn't do this themselves.

She looked over at Liz, who sat in the sand, as Gentle Water and Maria finished off the Magi in short order.

She loved her apprentice and felt so proud of everything she'd achieved.

Looking back at Echo, Amanda used some of her Magic to heal herself. She boosted her shields and readied her Magic once more.

Grunting with effort as she stood, Amanda's Magic flushed her system of pain and exhaustion as she approached Echo.

As she neared, Yasmin's Magic destroyed Echo's Aegis. Amanda picked her up by her neck and they locked eyes, but Echo just stared at her in defiance. Amanda threw her at the rock. She hit it and then fell unconscious. Amanda dove into her mind and ensured she wouldn't be waking up for a few hours at least.

As her friends finished off the remains of Mr Black's forces, Amanda turned to face the man himself. He stood within the strange metallic doorway that was recessed into the rock. He looked worried. Amanda approached him as he pulled out a Scroll from his pocket and unravelled it. He scanned the text in a panic, searching for something.

Amanda reached him, plucked the Scroll from his hands, and pulled him from the door by his collar.

"Sit down," she ordered him. He took a seat on a nearby rock.

Amanda looked through the doorway and saw the large metal room within.

"Wow. Now, that's an awful pretty room you have there," she said, marvelling at the space and the warheads that were arrayed about it. She could feel Temporal Magic emanating from the room and wondered what on earth Mr Black had been up to. She frowned and looked down at the man, and then at the room again. What was this thing and how did it fit into his plans?

She could maybe take a guess, but she couldn't quite believe it. Every time the words *time machine* passed through her head, she couldn't help but feel disbelief.

A woman suddenly popped up from behind one of the huge warheads. She pointed a gun at Amanda and immediately opened fire. Bullets bounced off her newly refreshed Aegis. They clattered to the metal floor of the device until she'd emptied her clip. Amanda noticed that the woman had her eyes closed for much of her clumsy attack, but opened them now.

Amanda raised an eyebrow at her. "Have you quite finished?"

The woman raised her arms in defeat and dropped the gun. "Uh, yes. Sorry," she said.

Amanda shook her head.

***

Standing on the beach, Amanda looked over the various figures who sat or were laid out before her. Most of the Initiated troops were alive and awake. Some were restrained while nursing injuries but otherwise, they were fine. The Magi and Scions who remained after the fight were all comatose. They couldn't be allowed to wake up lest they cause further issues and Maria stood guard over them making sure they didn't..

Amanda felt refreshed and calm, although her blood-stained clothes spoke volumes about the fight she'd just been in.

After some discussion, they'd chosen to leave the crew on the sub, but send them to sleep for the moment until Amanda and her friends had finished dealing with the situation.

Yasmin and Angel seemed to have disappeared, and no one had seen them since the fight had finished. Amanda felt grateful towards Yasmin. She had saved her life, again. This behaviour did not fit with her legends and seemed to be somewhat out of character for her. She had no idea why Yasmin kept saving her life and she wondered if she'd ever know the truth.

Dawn had broken about twenty minutes ago, and the heat from the sun had already started to beat down on them. Amanda really just wanted to lie on the beach and work on her tan, but that was merely a fantasy because she had too much to deal with.

Her friends were all healed and in relatively high spirits. Liz had broken her arm during the fight, but it had been easily fixed. Otherwise, there'd only been some cuts and bruises, which were quickly dealt with.

"So, what are we gonna do with them, then?" Liz asked.

"I'm still thinking about that," Amanda said. "I need to have a chat with Mr Black first, though. We have some things to discuss."

Liz nodded as Amanda turned and wandered over to Mr Black. He sat on a rock on a cushion made from a few coats and other items of clothing. His personal aid, Roxanne, sat next to him and whispered to him as she approached.

"The redhead's coming over again. Looks like she wants to talk to you," she said.

Amanda wasn't meant to hear that, but with her enhanced hearing, she could clearly make it out. She walked up to the old man and sat on a rock opposite, looking at him. He looked up at her, a look of defeat and sadness in his eyes, there seemed to be a hint of tears there, too.

"I'm sorry," he said.

"Well, that's a start, I suppose, to be sure. You have a lot to be sorry for, you know," Amanda answered.

"I'm quite aware of that," he said, hanging his head for a moment. "I sense you have questions for me."

"Indeed, I do."

"Ask them, I will answer them honestly."

"You planned to somehow destroy the Archons? Is that right?"

"I did. They are a menace and they need to be stopped. I will apologise for a lot of things, but not for wanting to save humanity from the whims of these creatures. My methods might have been…"

"Fecked up?" Amanda offered.

"Questionable," he finished. "But I still believe that the Archons are dangerous and need to be stopped."

"On that point, I agree with you, but sending a bunch of nukes into the vastness of the Abyss would not do that unless you could somehow place them right where you need them."

"Maybe. I still believe I had a chance, though," he said.

"I think we will have to agree to disagree on that point. I'm sure there are other, better ways to achieve your goal. I want it, too. The Archons and the Nomads are a scourge on this Earth, the sooner they're ended, the better. I'd like to work with you on that, but you would need to change your ways," Amanda said.

"We'll see," he answered.

Amanda sighed. "Has anybody ever told you that you're a difficult man?"

"You wouldn't be the first," he answered.

"I bet. Look, ever since meeting you in that power plant where you said you were my father…"

"I am your father."

"How can you say that? How can you be sure?"

"I'm sure," he said.

"Would you care to elaborate?" she asked, feeling a little exasperated by this verbal sparring.

"Maybe."

Anger bubbled up insider her. "Listen, gobshite, you're going to tell me what the bleedin' hell happened, how you got to be this way, and what the hell that metal room is. I want to know how and why you think you're my father, and what you want out of our relationship without me having to chase the answers out of you. Because believe me, you *don't* want me to rummage about in that head of yours at your age," she spat.

Mr Black didn't flinch. With her piece said, Amanda just stared at him and watched as he lowered his eyes and seemed to think for a moment.

"It all started twenty years ago. I'm actually only forty years old, despite what this body looks like. Twenty years ago, I was a fairly normal young man. Part of a wealthy family who were well-connected. I had a great future ahead of me, I suppose. But my family had been in service to an ancient and powerful Scion for over a thousand years. We knew nothing else other than to do his bidding, to run his enterprises, and to suffer his wrath. Serving Horlack was all we knew."

"Horlack?" Amanda asked, surprised.

"Yes, you know him?"

"I've had dealings with him. But that's not important. Please, continue."

Mr Black nodded. "For hundreds of years, my family had been searching for a way out, for a way to release ourselves from the bondage of being Horlack's slaves. Our salvation came in the form of a Scroll. The Lazarus Scroll, to be precise. After months of planning, my family used the Scroll to summon a true god and beg for his mercy and his help. This god, who referred to himself as 'Weaver', agreed to help us, asking us to choose one amongst the family to complete the mission and to reconvene on this tropical island that my family owned. My family chose me, and I felt elated that I would be the one to free our family from slavery. The night before the trip to the atoll, I celebrated, and paid a visit to a massage parlour, where I spent a couple of hours with an angel who called herself Sofia."

Mr Black looked up and gazed into Amanda's eyes. "She looked just like you. She had the same hair, identical features. I could swear you are her, but there's something different that I can't put my finger on."

Mr Black looked up at the sky and sighed. "That night, it felt like more than just sex. It felt transcendent, like nothing I've ever felt before. It's difficult to explain, other than to say nothing could ever feel like that again. Later, on the trip to the atoll on the seaplane, I couldn't help but think something more than just sex had happened that night. Something wonderful. But I wouldn't be sure until twenty years later," he said and looked up at Amanda, smiling.

"Continue," she said.

"The next day, on the island, in a cave that had been hollowed into this rock," he said, gesturing to the door of the strange device, "we enacted the ritual once more, summoning the one known as Weaver. He agreed to uphold his end of the deal, and around us, in that cave, the Weaver created the device. You may have already guessed its purpose. Most Magi can, after walking in there for the first time. It's a time travel device.

"The Weaver told us that the device would send one person, me, back in time to the day before Horlack first met our family, and through the use of a certain passage within the Lazarus Scroll, Horlack would be forced to miss the meeting with my family. The Weaver warned the family elders that there would be consequences, but they chose to go through with it anyway, believing the risk would be worth it." Mr Black took a breath; there were tears in his eyes again.

Amanda waited, feeling unsure how to take the story, it sounded crazy, even for her. But she'd been watching him with her Magical sight, and he'd been speaking the truth, at least as far as he knew.

With his emotions back under control, he took another breath before continuing. "The device was turned on and I stepped through the Portal it created, appearing in a forest somewhere, England or Scotland, maybe? I could never be sure. Before me, I could make out a fight through a copse of trees. Horlack and his armoured soldiers were fighting other soldiers and had basically won. They were moving through the clearing and killing anyone left alive.

"I took out the Scroll and read the passage -the Weaver had directed me to read. Green mist swirled around Horlack and the men. The soldiers all choked to death, while wounds appeared all over Horlack, badly wounding him.

"With my work done, I returned through the Portal and appeared back in that room. But, apart from Weaver and me, it was empty. I suddenly felt very weak and I was filled with aches and pains. I remember looking down at my hands," Mr Black said, holding his hands out in front of him, like he was looking at them for the very first time. "The backs of my hands looked old and frail. I asked the Weaver for an explanation, but I didn't like the answer."

Black lowered his hands and shook his head. "He'd said there would be consequences, and he hadn't lied. My family hadn't met with Horlack that fateful day, but had lived on, and died out during the Black Death. My parents, their parents, and so on back through the ages had never existed. My actions, according to the Weaver, had split the timeline, creating a new timeline where my family had died out.

"The Weaver had also aged me fifty years. At the time, I'd raged and shouted, angry at the price we'd paid, but the Weaver simply disappeared. Like this." He clicked his fingers, the sound a sharp thing that snapped Amanda out of whatever spell he'd cast over her with his story.

"That was nearly twenty-two years ago," Mr Black continued. "My family had gone, but it turned out that the Weaver had brought some things over to this timeline, including the yachts that still sat anchored off the island. I kept one, sold the rest and started to build my empire. In this timeline, I had never existed. There was no record of me anywhere. I was a ghost and I used that to my advantage.

"Nine months later, I heard of the disaster at Tārūt, the earthquake there and the reports of the red-haired angel who had saved the lives of hundreds of people, and I knew it had been Sofia, your mother. More recently, I heard a more personal account from a man who'd met Sofia earlier that day on Tārūt and helped her give birth to a baby girl. I believe that baby was you, Amanda. The timeline fits with both my night with Sofia, and with your birth."

Amanda had heard of the disaster at Tārūt in passing somewhere. She would be sure to look up the story once she was home, though. More importantly, she had a name for her mother now. Sofia. Her mother had been called Sofia, and it sounded like she'd been a Magus like her. She felt elated and yet she was still full of questions.

"So, you don't know why she gave me up? Why I grew up in an orphanage?" she asked.

Mr Black shook his head. "I'm sorry, no. I have no idea. I'd like to know that myself."

"You said you heard of a report by someone who met Sofia recently. Who made that report?"

"My aids found it on the Dark Web, made by someone going by the name of Edge. I wasn't able to track him down, and I had more pressing matters, anyway," he said, indicating the nukes that now sat on the beach a short distance away.

Amanda looked over to the warheads. "So, you never tried to contact the Weaver again, or go back through the device and undo what you did?"

"I vowed to never use that machine again, and kept the key to it hidden," he said, holding up a curious silver key on a chain around his neck. "As for the Weaver, sure, I tried to summon him again, but it never worked. After I lost the Scroll, that became impossible, anyway."

"I'll take that key," she said, holding her hand out. Mr Black took the key from around his neck and passed it to Amanda. She looked at it before placing it in her pocket. "You lost the Scroll?"

"The Scroll seems to have a life of its own, appearing where it needs to be all by itself. One day it was in my safe, the next day it had gone, and no one had been in the room, let alone in the safe. Like I said, a life of its own."

Amanda put her hand to her back pocket, making sure the Lazarus Scroll hadn't vanished. It hadn't, for now at least.

"So, why do you want to destroy the Archons?" she asked.

"Like the rest of my family, I hated being under the control of the Scion, Horlack. We knew a good amount about the supernatural world already. After time travelling, I started to recruit Magi and Scions to my cause, wanting to save others from the life I had lived. Naturally, I discovered more about the Archons and started to see their influence everywhere. They direct and shape this world of ours even now, corrupting it and those who live in it, every day. I will not stand by and let that happen while I have the power to do something."

"A noble goal, even if your methods leave something to be desired," she said as she stood up. She looked down at Echo, unconscious a few feet away. "And her? Is she really my sister?"

"Echo is my adopted daughter. I discovered her at the age of four, living as a dangerous curiosity in a government care home that had basically locked her away. Already a child prodigy and a Magus, I took her in and raised her as my own."

"She's very powerful."

"She's been everything to me, and I love her dearly, although, I think she's a little jealous of you."

"Understandable, to be sure," Amanda said, half-joking.

"Will I see you again, after today? I'd… I'd like to get to know you a little better. You are my daughter, after all."

Amanda looked down at him and at Echo. She'd heard of dysfunctional families before, but this felt like one step beyond.

A time-travelling prematurely-aged father and a psycho sister didn't sound like happy fun times to her. But they were her only link to her past and to her mother. She would need time to think, she couldn't make a choice like that now.

"I need time," she said.

"Of course, you do. I understand. Take as much time as you need. I have a card in my top pocket, take it, and call me sometime."

Amanda reached down and pulled the business card from his jacket pocket. It only had the word Black and a phone number printed on it. She stuffed it in her back pocket and turned away, leaving Mr Black where he sat. She had a lot to think about.

***

Angel stood atop the submarine just behind the conning tower, hidden from the beach. She was leaning against the tower, playing with a lock of hair that had come loose during the fight, and she was unbearably bored. She'd been watching events unfold for nearly an hour now and after the excitement of the fight, she just wanted to get on with it and finish this.

Mr Black, his flunkies, and the Arcadians were all sitting ducks. All they would have to do would be to launch a missile and blow it up the moment it launched, boom, dead Arcadians everywhere.

But Yasmin had insisted that they wait and watch and then Yasmin had disappeared somewhere for a better view. She wasn't sure where Yasmin was right now, but given her interest in this affair, she doubted she was far.

The fight had been good. She'd enjoyed it, and turning the tables on Mr Black had been a moment of great satisfaction for her. She'd grown bored of her mission with the Syndicate anyway, and wanted to return to her own businesses. She didn't feel totally comfortable siding with the Arcadians, but Mr Black's plan did have some merit, and there had always been the tiniest possibility that it might have succeeded. She had no desire to have any of the Archons destroyed by a mortal, so needs must, she supposed. But now that the threat had been averted, surely the time had come for them to deal with the Arcadians.

What was it about Amanda that had Yasmin acting so strangely? What kind of hold did that redhead have over her? She wished she knew. She hated Yasmin. She'd tortured her and forced her to give her allegiance to her, and that wasn't an easy pill to swallow. So, she followed orders, outwardly, at least, but deep down, she nursed her hatred of Yasmin and hoped to express it one day in a glorious act of revenge.

Angel pursed her lips. She looked around the side of the conning tower at the beach and saw the Arcadians cleaning up and dealing with Mr Black's forces. She glanced to her left at the open missile tubes, and then at the closed ones with their nuclear payload still sitting there, waiting to be deployed by someone with the balls to do so.

"Fuck it," she said to herself. She'd had enough of Yasmin's shit. She had a chance to strike a huge blow for the Archons, and watching it slip through her fingers was something she simply couldn't do.

She climbed back inside the sub, sliding down the railings of the ladder into the belly of the beast. She thought better than to Port inside. Too risky. It would give away her position to the Arcadians.

Before all this had kicked off on the island with the Arcadians showing up, Angel had found time to locate the missile operators, pull all the information she needed from their heads, and procure the keys she would need to launch the nukes.

Once in the missile control room, she went to work preparing one of the missiles for launch and setting its target so that it would detonate seconds after its launch. Moments later, with everything set and her Aegis up to full strength, she placed first one key, then the other in the control panels, and with a bit of Magic, turned both at the same time.

"Fuck Yasmin's rules," she said to herself.

***

Amanda wandered over the beach, turning the strange-looking silver key over in her hand as she approached her friends.

"How'd it go?" Maria asked as Amanda reached them.

"As well as could be expected. He ended up being quite forthcoming in the end, and I believe he was honest with me, even though his story turned out to be a little crazy."

"We're standing on a deserted island with Magical nukes, we've fought Sea Monsters and Were-creatures, and I think that's a time machine over in that rock—I think I'd be surprised if his story wasn't a little crazy."

Amanda smiled at Maria, her comments putting everything neatly into perspective. "You're right," she said.

"What's that you have there?" Liz asked.

"It's the key to that device," she said, indicating the doorway in the nearby rock. "I thought it best if he didn't have it anymore," she said.

"Good idea," Liz answered.

The explosion of sound from the ignition of the nuclear missile's boosters took Amanda by complete surprise. She flinched, ducking as if something had been thrown at her. Turning to the atoll's lagoon, she saw the smoke rising from the top of the submarine. For a second or two, all she could do was stare at the vast plume of smoke that rose from the boat, when suddenly the missile rose up from its tube, its boosters shooting flame and smoke from its rear end as it took flight, slowly at first. The shock passed and Amanda became intensely aware of the danger they were all in should that thing explode here and now. Within a fraction of a second, she weighed up their options and thought better of fumbling about trying to disarm or get rid of the missile when it could explode at any moment.

"SHIELD!" Amanda shouted and concentrated on her Magic. An Aegis, maybe thirty meters across sprang up around them that covered her friends and Mr Black's party. She and her friends pulled on as much Essentia as they could and forced it into the shield, strengthening their protection as much as they could.

A couple of seconds later as the tactical nuclear missile streaked upwards, it exploded with a blinding flash of light. Amanda had already crouched down and covered her head and face with her arms, but the light seemed to pass right through her, lighting her up. The noise from the blast made her ears bleed while the world around her shook as if from an earthquake.

Their Aegis strained from the force and power of the Magical nuclear reaction. She continued to force more energy into the Shield and sensed her friends doing the same, keeping the Aegis from failing altogether.

The chaos seemed to last forever, as if the most powerful and destructive storm the world had ever seen had been centred on the island, ruining the landscape around them.

Amanda stayed crouched on the sand, with no idea how much time had passed, but slowly, as she healed her ears and the sound of the thunderous explosion faded, she sat up and brushed the sand off her that had been thrown around inside the protective shield.

The scene that greeted them looked deceptively calm at first, with a circle of almost untouched beach, maybe thirty meters across, all about them that included the forces of Mr Black, the time device, and most of the warheads. She realised that one had been caught outside.

Beyond the few included palm trees and beach, the world outside of the shield appeared to be obscured by a misty grey and tan haze, like a sandstorm had been kicked up all around them. As they watched, the cloud of debris, dust, and dirt started the fade and settle, revealing the decimated landscape.

Their shielded circle of calm sat within a huge crater formed by the nuke that, for the moment, appeared to be nearly devoid of water. As they watched, the sea started to pour back in over the sides of the crater wall and fill this new lagoon. Looking around, Amanda noticed that one of her quick-thinking friends had somehow managed to teleport the unconscious crew of the sub, which had apparently disappeared or been destroyed, onto the beach inside of their Shield.

Amanda got up and looked over to Mr Black. But he wasn't there. She looked around, but it seemed like he'd disappeared. Nearby, her friends started to pick themselves up, with expressions of shock and almost hysterical sounds of laughter from Liz as she realised they'd just survived a nuclear bomb.

Feeling confused and unsure as to what to do next, Amanda only just registered the sound of another explosion, like a sonic boom that came from above. Amanda looked up in time to see a bright and powerful golden light, like a lightning strike that seemed to be growing in size and noise, when suddenly it passed through the Aegis, apparently unhindered by it, and struck Amanda on the top of her back with a strength that threw her to the beach. The pain was intense, beyond anything she had ever felt before as this energy bolt arced from the heavens and seared her back in a torrent of light and energy and fire that had her screaming in agony.

***

Liz fell on her rear as the golden lightning blast threw Amanda to the sand and continued to surge down onto her mentor from the heavens above. The sustained stream of energy seemed to be burning Amanda's back and it caused Liz to hold her hands up to her face to keep the intense light from her eyes as her friend screamed.

"Amanda!" Liz shouted in vain.

Liz felt helpless, she could only watch as this powerful force pummelled Amanda to the ground as if it was trying to kill her.

She could see some of her friends had a similar reaction, looking on in both horror and fascination at what was happening. She saw and felt Maria try to work some Magic, but the winds that flew out from this energy just blew the Magic away, like a strong wind would do to smoke.

Then, as suddenly as it had started, it stopped. The last of the energy bolt flowed into Amanda's body as everything fell into relative silence again.

All around them, things continued as they were—the new lagoon continued to fill up with seawater while the winds made the palms trees sway lazily.

Liz looked around at her friends and back at her mentor, wondering what she should do. Steam rose from Amanda's back, obscuring Liz's view, but she could see with her Magical sight that Amanda had survived, that her heartbeat remained strong and vital.

Liz sighed with relief.

"Amanda," she called, but her mentor didn't move. Liz looked about her again and slowly came to her feet. Gentle Water and Maria were reasonably close by, looking at Amanda and at each other, unsure of what they'd just witnessed.

"Do you think it's... safe?" Liz asked.

"I think so," said Maria. "But I've never seen anything like that before."

"Any ideas what it could have been?"

"Your guess is as good as mine, I think," Maria said.

Liz nodded and started to walk over the sand and approach where Amanda lay. As she drew near, the steam steadily rising from Amanda's back started to fade. What Liz saw made her catch her breath as Amanda began to stir.

***

I must have passed out briefly, thought Amanda as she woke up with her face in the sand; its gritty, salty taste filled her mouth. She could make out voices, someone was calling her name. Might that be Liz? She coughed and tried to move. She felt stiff and ached all over as if she'd just spent an entire day in the gym working on every part of her body.

Then, she felt the burning pain as her mind suddenly registered the sensation that her brain seemed to have been hiding from her. She pulled herself up to her knees, pushing up with her hands and grunting from the feeling of fire that covered her back. The skin on her entire back and upper arms felt taught and tender like she'd been sunburnt. She remembered the bolt of energy that had hit her and while that explained the pain, she wondered what on earth it had been and why it had hit her.

She sat back on her feet, kneeling on the sand as Liz and Maria appeared in her field of view, followed by Gentle Water just behind them. She had to blink a few times to bring her vision back into focus so she could see them properly.

"Amanda. Amanda, are you alright?" Liz asked.

"I'm grand. A little groggy, and I feel like I've been burnt to shite, but I'm good. Is everyone okay? What happened?"

"We're fine, Mandy," Maria said. "But take it easy, we have no idea what just happened to you."

"What do you mean?" Amanda answered.

"Um, best you look for yourself," Liz answered and pointed to Amanda's upper arm.

Amanda looked down and had two surprises as she did so. Firstly, she realised she was topless. Her vest top had been burnt off leaving her chest exposed to the world. She quickly put her arms across her bosom, and immediately noticed the strange flowing black tattoo-like markings on both of her upper arms.

They wrapped around her arm, about halfway between her shoulder and her elbow on both sides and flowed up over her shoulders and onto her back. She couldn't see much, but it looked like it grew into a huge design all over her back. She could see parts of it spilling around her ribs to the sides of her breasts and over her hips as well.

"What in the bleeding hell?" she exclaimed as she pulled on her Magic and created another set of senses that she used to look at her back more clearly. The tattoo covered her whole back, from shoulder to shoulder, up to her hairline on the back of her neck and down to her hips and the top of her bum. It was a flowing tribal design of black lines that circled about each other creating spirals and graceful points. In the centre of it, though, surrounded by the tribal pattern and covering about half of her back, were several circles that interlocked which looked like some kind of Magical summoning circles. These circles were filled with curious-looking runes, like writing, but in a language she'd never seen before.

She cancelled the Magical effect and paused suddenly, concentrating. She felt different. Somehow, more connected to the ebb and flow of Essentia and as she pulled at the threads of Magical energy again, she found she could direct it more easily. It responded to her and did her bidding as it had never done before. She looked at her hands, forgetting her nudity for a moment, fascinated with the ease at which Essentia flowed about them with hardly a thought at all. "What's happened to me?" she whispered.

"What is it?" Gentle Water asked.

"I've...I mean, I think I'm more powerful. I can pull this Essentia about like it's nothing... and... I think I've gone up a rank in skill as well."

"From Knight to Sage?" Gentle Water questioned her.

Amanda looked up. "Yes, I think so," she replied, seeing Maya, Yoh, Orion, and Xain gingerly approaching her.

She sensed the quick Magical effect that Gentle Water used, knowing he'd just changed his perception.

"Your aura's changed, too," he said.

"How?" Amanda asked as she watched Liz and Maria look at her with the same effect Gentle Water had just used and saw their expressions change, looking surprised and confused in equal measure.

"Your Aura has a mottled effect of both a golden and a deep violet colour, the colours of a newborn and of someone on the edge of death. The colours of life and death."

She saw realisation pass over Maria's face, but Amanda still felt confused, as did Liz from the looks of things.

"Meaning?" Amanda pressed.

"It's the prophecy. The Prophecy of Helene. It's you," Maria said.

Amanda covered her nakedness, feeling exposed again. She didn't like this talk of prophecy. It put her on edge, made her the centre of attention, and made her feel like people expected something from her. She stood up and, with a quick working of Magic, conjured a brand new fitted crop top on her body.

"We'll talk about this later," she said, wanting to change the subject. She looked about her, ignoring the looks of concern on her friend's faces and realised she still couldn't see Mr Black, Roxanne, or Echo. "Has anyone seen Mr Black?" she asked.

***

Angel stood on a rock as the sea surged past her into the new lagoon with the small island in the middle where the time device and the Arcadians were. A new atoll had been created by the nuclear blast, the circle of islands formed by the raised ridge of the crater. In the centre of the new lagoon on the small island there, the Magi Angel had wanted to kill, had managed to survive the nuclear blast.

Angel felt cheated, but having just watched the strange energy that had flowed into Amanda and marked her, Angel didn't feel too bad. At least, some interesting information had come out of this that she could use. She could hear the voices of the Arcadians as they talked to Amanda, discussing the prophecy. There would be plenty of people who would be interested to hear of this bit of news, and she would be sure to let them know.

With a smile, she worked her Magic and Ported from the island.

- Nowhere

Alicia laughed hysterically as she swung the dagger again and again. Blood from the corpse flew with every strike, and as she calmed down and looked down at the remains, she noted with fascination that you really couldn't tell who this had been just an hour earlier.

These past few days, Yasmin had given her a couple of new playthings every day, asking only that she amuse Yasmin. Alicia knew what that meant, and she had come to enjoy what she did. As long as her mistress was happy, she was happy.

Today's had been a beautiful teenage boy, innocent and scared, and Alicia had made sure to string this out to give her mistress as much amusement as she could. These shows of loyalty always had to come to an end eventually, and Alicia wanted to end it on a high note, so she really went for it, going a little crazy as she hacked this boy into tiny pieces.

She turned her naked body, covered in blood that dripped to the floor and tasted salty in her mouth, towards her mistress, who sat nearby with a huge grin on her face.

"You've done well, Alicia, I'm proud of you," Yasmin said.

Epilogue 1
Reawakening

The Atoll, Pacific Ocean

The sun slowly sank towards the horizon, looking like it might extinguish itself by dropping into the vast ocean surrounding the small island on the edge of the new atoll.

Yellow and orange light spread over the sky, creating a beautiful panorama that would make an artist weep.

The small island had only been formed for a day. It was small and unassuming and only one of many that made up the ring of small islands that encircled the new lagoon created by the nuclear blast that morning.

Devoid of any indigenous life for the time being, nothing should have moved, but as the orange light that filled the sky slowly turned red, the earth on the island shifted, and a form rose from the ground.

It sat up at first, looking around. Seeing something half-buried next to it, it reached down and picked it up.

The huge thing stood, raising itself up to stand on its two huge legs and looked out to sea, and then down at the figure it held in its arms.

"Echo," it said in a deep rumbling voice, addressing the unmoving, but still alive girl it held in its arms. Echo didn't move, but it knew she was alive. The thing looked about itself once more.

"Roxanne?" it said, its voice a little louder this time.

"Yes, sir?" came the reply. It sounded odd and reverberated about its ribs. The thing looked down to see a face on the left side of its chest, just below its collar bone. Its whole body had been transformed, mutated. No longer was he an aged old man, now he had been changed, enhanced. He felt like he maybe stood about double the height he had before, but his skin looked terrible. Like some kind of infected mutant. He could feel Roxanne's thoughts as part of his own and knew he'd somehow been fused with her. She'd been melted into him to become a part of him, but something else caught his attention when he looked down. Right there in the centre of his chest, buried in his flesh and ribs, glowed the green Orb. It throbbed and pulsated with his heartbeat and filled his body with power. He could feel the energy that flowed into him, the strength that it gave him, and he knew he'd been reborn.

Emotions churned inside him. He felt elated that he'd somehow survived the nuclear explosion, but he also felt rage and injustice at his failure to destroy the Archons. He thought of the reason for his failure. He thought of Amanda, his daughter, and then looked down at Echo.

She was more of a daughter to him than Amanda was. He could feel the rage inside him. He'd always had that drive, that anger, but it had grown along with his body and become something strong and powerful that he could no longer ignore. Thinking of Amanda now, at how she had failed to understand his mission, at how she'd stood against him, fought his men, and defeated him only made his rage grow.

He tried to keep it under control, to moderate it, but he was past that now, and the anger washed through him like a torrent of energy as he breathed harder and harder before he had to let it out and he roared to the heavens.

His inhuman voice carried over the sea and could be heard on all parts of the atoll. As he reined in his emotions he thought only of how he could hurt those who had wronged him. He heard voices then, from the small island behind him in the centre of the lagoon. Turning to look, he noticed a smallish ship that had probably been there for a while.

With his enhanced sight, he could make out movement on the ship and beach. It looked like a military boat, and as he moved over the island to get a better look, he noticed another, much larger naval frigate that had been hidden behind the rocks of his small island. The soldiers were being picked up. Maybe they had a boat he could use to get back to the mainland.

Epilogue 2
Taking stock

New York

Amanda sat on her sofa, her bare feet up on the seat as she leaned back into Maria. She sat behind her with her right arm around Amanda's body, her left tracing gentle lines over her skin, following the lines of the tattoo.

After the chaos of the last few days, sitting here relaxing with someone she loved and not having to answer questions or deal with people felt amazing. She leant her head to her right, enjoying the softness of the sofa against her head and the gentle touch of Maria's fingers.

Back on the island, after the energy had hit her and burnt the tattoo onto her back, the pain had soon subsided to a dull ache, and then became just a tightness of her skin, before that went too.

They'd known they had a lot to do, but they also knew their time on the Island was limited. There would almost certainly be military aircraft on the way. Working quickly, they'd made sure they cleaned up the radiation from the bomb, scrubbing the land, sea, and air of the lethal contamination before releasing the Shield they had created to protect themselves.

Following that, they needed to deal with the other people on the island, and after some discussion, they felt it best to put the word out to the US military that their sailors would need to be picked up. They quickly contacted Shaun, who confirmed that an aircraft was on its way, so they redoubled their efforts.

The Initiated, Scions, and Magi who had worked for Mr Black had been Ported to a place where the Magi Council could deal with them. As for Mr Black himself, the brief hunt they conducted for him turned up nothing, but they were pushed for time. He had not been inside the Aegis during the explosion, and Amanda feared the worst. At the time, it had slipped her mind, but she had since remembered that Mr Black had also used the green Orb he had found at the Antarctic dig and realised she'd never found any sign of it. Had Mr Black had it? Maybe he'd hidden it somewhere, which could in turn, mean that the item had been destroyed in the blast as well. Although, Amanda had her doubts about that.

Finally, before they left, Amanda realised she had misplaced the key to the device and the Lazarus Scroll, even though she knew she had them a short time earlier, just before the energy blast.

They had hunted for them, but without any luck, and Amanda remembered the words of Mr Black, that the Scroll had a mind of its own and would disappear all by itself. She wondered if that had happened here. She'd kept both items in the same pocket, would that have had an influence? Did the energy blast have anything to do with it? She had no idea.

They left the island moments before the first military planes were on the scene and were back in New York in no time.

Since then, Gentle Water had spoken with her about the prophecy, almost insisting that Amanda try to cross into the Abyss, but Amanda felt tired and apologised to Gentle Water, saying she would speak to him soon, but that she just needed some time to herself.

Today, after a fitful night's rest, Maria had come over. Other than a few pleasantries they hardly spoke before getting a drink and sitting in the living room. Amanda felt no pressure from Maria. She seemed to know that Amanda needed to think. Questions and fuss could wait.

They'd sat for over an hour now as Amanda thought about what Mr Black had said about her mother, Sofia and how she had been working in a manner very similar to what Amanda had done on the streets of New York a couple of years ago. She wondered why Sofia had abandoned her at that orphanage, what reason would she have to do that? It sounded like she would have been a single mother. Mr Black, at least at the time, had no interest in her upbringing, and who knew what other pressures she would have had.

Could she have been a Magi as well? She didn't have much to go on other than a name, Sofia, and a report written online by someone going by the name of Edge.

She would have to do some digging.

She also knew she would have to spend some time with Gentle Water soon and test out if what this Prophecy said about her was true or not.

Glancing at the table, lying next to a crumb-covered plate that she'd eaten a slice of baked Vanilla cheesecake off of, she noticed the leaflet she'd placed there that she'd fished out of the usual junk mail. It seemed to be an announcement of the reopening of the Pit Club.

It was under new management, apparently. As Lucian's former home, she felt unsure about this and vowed to pay the club a visit soon.

But not right now. For now, she just wanted to enjoy the quiet and the presence of someone who cared for her. She would return to the chaos of the Magi world soon enough.

Author Note

I always look forward to creating the cover for book 3. Mainly, because this is the book where Amanda first wears THE Red Dress.

I've been drawing Amanda for years, and the idea of the sheer red dress has been a look I have returned to time and time again. So, when it came to writing the books, I just had to get this dress into the narrative somewhere.

The ball in this book seemed like the perfect place, it also was the part of the book where she learns something about herself and the world she lives in that changes her view on things a little. Having that happen in the red dress seemed perfect to me.

The original versions of the first four books had Amanda wearing the same thing on every cover. But, I was keen to switch that up and have Amanda wearing different stuff.

Her favourite clothes are her scruffy ripped jeans, strappy tops, and trainers, but I wanted to show more to her than that as Amanda does like wearing other things. So, you will notice that she has a different outfit on nearly every cover.

Doing these shoots and creating these covers is very much a labour of love. I'm a creative, a storyteller, and an artist at heart, and writing books really does bring all those things together into one product.

I'm looking forward to creating and sharing more art with you soon.

I hope you're enjoying the Magi Saga.

Other stuff:
I have a Facebook Group which you might like to join here;
https://www.facebook.com/groups/MagiSagaFans/

Check out my other books on the next page.
Many Thanks
Andrew

Review

If you enjoyed this book, please consider leaving a review.

Booklist

For full list of Andrew Dobell's Books, visit his website at;
www.andrewdobellauthor.co.uk/booklist

Printed in Great Britain
by Amazon

19600695R00202